War & Travel By Edith Wharton

Edith Newbold Jones was born in New York on January 24, 1862. Born into wealth, this background of privilege gave her a wealth of experience to eventually, after several false starts, produce many works based on it culminating in her Pulitzer Prize winning novel 'The Age Of Innocence'

Marriage to Edward Robbins Wharton, who was 12 years older in 1885 seemed to offer much and for some years they travelled extensively. After some years it was apparent that her husband suffered from acute depression and so the travelling ceased and they retired to The Mount, their estate designed by Edith. By 1908 his condition was said to be incurable and prior to divorcing Edward in 1913 she began an affair, in 1908, with Morton Fullerton, a Times journalist, who was her intellectual equal and allowed her writing talents to push forward and write the novels for which she is so well known.

Acknowledged as one of the great American writers with novels such as Ethan Frome and the House of Mirth among many. Wharton also wrote many short stories, including ghost stories and poems which we are pleased to publish.

Edith Wharton died of a stroke in 1937 at the Domaine Le Pavillon Colombe, her 18th-century house on Rue de Montmorency in Saint-Brice-sous-Forêt.

Index of Contents
FIGHTING FRANCE – FROM DUNKERQUE TO BELPORT
THE LOOK OF PARIS - (AUGUST, 1914—FEBUARY, 1915)
I - AUGUST
II
III - FEBRUARY
IN ARGONNE
I
II
IN LORRAINE AND THE VOSGES
NANCY, May 13th, 1915
May 14th.
May 15th.
May 16th.
May 17th.
IN THE NORTH
June 19th, 1915.
June 20th.
June 21st.
June 22nd.
June 23rd LA PANNE.
June 24th.
IN ALSACE
August 13th, 1915.
August 14th.
August 15th.

August 16th.
August 17th.
August 18th.
THE TONE OF FRANCE

IN MOROCCO

PREFACE
I
II
NOTE

I - RABAT AND SALE

I - LEAVING TANGIER
II - THE TRAIL TO EL-KSAR
III - EL-KSAR TO RABAT
IV - THE KASBAH OF THE OUDAYAS
V - ROBINSON CRUSOE'S "SALLEE"
VI - CHELLA AND THE GREAT MOSQUE

II - VOLUBILIS, MOULAY IDRISS AND MEKNEZ

I - VOLUBILIS
II - MOULAY IDRISS
III - MEKNEZ

III - FEZ

I - THE FIRST VISION
II - FEZ ELDJID
III - FEZ ELBALI
IV - EL ANDALOUS AND THE POTTERS' FIELD
V - MEDERSAS, BAZAARS AND AN OASIS
VI - THE LAST GLIMPSE

IV - MARRAKECH

I - THE WAY THERE
II - THE BAHIA
III - THE BAZAARS
IV - THE AGDAL
V - ON THE ROOFS
VI - THE SAADIAN TOMBS

V - HAREMS AND CEREMONIES

I - THE CROWD IN THE STREET
II - AID-EL-KEBIR
III - THE IMPERIAL MIRADOR
IV - IN OLD RABAT
V - IN FEZ
VI - IN MARRAKECH

VI - GENERAL LYAUTEY'S WORK IN MOROCCO

I
II
III
THE WORK OF THE FRENCH PROTECTORATE, 1912-1918
PORTS
COMMERCE

COMPARATIVE TABLES
JUSTICE
EDUCATION
MEDICAL AID

VII - A SKETCH OF MOROCCAN HISTORY

I - THE BERBERS
II - PHENICIANS, ROMANS AND VANDALS
III - THE ARAB CONQUEST
IV - ALMORAVIDS AND ALMOHADS
V - THE MERINIDS
VI - THE SAADIANS
VII - THE HASSANIANS

VIII - NOTE ON MOROCCAN ARCHITECTURE

I
II
III
IV
IX
BOOKS CONSULTED
Edith Wharton – A Short Biography
Edith Wharton – A Concise Bibliography

FIGHTING FRANCE – FROM DUNKERQUE TO BELPORT

THE LOOK OF PARIS

(AUGUST, 1914—FEBUARY, 1915)

I

AUGUST

On the 30th of July, 1914, motoring north from Poitiers, we had lunched somewhere by the roadside under apple-trees on the edge of a field. Other fields stretched away on our right and left to a border of woodland and a village steeple. All around was noonday quiet, and the sober disciplined landscape which the traveller's memory is apt to evoke as distinctively French. Sometimes, even to accustomed eyes, these ruled-off fields and compact grey villages seem merely flat and tame; at other moments the sensitive imagination sees in every thrifty sod and even furrow the ceaseless vigilant attachment of generations faithful to the soil. The particular bit of landscape before us spoke in all its lines of that attachment. The air seemed full of the long murmur of human effort, the rhythm of oft-repeated tasks, the serenity of the scene smiled away the war rumours which had hung on us since morning.

All day the sky had been banked with thunder-clouds, but by the time we reached Chartres, toward four o'clock, they had rolled away under the horizon, and the town was so saturated with sunlight that to pass into the cathedral was like entering the dense obscurity of a church in Spain. At first all detail was imperceptible; we were in a hollow night. Then, as the shadows gradually thinned and gathered themselves up into pier and vault and ribbing, there burst out of them great sheets and showers of colour. Framed by such depths of darkness, and steeped in a blaze of mid-summer sun, the familiar windows seemed singularly remote and yet overpoweringly vivid. Now they widened into dark-shored pools splashed with sunset, now glittered and menaced like the shields of fighting angels. Some were cataracts of sapphires, others roses dropped from a saint's tunic, others great carven platters strewn with heavenly regalia, others the sails of galleons bound for the Purple Islands; and in the western wall the scattered fires of the rose-window hung like a constellation in an African night. When one dropped one's eyes form these ethereal harmonies, the dark masses of masonry below them, all veiled and muffled in a mist pricked by a few altar lights, seemed to symbolize the life on earth, with its shadows, its heavy distances and its little islands of illusion. All that a great cathedral can be, all the meanings it can express, all the tranquilizing power it can breathe upon the soul, all the richness of detail it can fuse into a large utterance of strength and beauty, the cathedral of Chartres gave us in that perfect hour.

It was sunset when we reached the gates of Paris. Under the heights of St. Cloud and Suresnes the reaches of the Seine trembled with the blue-pink lustre of an early Monet. The Bois lay about us in the stillness of a holiday evening, and the lawns of Bagatelle were as fresh as June. Below the Arc de Triomphe, the Champs Elysees sloped downward in a sun-powdered haze to the mist of fountains and the ethereal obelisk; and the currents of summer life ebbed and flowed with a normal beat under the trees of the radiating avenues. The great city, so made for peace and art and all humanest graces, seemed to lie by her river-side like a princess guarded by the watchful giant of the Eiffel Tower.

The next day the air was thundery with rumours. Nobody believed them, everybody repeated them. War? Of course there couldn't be war! The Cabinets, like naughty children, were again dangling their feet over the edge; but the whole incalculable weight of things-as-they-were, of the daily necessary business of living, continued calmly and convincingly to assert itself against the bandying of diplomatic words. Paris went on steadily about her mid-summer business of feeding, dressing, and amusing the great army of tourists who were the only invaders she had seen for nearly half a century.

All the while, everyone knew that other work was going on also. The whole fabric of the country's seemingly undisturbed routine was threaded with noiseless invisible currents of preparation, the sense of them was in the calm air as the sense of changing weather is in the balminess of a perfect afternoon. Paris counted the minutes till the evening papers came.

They said little or nothing except what everyone was already declaring all over the country. "We don't want war—mais it faut que cela finisse!" "This kind of thing has got to stop": that was the only phase one heard. If diplomacy could still arrest the war, so much the better: no one in France wanted it. All who spent the first days of August in Paris will testify to the agreement of feeling on that point. But if war had to come, the country, and every heart in it, was ready.

At the dressmaker's, the next morning, the tired fitters were preparing to leave for their usual holiday. They looked pale and anxious—decidedly, there was a new weight of apprehension in the air. And in the rue Royale, at the corner of the Place de la Concorde, a few people had stopped to look at a little strip of white paper against the wall of the Ministere de la Marine. "General mobilization" they read—and an armed nation knows what that means. But the group about the paper was small and quiet. Passers by read the notice and went on. There were no cheers, no gesticulations: the dramatic sense of the race had already told them that the event was too great to be dramatized. Like a monstrous landslide it had fallen across the path of an orderly laborious nation, disrupting its routine, annihilating its industries, rending families apart, and burying under a heap of senseless ruin the patiently and painfully wrought machinery of civilization...

That evening, in a restaurant of the rue Royale, we sat at a table in one of the open windows, abreast with the street, and saw the strange new crowds stream by. In an instant we were being shown what mobilization was—a huge break in the normal flow of traffic, like the sudden rupture of a dyke. The street was flooded by the torrent of people sweeping past us to the various railway stations. All were on foot, and carrying their luggage; for since dawn every cab and taxi and motor—omnibus had disappeared. The War Office had thrown out its drag-net and caught them all in. The crowd that passed our window was chiefly composed of conscripts, the mobilisables of the first day, who were on the way to the station accompanied by their families and friends; but among them were little clusters of bewildered tourists, labouring along with bags and bundles, and watching their luggage pushed before them on hand-carts—puzzled inarticulate waifs caught in the cross-tides racing to a maelstrom.

In the restaurant, the befrogged and red-coated band poured out patriotic music, and the intervals between the courses that so few waiters were left to serve were broken by the ever-recurring obligation to stand up for the Marseillaise, to stand up for God Save the King, to stand up for the Russian National Anthem, to stand up again for the Marseillaise. "Et dire que ce sont des Hongrois qui jouent tout cela!" a humourist remarked from the pavement.

As the evening wore on and the crowd about our window thickened, the loiterers outside began to join in the war-songs. "Allons, debout! "—and the loyal round begins again. "La chanson du depart" is a frequent demand; and the chorus of spectators chimes in roundly. A sort of quiet humour was the note of the street. Down the rue Royale, toward the Madeleine, the bands of other restaurants were attracting other throngs, and martial refrains were strung along the Boulevard like its garlands of arc-lights. It was a night of singing and acclamations, not boisterous, but gallant and determined. It was Paris badauderie at its best.

Meanwhile, beyond the fringe of idlers the steady stream of conscripts still poured along. Wives and families trudged beside them, carrying all kinds of odd improvised bags and bundles. The impression disengaging itself from all this superficial confusion was that of a cheerful steadiness of spirit. The faces ceaselessly streaming by were serious but not sad; nor was there any air of bewilderment—the stare of driven cattle. All these lads and young men seemed to know what they were about and why they were about it. The youngest of them looked suddenly grown up and responsible; they understood their stake in the job, and accepted it.

The next day the army of midsummer travel was immobilized to let the other army move. No more wild rushes to the station, no more bribing of concierges, vain quests for invisible cabs, haggard hours of waiting in the queue at Cook's. No train stirred except to carry soldiers, and the civilians who had not bribed and jammed their way into a cranny of the thronged carriages leaving the first night could only creep back through the hot streets to their hotel and wait. Back they went, disappointed yet half-relieved, to the resounding emptiness of porterless halls, waiterless restaurants, motionless lifts: to the queer disjointed life of fashionable hotels suddenly reduced to the intimacies and make-shift of a Latin Quarter pension. Meanwhile it was strange to watch the gradual paralysis of the city. As the motors, taxis, cabs and vans had vanished from the streets, so the lively little steamers had left the Seine. The canal-boats too were gone, or lay motionless: loading and unloading had ceased. Every great architectural opening framed an emptiness; all the endless avenues stretched away to desert distances. In the parks and gardens no one raked the paths or trimmed the borders. The fountains slept in their basins, the worried sparrows fluttered unfed, and vague dogs, shaken out of their daily habits, roamed unquietly, looking for familiar eyes.

Paris, so intensely conscious yet so strangely entranced, seemed to have had curare injected into all her veins.

The next day—the 2nd of August—from the terrace of the Hotel de Crillon one looked down on a first faint stir of returning life. Now and then a taxi-cab or a private motor crossed the Place de la Concorde, carrying soldiers to the stations. Other conscripts, in detachments, tramped by on foot with bags and banners. One detachment stopped before the black-veiled statue of Strasbourg and laid a garland at her feet. In ordinary times this demonstration would at once have attracted a crowd; but at the very moment when it might have been expected to provoke a patriotic outburst it excited no more attention than if one of the soldiers had turned aside to give a penny to a beggar. The people crossing the square did not even stop to look. The meaning of this apparent indifference was obvious. When an armed nation mobilizes, everybody is busy, and busy in a definite and pressing way. It is not only the fighters that mobilize: those who stay behind must do the same. For each French household, for each individual man or woman in France, war means a complete reorganization of life. The detachment of conscripts, unnoticed, paid their tribute to the Cause and passed on...

Looked back on from these sterner months those early days in Paris, in their setting of grave architecture and summer skies, wear the light of the ideal and the abstract. The sudden flaming up of national life, the abeyance of every small and mean preoccupation, cleared the moral air as the streets had been cleared, and made the spectator feel as though he were reading a great poem on War rather than facing its realities.

Something of this sense of exaltation seemed to penetrate the throngs who streamed up and down the Boulevards till late into the night. All wheeled traffic had ceased, except that of the rare taxi-cabs impressed to carry conscripts to the stations; and the middle of the Boulevards was as thronged with foot-passengers as an Italian market-place on a Sunday morning. The vast tide swayed up and down at a slow pace, breaking now and then to make room for one of the volunteer "legions" which were forming at every corner: Italian, Roumanian, South American, North American, each headed by its national flag and hailed with cheering as it passed. But even the cheers were sober: Paris was not to be shaken out of her self-imposed serenity. One felt something nobly conscious and voluntary in the mood of this quiet multitude. Yet it was a mixed throng, made up of every class, from the scum of the Exterior Boulevards to the cream of the fashionable restaurants. These people, only two days ago, had been leading a thousand different lives, in indifference or in antagonism to each other, as alien as enemies across a frontier: now workers and idlers, thieves, beggars, saints, poets, drabs and sharpers, genuine people and showy shams, were all bumping up against each other in an instinctive community of emotion. The "people," luckily, predominated; the faces of workers look best in such a crowd, and there were thousands of them, each illuminated and singled out by its magnesium-flash of passion.

I remember especially the steady-browed faces of the women; and also the small but significant fact that every one of them had remembered to bring her dog. The biggest of these amiable companions had to take their chance of seeing what they could through the forest of human legs; but every one that was portable was snugly lodged in the bend of an elbow, and from this safe perch scores and scores of small serious muzzles, blunt or sharp, smooth or woolly, brown or grey or white or black or brindled, looked out on the scene with the quiet awareness of the Paris dog. It was certainly a good sign that they had not been forgotten that night.

II

We had been shown, impressively, what it was to live through a mobilization; now we were to learn that mobilization is only one of the concomitants of martial law, and that martial law is not comfortable to live under—at least till one gets used to it.

At first its main purpose, to the neutral civilian, seemed certainly to be the wayward pleasure of complicating his life; and in that line it excelled in the last refinements of ingenuity. Instructions began to shower on us after the lull of the first days: instructions as to what to do, and what not to do, in order to make our presence tolerable and our persons secure. In the first place, foreigners could not remain in France without satisfying the authorities as to their nationality and antecedents; and to do this necessitated repeated ineffective visits to chanceries, consulates and police stations, each too densely thronged with flustered applicants to permit the entrance of one more. Between these vain pilgrimages, the traveller impatient to leave had to toil on foot to distant railway stations, from which he returned baffled by vague answers and disheartened by the declaration that tickets, when achievable, must also be vises by the police. There was a moment when it seemed that ones inmost thoughts had to have that unobtainable visa—to obtain which, more fruitless hours must be lived on grimy stairways between perspiring layers of fellow-aliens. Meanwhile one's money was probable running short, and one must cable or telegraph for more. Ah—but cables and telegrams must be vises too—and even when they were, one got no guarantee that they would be sent! Then one could not use code addresses, and the ridiculous number of words contained in a New York address seemed to multiply as the francs in one's pockets diminished. And when the cable was finally dispatched it was either lost on the way, or reached its destination only to call forth, after anxious days, the disheartening response: "Impossible at present. Making every effort." It is fair to add that, tedious and even irritating as many of these transactions were, they were greatly eased by the sudden uniform good-nature of the French functionary, who, for the first time, probably, in the long tradition of his line, broke through its fundamental rule and was kind.

Luckily, too, these incessant comings and goings involved much walking of the beautiful idle summer streets, which grew idler and more beautiful each day. Never had such blue-grey softness of afternoon brooded over Paris, such sunsets turned the heights of the Trocadero into Dido's Carthage, never, above all, so rich a moon ripened through such perfect evenings. The Seine itself had no small share in this mysterious increase of the city's beauty. Released from all traffic, its hurried ripples smoothed themselves into long silken reaches in which quays and monuments at last saw their unbroken images. At night the fire-fly lights of the boats had vanished, and the reflections of the street lamps were lengthened into streamers of red and gold and purple that slept on the calm current like fluted water-weeds. Then the moon rose and took possession of the city, purifying it of all accidents, calming and enlarging it and giving it back its ideal lines of strength and repose. There was something strangely moving in this new Paris of the August evenings, so exposed yet so serene, as though her very beauty shielded her.

So, gradually, we fell into the habit of living under martial law. After the first days of flustered adjustment the personal inconveniences were so few that one felt almost ashamed of their not being more, of not being called on to contribute some greater sacrifice of comfort to the Cause. Within the first week over two thirds of the shops had closed—the greater number bearing on their shuttered windows the notice "Pour cause de mobilisation," which showed that the "patron" and staff were at the front. But enough remained open to satisfy every ordinary want, and the closing of the others served to prove how much one could do without. Provisions were as cheap and plentiful as ever, though for a while it was easier to buy food than to have it cooked. The restaurants were closing rapidly, and one often had to wander a long way for a meal, and wait a longer time to get it. A few hotels still carried on a halting life, galvanized by an occasional inrush of travel from Belgium and Germany; but most of them had closed or were being hastily transformed into hospitals.

The signs over these hotel doors first disturbed the dreaming harmony of Paris. In a night, as it seemed, the whole city was hung with Red Crosses. Every other building showed the red and white band across its front, with "Ouvroir" or "Hopital" beneath; there was something sinister in these preparations for horrors in which one could not yet believe, in the making of bandages for limbs yet sound and whole, the spreading of pillows for heads yet carried high. But insist as they would on the woe to come, these warning signs did not deeply stir the trance of Paris. The first days of the war were full of a kind of unrealizing confidence, not boastful or fatuous, yet as different as possible from the clear-headed tenacity of purpose that the experience of the next few months was to develop. It is hard to evoke, without seeming to exaggerate it, that the mood of early August: the assurance, the balance, the kind of smiling fatalism with which Paris moved to her task. It is not impossible that the beauty of the season and the silence of the city may have helped to produce this mood. War, the shrieking fury, had announced herself by a great wave of stillness. Never was desert hush more complete: the silence of a street is always so much deeper than the silence of wood or field.

The heaviness of the August air intensified this impression of suspended life. The days were dumb enough; but at night the hush became acute. In the quarter I inhabit, always deserted in summer, the shuttered streets were mute as catacombs, and the faintest pin-prick of noise seemed to tear a rent in a black pall of silence. I could hear the tired tap of a lame hoof half a mile away, and the tread of the policeman guarding the Embassy across the street beat against the pavement like a series of detonations. Even the variegated noises of the city's waking-up had ceased. If any sweepers, scavengers or rag-pickers still plied their trades they did it as secretly as ghosts. I remember one morning being roused out of a deep sleep by a sudden explosion of noise in my room. I sat up with a start, and found I had been waked by a low-voiced exchange of "Bonjours" in the street...

Another fact that kept the reality of war from Paris was the curious absence of troops in the streets. After the first rush of conscripts hurrying to their military bases it might have been imagined that the reign of peace had set in. While smaller cities were swarming with soldiers no glitter of arms was reflected in the empty avenues of the capital, no military music sounded through them. Paris scorned all show of war, and fed the patriotism of her children on the mere sight of her beauty. It was enough.

Even when the news of the first ephemeral successes in Alsace began to come in, the Parisians did not swerve from their even gait. The newsboys did all the shouting—and even theirs was presently silenced by decree. It seemed as though it had been unanimously, instinctively decided that the Paris of 1914 should in no respect resemble the Paris of 1870, and as though this resolution had passed at birth into the blood of millions born since that fatal date, and ignorant of its bitter lesson. The unanimity of self-restraint was the notable characteristic of this people suddenly plunged into an unsought and unexpected war. At first their steadiness of spirit might have passed for the bewilderment of a generation born and bred in peace, which did not yet understand what war implied. But it is precisely on such a mood that easy triumphs might have been supposed to have the most disturbing effect. It was the crowd in the street that shouted "A Berlin!" in 1870; now the crowd in the street continued to mind its own business, in spite of showers of extras and too-sanguine bulletins.

I remember the morning when our butcher's boy brought the news that the first German flag had been hung out on the balcony of the Ministry of War. Now I thought, the Latin will boil over! And I wanted to be there to see. I hurried down the quiet rue de Martignac, turned the corner of the Place Sainte Clotilde, and came on an orderly crowd filling the street before the Ministry of War. The crowd was so orderly that the few pacific gestures of the police easily cleared a way for passing cabs, and for the military motors perpetually dashing up. It was composed of all classes, and there were many family groups, with little boys straddling their mothers' shoulders, or lifted up by the policemen when they were too heavy for their mothers. It is safe to say that there was hardly a man or woman of that crowd who had not a soldier at the front; and there before them hung the enemy's first flag—a splendid silk flag, white and black and crimson, and embroidered in gold. It was the flag of an Alsatian regiment—a regiment of Prussianized Alsace. It symbolized all they most abhorred in the whole abhorrent job that lay ahead of them; it symbolized also their finest ardour and their noblest hate, and the reason why, if every other reason failed, France could never lay down arms till the last of such flags was low. And there they stood and looked at it, not dully or uncomprehendingly, but consciously, advisedly, and in silence; as if already foreseeing all it would cost to keep that flag and add to it others like it; forseeing the cost and accepting it. There seemed to be men's hearts even in the children of that crowd, and in the mothers whose weak arms held them up. So they gazed and went on, and made way for others like them, who gazed in their turn and went on too. All day the crowd renewed itself, and it was always the same crowd, intent and understanding and silent, who looked steadily at the flag, and knew what its being there meant. That, in August, was the look of Paris.

III

FEBRUARY

February dusk on the Seine. The boats are plying again, but they stop at nightfall, and the river is inky-smooth, with the same long weed-like reflections as in August. Only the reflections are fewer and paler; bright lights are muffled everywhere. The line of the quays is scarcely discernible, and the heights of the Trocadero are lost in the blur of night, which presently effaces even the firm tower-tops of Notre-Dame. Down the damp pavements only a few street lamps throw their watery zigzags. The shops are shut, and the windows above them thickly curtained. The faces of the houses are all blind.

In the narrow streets of the Rive Gauche the darkness is even deeper, and the few scattered lights in courts or "cites" create effects of Piranesi-like mystery. The gleam of the chestnut-roaster's brazier at a street corner deepens the sense of an old adventurous Italy, and the darkness beyond seems full of cloaks and conspiracies. I turn, on my way home, into an empty street between high garden walls, with a single light showing far off at its farther end. Not a soul is in sight between me and that light: my steps echo endlessly in the silence. Presently a dim figure comes around the corner ahead of me. Man or woman? Impossible to tell till I overtake it. The February fog deepens the darkness, and the faces one passes are indistinguishable. As for the numbers of the houses, no one thinks of looking for them. If you know the quarter you count doors from the corner, or try to puzzle out the familiar outline of a balcony or a pediment; if you are in a strange street, you must ask at the nearest tobacconist's—for, as for finding a policeman, a yard off you couldn't tell him from your grandmother!

Such, after six months of war, are the nights of Paris; the days are less remarkable and less romantic.

Almost all the early flush and shiver of romance is gone; or so at least it seems to those who have watched the gradual revival of life. It may appear otherwise to observers from other countries, even from those involved in the war. After London, with all her theaters open, and her machinery of amusement almost unimpaired, Paris no doubt seems like a city on whom great issues weigh. But to those who lived through that first sunlit silent month the streets to-day show an almost normal activity. The vanishing of all the motorbuses, and of the huge lumbering commercial vans, leaves many a forgotten perspective open and reveals many a lost grace of architecture; but the taxi-cabs and private motors are almost as abundant as in peace-time, and the peril of pedestrianism is kept at its normal pitch by the incessant dashing to and fro of those unrivalled engines of destruction, the hospital and War Office motors. Many shops have reopened, a few theatres are tentatively producing patriotic drama or mixed programmes seasonal with sentiment and mirth, and the cinema again unrolls its eventful kilometres.

For a while, in September and October, the streets were made picturesque by the coming and going of English soldiery, and the aggressive flourish of British military motors. Then the fresh faces and smart uniforms disappeared, and now the nearest approach to "militarism" which Paris offers to the casual sight-seer is the occasional drilling of a handful of piou-pious on the muddy reaches of the Place des Invalides. But there is another army in Paris. Its first detachments came months ago, in the dark September days—lamentable rear-guard of the Allies' retreat on Paris. Since then its numbers have grown and grown, its dingy streams have percolated through all the currents of Paris life, so that wherever one goes, in every quarter and at every hour, among the busy confident strongly-stepping Parisians one sees these other people, dazed and slowly moving—men and women with sordid bundles on their backs, shuffling along hesitatingly in their tattered shoes, children dragging at their hands and tired-out babies pressed against their shoulders: the great army of the Refugees. Their faces are unmistakable and unforgettable. No one who has ever caught that stare of dumb bewilderment—or that other look of concentrated horror, full of the reflection of flames and ruins— can shake off the obsession of the Refugees. The look in their eyes is part of the look of Paris. It is the dark shadow on the brightness of the face she turns to the enemy. These poor people cannot look across the borders to eventual triumph. They belong mostly to a class whose knowledge of the world's affairs is measured by the shadow of their village steeple. They are no more curious of the laws of causation than the thousands overwhelmed at Avezzano. They were ploughing and sowing, spinning and weaving and minding their business, when suddenly a great darkness full of fire and blood came down on them. And now they are here, in a strange country, among unfamiliar faces and new ways, with nothing left to them in the world but the memory of burning homes and massacred children and young men dragged to slavery, of infants torn from their mothers, old men trampled by drunken heels and priests slain while they prayed beside the dying. These are the people who stand in hundreds every day outside the doors of the shelters improvised to rescue them, and who receive, in return for the loss of everything that makes life sweet, or intelligible, or at least endurable, a cot in a dormitory, a meal-ticket—and perhaps, on lucky days, a pair of shoes...

What are the Parisians doing meanwhile? For one thing—and the sign is a good one—they are refilling the shops, and especially, of course, the great "department stores." In the early war days there was no stranger sight than those deserted palaces, where one strayed between miles of unpurchased wares in quest of vanished salesmen. A few clerks, of course, were left: enough, one would have thought, for the rare purchasers who disturbed their meditations. But the few there were did not care to be disturbed: they lurked behind their walls of sheeting, their bastions of flannelette, as if ashamed to be discovered. And when one had coaxed them out they went through the necessary gestures automatically, as if mournfully wondering that any one should care to buy. I remember once, at the Louvre, seeing the whole force of a "department," including the salesman I was trying to cajole into showing me some medicated gauze, desert their posts simultaneously to gather about a motor-cyclist in a muddy uniform who had dropped in to see his pals with tales from the front. But after six months the pressure of normal appetites has begun to reassert itself—and to shop is one of the normal appetites of woman. I say "shop" instead of buy, to distinguish between the dull purchase of necessities and the voluptuousness of acquiring things one might do without. It is evident that many of the thousands now fighting their way into the great shops must be indulging in the latter delight. At a moment when real wants are reduced to a minimum, how else account for the congestion of the department store? Even allowing for the immense, the perpetual buying of supplies for hospitals and work-rooms, the incessant stoking-up of the innumerable centres of charitable production, there is no explanation of the crowding of the other departments except the fact that woman, however valiant, however tried, however suffering and however self-denying, must eventually, in the long run, and at whatever cost to her pocket and her ideals, begin to shop again. She has renounced the theatre, she denies herself the teo-rooms, she goes apologetically and furtively (and economically) to concerts—but the swinging doors of the department stores suck her irresistibly into their quicksand of remnants and reductions.

No one, in this respect, would wish the look of Paris to be changed. It is a good sign to see the crowds pouring into the shops again, even though the sight is less interesting than that of the other crowds streaming daily—and on Sunday in immensely augmented numbers—across the Pont Alexandre III to the great court of the Invalides where the German trophies are displayed. Here the heart of France beats with a richer blood, and something of its glow passes into foreign veins as one watches the perpetually renewed throngs face to face with the long triple row of German guns. There are few in those throngs to whom one of the deadly pack has not dealt a blow; there are personal losses, lacerating memories, bound up with the sight of all those evil engines. But personal sorrow is the sentiment least visible in the look of Paris. It is not fanciful to say that the Parisian face, after six months of trial, has acquired a new character. The change seems to have affected the very stuff it is moulded of, as though the long ordeal had hardened the poor human clay into some dense commemorative substance. I often pass in the street women whose faces look like memorial medals—idealized images of what they were in the flesh. And the masks of some of the men—those queer tormented Gallic masks, crushed-in and squat and a little satyr-like—look like the bronzes of the Naples Museum, burnt and twisted from their baptism of fire. But none of these faces reveals a personal preoccupation: they are looking, one and all, at France erect on her borders. Even the women who are comparing different widths of Valenciennes at the lace-counter all have something of that vision in their eyes—or else one does not see the ones who haven't.

It is still true of Paris that she has not the air of a capital in arms. There are as few troops to be seen as ever, and but for the coming and going of the orderlies attached to the War Office and the Military Government, and the sprinkling of uniforms about the doors of barracks, there would be no sign of war in the streets—no sign, that is, except the presence of the wounded. It is only lately that they have begun to appear, for in the early months of the war they were not sent to Paris, and the splendidly appointed hospitals of the capital stood almost empty, while others, all over the country, were overcrowded. The motives for the disposal of the wounded have been much speculated upon and variously explained: one of its results may have been the maintaining in Paris of the extraordinary moral health which has given its tone to the whole country, and which is now sound and strong enough to face the sight of any misery.

And miseries enough it has to face. Day by day the limping figures grow more numerous on the pavement, the pale bandaged heads more frequent in passing carriages. In the stalls at the theatres and concerts there are many uniforms; and their wearers usually have to wait till the hall is emptied before they hobble out on a supporting arm. Most of them are very young, and it is the expression of their faces which I should like to picture and interpret as being the very essence of what I have called the look of Paris. They are grave, these young faces: one hears a great deal of the gaiety in the trenches, but the wounded are not gay. Neither are they sad, however. They are calm, meditative, strangely purified and matured. It is as though their great experience had purged them of pettiness, meanness and frivolity, burning them down to the bare bones of character, the fundamental substance of the soul, and shaping that substance into something so strong and finely tempered that for a long time to come Paris will not care to wear any look unworthy of the look on their faces.

I

The permission to visit a few ambulances and evacuation hospitals behind the lines gave me, at the end of February, my first sight of War.

Paris is no longer included in the military zone, either in fact or in appearance. Though it is still manifestly under the war-cloud, its air of reviving activity produces the illusion that the menace which casts that cloud is far off not only in distance but in time. Paris, a few months ago so alive to the nearness of the enemy, seems to have grown completely oblivious of that nearness; and it is startling, not more than twenty miles from the gates, to pass from such an atmosphere of workaday security to the imminent sense of war.

Going eastward, one begins to feel the change just beyond Meaux. Between that quiet episcopal city and the hill-town of Montmirail, some forty miles farther east, there are no sensational evidences of the great conflict of September—only, here and there, in an unploughed field, or among the fresh brown furrows, a little mound with a wooden cross and a wreath on it. Nevertheless, one begins to perceive, by certain negative signs, that one is already in another world. On the cold February day when we turned out of Meaux and took the road to the Argonne, the change was chiefly shown by the curious absence of life in the villages through which we passed. Now and then a lonely ploughman and his team stood out against the sky, or a child and an old woman looked from a doorway; but many of the fields were fallow and most of the doorways empty. We passed a few carts driven by peasants, a stray wood-cutter in a copse, a road-mender hammering at his stones; but already the "civilian motor" had disappeared, and all the dust-coloured cars dashing past us were marked with the Red Cross or the number of an army division. At every bridge and railway-crossing a sentinel, standing in the middle of the road with lifted rifle, stopped the motor and examined our papers. In this negative sphere there was hardly any other tangible proof of military rule; but with the descent of the first hill beyond Montmirail there came the positive feeling: This is war!

Along the white road rippling away eastward over the dimpled country the army motors were pouring by in endless lines, broken now and then by the dark mass of a tramping regiment or the clatter of a train of artillery. In the intervals between these waves of military traffic we had the road to ourselves, except for the flashing past of despatch-bearers on motor-cycles and of hideously hooting little motors carrying goggled officers in goat-skins and woollen helmets.

The villages along the road all seemed empty—not figuratively but literally empty. None of them has suffered from the German invasion, save by the destruction, here and there, of a single house on which some random malice has wreaked itself; but since the general flight in September all have remained abandoned, or are provisionally occupied by troops, and the rich country between Montmirail and Chalons is a desert.

The first sight of Chame is extraordinarily exhilarating. The old town lying so pleasantly between canal and river is the Head-quarters of an army—not of a corps or of a division, but of a whole army—and the network of grey provincial streets about the Romanesque towers of Notre Dame rustles with the movement of war. The square before the principal hotel—the incomparably named

"Haute Mere-Dieu"—is as vivid a sight as any scene of modern war can be. Rows of grey motor-lorries and omnibuses do not lend themselves to as happy groupings as a detachment of cavalry, and spitting and spurting motor-cycles and "torpedo" racers are no substitute for the glitter of helmets and the curvetting of chargers; but once the eye has adapted itself to the ugly lines and the neutral tints of the new warfare, the scene in that crowded clattering square becomes positively brilliant. It is a vision of one of the central functions of a great war, in all its concentrated energy, without the saddening suggestions of what, on the distant periphery, that energy is daily and hourly resulting in. Yet even here such suggestions are never long out of sight; for one cannot pass through Chalons without meeting, on their way from the station, a long line of "eclopes"—the unwounded but battered, shattered, frost-bitten, deafened and half-paralyzed wreckage of the awful struggle. These poor wretches, in their thousands, are daily shipped back from the front to rest and be restored; and it is a grim sight to watch them limping by, and to meet the dazed stare of eyes that have seen what one dare not picture.

If one could think away the "'eclopes" in the streets and the wounded in their hospitals, Chalons would be an invigorating spectacle. When we drove up to the hotel even the grey motors and the sober uniforms seemed to sparkle under the cold sky. The continual coming and going of alert and busy messengers, the riding up of officers (for some still ride!), the arrival of much-decorated military personages in luxurious motors, the hurrying to and fro of orderlies, the perpetual depleting and refilling of the long rows of grey vans across the square, the movements of Red Cross ambulances and the passing of detachments for the front, all these are sights that the pacific stranger could forever gape at. And in the hotel, what a clatter of swords, what a piling up of fur coats and haversacks, what a grouping of bronzed energetic heads about the packed tables in the restaurant! It is not easy for civilians to get to Chalons, and almost every table is occupied by officers and soldiers—for, once off duty, there seems to be no rank distinction in this happy democratic army, and the simple private, if he chooses to treat himself to the excellent fare of the Haute Mere-Dieu, has as good a right to it as his colonel.

The scene in the restaurant is inexhaustibly interesting. The mere attempt to puzzle out the different uniforms is absorbing. A week's experience near the front convinces me that no two uniforms in the French army are alike either in colour or in cut. Within the last two years the question of colour has greatly preoccupied the French military authorities, who have been seeking an invisible blue; and the range of their experiments is proved by the extraordinary variety of shades of blue, ranging from a sort of greyish robin's-egg to the darkest navy, in which the army is clothed. The result attained is the conviction that no blue is really inconspicuous, and that some of the harsh new slaty tints are no less striking than the deeper shades they have superseded. But to this scale of experimental blues, other colours must be added: the poppy-red of the Spahis' tunics, and various other less familiar colours—grey, and a certain greenish khaki—the use of which is due to the fact that the cloth supply has given out and that all available materials are employed. As for the differences in cut, the uniforms vary from the old tight tunic to the loose belted jacket copied from the English, and the emblems of the various arms and ranks embroidered on these diversified habits add a new element of perplexity. The aviator's wings, the motorist's wheel, and many of the newer symbols, are easily recognizable—but there are all the other arms, and the doctors and the stretcher-bearers, the sappers and miners, and heaven knows how many more ramifications of this great host which is really all the nation.

The main interest of the scene, however, is that it shows almost as many types as uniforms, and that almost all the types are so good. One begins to understand (if one has failed to before) why the French say of themselves: "La France est une nation guerriere." War is the greatest of paradoxes: the most senseless and disheartening of human retrogressions, and yet the stimulant of qualities of soul which, in every race, can seemingly find no other means of renewal. Everything depends, therefore, on the category of impulses that war excites in a people. Looking at the faces at Chalons, one sees at once in which [Page 54] sense the French are "une nation guerriere." It is not too much to say that war has given beauty to faces that were interesting, humorous, acute, malicious, a hundred vivid and expressive things, but last and least of all beautiful. Almost all the faces about these crowded tables—young or old, plain or handsome, distinguished or average—have the same look of quiet authority: it is as though all "nervosity," fussiness, little personal oddities, meannesses and vulgarities, had been burnt away in a great flame of self-dedication. It is a wonderful example of the rapidity with which purpose models the human countenance. More than half of these men were probably doing dull or useless or unimportant things till the first of last August; now each one of them, however small his job, is sharing in a great task, and knows it, and has been made over by knowing it.

Our road on leaving Chalons continued to run northeastward toward the hills of the Argonne.

We passed through more deserted villages, with soldiers lounging in the doors where old women should have sat with their distaffs, soldiers watering their horses in the village pond, soldiers cooking over gypsy fires in the farm-yards. In the patches of woodland along the road we came upon more soldiers, cutting down pine saplings, chopping them into even lengths and loading them on hand-carts, with the green boughs piled on top. We soon saw to what use they were put, for at every cross-road or railway bridge a warm sentry-box of mud and straw and plaited pine-branches was plastered against a bank or tucked like a swallow's nest into a sheltered corner. A little farther on we began to come more and more frequently on big colonies of "Seventy-fives." Drawn up nose to nose, usually against a curtain of woodland, in a field at some distance from the road, and always attended by a cumbrous drove of motor-vans, they looked like giant gazelles feeding among elephants; and the stables of woven pine-boughs which stood near by might have been the huge huts of their herdsmen.

The country between Marne and Meuse is one of the regions on which German fury spent itself most bestially during the abominable September days. Half way between Chalons and Sainte Menehould we came on the first evidence of the invasion: the lamentable ruins of the village of Auve. These pleasant villages of the Aisne, with their one long street, their half-timbered houses and high-roofed granaries with espaliered gable-ends, are all much of one pattern, and one can easily picture what Auve must have been as it looked out, in the blue September weather, above the ripening pears of its gardens to the crops in the valley and the large landscape beyond. Now it is a mere waste of rubble [Page 58] and cinders, not one threshold distinguishable from another. We saw many other ruined villages after Auve, but this was the first, and perhaps for that reason one had there, most hauntingly, the vision of all the separate terrors, anguishes, uprootings and rendings apart involved in the destruction of the obscurest of human communities. The photographs on the walls, the twigs of withered box above the crucifixes, the old wedding-dresses in brass-clamped trunks, the bundles of letters laboriously written and as painfully deciphered, all the thousand and one bits of the past that give meaning and continuity to the present—of all that accumulated warmth nothing was left but a brick-heap and some twisted stove-pipes!

As we ran on toward Sainte Menehould the names on our map showed us that, just beyond the parallel range of hills six or seven miles to the north, the two armies lay interlocked. But we heard no cannon yet, and the first visible evidence of the nearness of the struggle was the encounter, at a bend of the road, of a long line of grey-coated figures tramping toward us between the bayonets of their captors. They were a sturdy lot, this fresh "bag" from the hills, of a fine fighting age, and much less famished and war-worn than one could have wished. Their broad blond faces were meaningless, guarded, but neither defiant nor unhappy: they seemed none too sorry for their fate.

Our pass from the General Head-quarters carried us to Sainte Menehould on the edge of the Argonne, where we had to apply to the Head-quarters of the division for a farther extension. The Staff are lodged in a house considerably the worse for German occupancy, where offices have been improvised by means of wooden hoardings, and where, sitting in a bare passage on a frayed damask sofa surmounted by theatrical posters and faced by a bed with a plum-coloured counterpane, we listened for a while to the jingle of telephones, the rat-tat of typewriters, the steady hum of dictation and the coming and going of hurried despatch-bearers and orderlies. The extension to the permit was presently delivered with the courteous request that we should push on to Verdun as fast as possible, as civilian motors were not wanted on the road that afternoon; and this request, coupled with the evident stir of activity at Head-quarters, gave us the impression that there must be a good deal happening beyond the low line of hills to the north. How much there was we were soon to know.

We left Sainte Menehould at about eleven, and before twelve o'clock we were nearing a large village on a ridge from which the land swept away to right and left in ample reaches. The first glimpse of the outlying houses showed nothing unusual; but presently the main street turned and dipped downward, and below and beyond us lay a long stretch of ruins: the calcined remains of Clermont-en-Argonne, destroyed by the Germans on the 4th of September. The free and lofty situation of the little town—for it was really a good deal more than a village—makes its present state the more lamentable. One can see it from so far off, and through the torn traceries of its ruined church the eye travels over so lovely a stretch of country! No doubt its beauty enriched the joy of wrecking it.

At the farther end of what was once the main street another small knot of houses has survived. Chief among them is the Hospice for old men, where Sister Gabrielle Rosnet, when the authorities of Clermont took to their heels, stayed behind to defend her charges, and where, ever since, she has nursed an undiminishing stream of wounded from the eastern front. We found Soeur Rosnet, with her Sisters, preparing the midday meal of her patients in the little kitchen of the Hospice: the kitchen which is also her dining-room and private office. She insisted on our finding time to share the filet and fried potatoes that were just being taken off the stove, and while we lunched she told us the story of the invasion—of the Hospice doors broken down "a coups de crosse" and the grey officers bursting in with revolvers, and finding her there before them, in the big vaulted vestibule, "alone with my old men and my Sisters." Soeur Gabrielle Rosnet is a small round active woman, with a shrewd and ruddy face of the type that looks out calmly from the dark background of certain Flemish pictures. Her blue eyes are full of warmth and humour, and she puts as much gaiety as wrath into her tale. She does not spare epithets in talking of "ces satanes Allemands"—these Sisters and nurses of the front have seen sights to dry up the last drop of sentimental pity—but through all the horror of those fierce September days, with Clermont blazing about her and the helpless remnant of its inhabitants under the perpetual threat of massacre, she retained her sense of the little inevitable absurdities of life, such as her not knowing how to address the officer in command "because he was so tall that I couldn't see up to his shoulder-straps."—"Et ils etaient tous comme ca," she added, a sort of reluctant admiration in her eyes.

A subordinate "good Sister" had just cleared the table and poured out our coffee when a woman came in to say, in a matter-of-fact tone, that there was hard fighting going on across the valley. She added calmly, as she dipped our plates into a tub, that an obus had just fallen a mile or two off, and that if we liked we could see the fighting from a garden over the way. It did not take us long to reach that garden! Soeur Gabrielle showed the way, bouncing up the stairs of a house across the street, and flying at her heels we came out on a grassy terrace full of soldiers.

The cannon were booming without a pause, and seemingly so near that it was bewildering to look out across empty fields at a hillside that seemed like any other. But luckily somebody had a field-glass, and with its help a little corner of the battle of Vauquois was suddenly brought close to us—the rush of French infantry up the slopes, the feathery drift of French gun-smoke lower down, and, high up, on the wooded crest along the sky, the red lightnings and white puffs of the German artillery. Rap, rap, rap, went the answering guns, as the troops swept up and disappeared into the fire-tongued wood; and we stood there dumbfounded at the accident of having stumbled on this visible episode of the great subterranean struggle.

Though Soeur Rosnet had seen too many such sights to be much moved, she was full of a lively curiosity, and stood beside us, squarely planted in the mud, holding the field-glass to her eyes, or passing it laughingly about among the soldiers. But as we turned to go she said: "They've sent us word to be ready for another four hundred to-night"; and the twinkle died out of her good eyes.

Her expectations were to be dreadfully surpassed; for, as we learned a fortnight later from a three column communique, the scene we had assisted at was no less than the first act of the successful assault on the high-perched village of Vauquois, a point of the first importance to the Germans, since it masked their operations to the north of Varennes and commanded the railway by which, since September, they have been revictualling and reinforcing their army in the Argonne. Vauquois had been taken by them at the end of September and, thanks to its strong position on a rocky spur, had been almost impregnably fortified; but the attack we looked on at from the garden of Clermont, on Sunday, February 28th, carried the victorious French troops to the top of the ridge, and made them masters of a part of the village. Driven from it again that night, they were to retake it after a five days' struggle of exceptional violence and prodigal heroism, and are now securely established there in a position described as "of vital importance to the operations." "But what it cost!" Soeur Gabrielle said, when we saw her again a few days later.

II

The time had come to remember our promise and hurry away from Clermont; but a few miles farther our attention was arrested by the sight of the Red Cross over a village house. The house was little more than a hovel, the village—Blercourt it was called—a mere hamlet of scattered cottages and cow-stables: a place so easily overlooked that it seemed likely our supplies might be needed there.

An orderly went to find the medecin-chef, and we waded after him through the mud to one after another of the cottages in which, with admirable ingenuity, he had managed to create out of next to nothing the indispensable requirements of a second-line ambulance: sterilizing and disinfecting appliances, a bandage-room, a pharmacy, a well-filled wood-shed, and a clean kitchen in which "tisanes" were brewing over a cheerful fire. A detachment of cavalry was quartered in the village, which the trampling of hoofs had turned into a great morass, and as we picked our way from cottage to cottage in the doctor's wake he told us of the expedients to which he had been put to secure even the few hovels into which his patients were crowded. It was a complaint we were often to hear repeated along this line of the front, where troops and wounded are packed in thousands into villages meant to house four or five hundred; and we admired the skill and devotion with which he had dealt with the difficulty, and managed to lodge his patients decently.

We came back to the high-road, and he asked us if we should like to see the church. It was about three o'clock, and in the low porch the cure was ringing the bell for vespers. We pushed open the inner doors and went in. The church was without aisles, and down the nave stood four rows of wooden cots with brown blankets. In almost every one lay a soldier—the doctor's "worst cases"—few of them wounded, the greater number stricken with fever, bronchitis, frost-bite, pleurisy, or some other form of trench-sickness too severe to permit of their being carried farther from the front. One or two heads turned on the pillows as we entered, but for the most part the men did not move.

The cure, meanwhile, passing around to the sacristy, had come out before the altar in his vestments, followed by a little white acolyte. A handful of women, probably the only "civil" inhabitants left, and some of the soldiers we had seen about the village, had entered the church and stood together between the rows of cots; and the service began. It was a sunless afternoon, and the picture was all in monastic shades of black and white and ashen grey: the sick under their earth-coloured blankets, their livid faces against the pillows, the black dresses of the women (they seemed all to be in mourning) and the silver haze floating out from the little acolyte's censer. The only light in the scene—the candle-gleams on the altar, and their reflection in the embroideries of the cure's chasuble—were like a faint streak of sunset on the winter dusk. For a while the long Latin cadences sounded on through the church; but presently the cure took up in French the Canticle of the Sacred Heart, composed during the war of 1870, and the little congregation joined their trembling voices in the refrain:

"Sauvez, sauvez la France, Ne l'abandonnez pas!"

The reiterated appeal rose in a sob above the rows of bodies in the nave: "Sauvez, sauvez la France," the women wailed it near the altar, the soldiers took it up from the door in stronger tones; but the bodies in the cots never stirred, and more and more, as the day faded, the church looked like a quiet grave-yard in a battle-field.

After we had left Sainte Menehould the sense of the nearness and all-pervadingness of the war became even more vivid. Every road branching away to our left was a finger touching a red wound: Varennes, le Four de Paris, le Bois de la Grurie, were not more than eight or ten miles to the north. Along our own road the stream of motor-vans and the trains of ammunition grew longer and more frequent. Once we passed a long line of "Seventy-fives" going single file up a hillside, farther on we watched a big detachment of artillery galloping across a stretch of open country. The movement of supplies was continuous, and every village through which we passed swarmed with soldiers busy loading or unloading the big vans, or clustered about the commissariat motors while hams and quarters of beef were handed out. As we approached Verdun the cannonade had grown louder again; and when we reached the walls of the town and passed under the iron teeth of the portcullis we felt ourselves in one of the last outposts of a mighty line of defense. The desolation of Verdun is as impressive as the feverish activity of Chalons. The civil population was evacuated in September, and only a small percentage have returned. Nine-tenths of the shops are closed, and as the troops are nearly all in the trenches there is hardly any movement in the streets.

The first duty of the traveller who has successfully passed the challenge of the sentinel at the gates is to climb the steep hill to the citadel at the top of the town. Here the military authorities inspect one's papers, and deliver a "permis de sejour" which must be verified by the police before lodgings can be obtained. We found the principal hotel much less crowded than the Haute Mere-Dieu at Chalons, though many of the officers of the garrison mess there. The whole atmosphere of the place was different: silent, concentrated, passive. To the chance observer, Verdun appears to live only in its hospitals; and of these there are fourteen within the walls alone. As darkness fell, the streets became completely deserted, and the cannonade seemed to grow nearer and more incessant. That first night the hush was so intense that every reverberation from the dark hills beyond the walls brought out in the mind its separate vision of destruction; and then, just as the strained imagination could bear no more, the thunder ceased. A moment later, in a court below my windows, a pigeon began to coo; and all night long the two sounds strangely alternated...

On entering the gates, the first sight to attract us had been a colony of roughly-built bungalows scattered over the miry slopes of a little park adjoining the railway station, and surmounted by the sign: "Evacuation Hospital No. 6." The next morning we went to visit it. A part of the station buildings has been adapted to hospital use, and among them a great roofless hall, which the surgeon in charge has covered in with canvas and divided down its length into a double row of tents. Each tent contains two wooden cots, scrupulously clean and raised high above the floor; and the immense ward is warmed by a row of stoves down the central passage. In the bungalows across the road are beds for the patients who are to be kept for a time before being transferred to the hospitals in the town. In one bungalow an operating-room has been installed, in another are the bathing arrangements for the newcomers from the trenches. Every possible device for the relief of the wounded has been carefully thought out and intelligently applied by the surgeon in charge and the infirmiere major who indefatigably seconds him. Evacuation Hospital No. 6 sprang up in an hour, almost, on the dreadful August day when four thousand wounded lay on stretchers between the railway station and the gate of the little park across the way; and it has gradually grown into the model of what such a hospital may become in skilful and devoted hands.

Verdun has other excellent hospitals for the care of the severely wounded who cannot be sent farther from the front. Among them St. Nicolas, in a big airy building on the Meuse, is an example of a great French Military Hospital at its best; but I visited few others, for the main object of my journey was to get to some of the second-line ambulances beyond the town. The first we went to was in a small village to the north of Verdun, not far from the enemy's lines at Cosenvoye, and was fairly representative of all the others. The dreary muddy village was crammed with troops, and the ambulance had been installed at haphazard in such houses as the military authorities could spare. The arrangements were primitive but clean, and even the dentist had set up his apparatus in one of the rooms. The men lay on mattresses or in wooden cots, and the rooms were heated by stoves. The great need, here as everywhere, was for blankets and clean underclothing; for the wounded are brought in from the front encrusted with frozen mud, and usually without having washed or changed for weeks. There are no women nurses in these second-line ambulances, but all the army doctors we saw seemed intelligent, and anxious to do the best they could for their men in conditions of unusual hardship. The principal obstacle in their way is the over-crowded state of the villages. Thousands of soldiers are camped in all of them, in hygienic conditions that would be bad enough for men in health; and there is also a great need for light diet, since the hospital commissariat of the front apparently supplies no invalid foods, and men burning with fever have to be fed on meat and vegetables.

In the afternoon we started out again in a snow-storm, over a desolate rolling country to the south of Verdun. The wind blew fiercely across the whitened slopes, and no one was in sight but the sentries marching up and down the railway lines, and an occasional cavalryman patrolling the lonely road. Nothing can exceed the mournfulness of this depopulated land: we might have been wandering over the wilds of Poland. We ran some twenty miles down the steel-grey Meuse to a village about four miles west of Les Eparges, the spot where, for weeks past, a desperate struggle had been going on. There must have been a lull in the fighting that day, for the cannon had ceased; but the scene at the point where we left the motor gave us the sense of being on the very edge of the conflict. The long straggling village lay on the river, and the trampling of cavalry and the hauling of guns had turned the land about it into a mud-flat. Before the primitive cottage where the doctor's office had been installed were the motors of the surgeon and the medical inspector who had accompanied us. Near by stood the usual flock of grey motor-vans, and all about was the coming and going of cavalry remounts, the riding up of officers, the unloading of supplies, the incessant activity of mud-splashed sergeants and men.

The main ambulance was in a grange, of which the two stories had been partitioned off into wards. Under the cobwebby rafters the men lay in rows on clean pallets, and big stoves made the rooms dry and warm. But the great superiority of this ambulance was its nearness to a canalboat which had been fitted up with hot douches. The boat was spotlessly clean, and each cabin was shut off by a gay curtain of red-flowered chintz. Those curtains must do almost as much as the hot water to make over the morale of the men: they were the most comforting sight of the day.

Farther north, and on the other bank of the Meuse, lies another large village which has been turned into a colony of eclopes. Fifteen hundred sick or exhausted men are housed there—and there are no hot douches or chintz curtains to cheer them! We were taken first to the church, a large featureless building at the head of the street. In the doorway our passage was obstructed by a mountain of damp straw which a gang of hostler-soldiers were pitch-forking out of the aisles. The interior of the church was dim and suffocating. Between the pillars hung screens of plaited straw, forming little enclosures in each of which about a dozen sick men lay on more straw, without mattresses or blankets. No beds, no tables, no chairs, no washing appliances—in their muddy clothes, as they come from the front, they are bedded down on the stone floor like cattle till they are well enough to go back to their job. It was a pitiful contrast to the little church at Blercourt, with the altar lights twinkling above the clean beds; and one wondered if even so near the front, it had to be. "The African village, we call it," one of our companions said with a laugh: but the African village has blue sky over it, and a clear stream runs between its mud huts.

We had been told at Sainte Menehould that, for military reasons, we must follow a more southerly direction on our return to Chalons; and when we left Verdun we took the road to Bar-le-Duc. It runs southwest over beautiful broken country, untouched by war except for the fact that its villages, like all the others in this region, are either deserted or occupied by troops. As we left Verdun behind us the sound of the cannon grew fainter and died out, and we had the feeling that we were gradually passing beyond the flaming boundaries into a more normal world; but suddenly, at a cross-road, a sign-post snatched us back to war: St. Mihiel, 18 Kilometres. St. Mihiel, the danger-spot of the region, the weak joint in the armour! There it lay, up that harmless-looking bye-road, not much more than ten miles away—a ten minutes' dash would have brought us into the thick of the grey coats and spiked helmets! The shadow of that sign-post followed us for miles, darkening the landscape like the shadow from a racing storm-cloud.

Bar-le-Duc seemed unaware of the cloud. The charming old town was in its normal state of provincial apathy: few soldiers were about, and here at last civilian life again predominated. After a few days on the edge of the war, in that intermediate region under its solemn spell, there is something strangely lowering to the mood in the first sight of a busy unconscious community. One looks instinctively, in the eyes of the passers by, for a reflection of that other vision, and feels diminished by contact with people going so indifferently about their business.

A little way beyond Bar-le-Duc we came on another phase of the war-vision, for our route lay exactly in the track of the August invasion, and between Bar-le-Duc and Vitry-le-Francois the high-road is lined with ruined towns. The first we came to was Laimont, a large village wiped out as if a cyclone had beheaded it; then comes Revigny, a town of over two thousand inhabitants, less completely levelled because its houses were more solidly built, but a spectacle of more tragic desolation, with its wide streets winding between scorched and contorted fragments of masonry, bits of shop-fronts, handsome doorways, the colonnaded court of a public building. A few miles farther lies the most piteous of the group: the village of Heiltz-le-Maurupt, once pleasantly set in gardens and orchards, now an ugly waste like the others, and with a little church so stripped and wounded and dishonoured that it lies there by the roadside like a human victim.

In this part of the country, which is one of many cross-roads, we began to have unexpected difficulty in finding our way, for the names and distances on the milestones have all been effaced, the sign-posts thrown down and the enamelled plaques on the houses at the entrance to the villages removed. One report has it that this precaution was taken by the inhabitants at the approach of the invading army, another that the Germans themselves demolished the sign-posts and plastered over the mile-stones in order to paint on them misleading and encouraging distances. The result is extremely bewildering, for, all the villages being either in ruins or uninhabited, there is no one to question but the soldiers one meets, and their answer is almost invariably "We don't know—we don't belong here." One is in luck if one comes across a sentinel who knows the name of the village he is guarding.

It was the strangest of sensations to find ourselves in a chartless wilderness within sixty or seventy miles of Paris, and to wander, as we did, for hours across a high heathery waste, with wide blue distances to north and south, and in all the scene not a landmark by means of which we could make a guess at our whereabouts. One of our haphazard turns at last brought us into a muddy bye-road with long lines of "Seventy-fives" ranged along its banks like grey ant-eaters in some monstrous menagerie. A little farther on we came to a bemired village swarming with artillery and cavalry, and found ourselves in the thick of an encampment just on the move. It seems improbable that we were meant to be there, for our arrival caused such surprise that no sentry remembered to challenge us, and obsequiously saluting sous-officiers instantly cleared a way for the motor. So, by a happy accident, we caught one more war-picture, all of vehement movement, as we passed out of the zone of war.

We were still very distinctly in it on returning to Chalons, which, if it had seemed packed on our previous visit, was now quivering and cracking with fresh crowds. The stir about the fountain, in the square before the Haute Mere-Dieu, was more melodramatic than ever. Every one was in a hurry, every one booted and mudsplashed, and spurred or sworded or despatch-bagged, or somehow labelled as a member of the huge military beehive. The privilege of telephoning and telegraphing being denied to civilians in the war-zone, it was ominous to arrive at night-fall on such a crowded scene, and we were not surprised to be told that there was not a room left at the Haute Mere-Dieu, and that even the sofas in the reading-room had been let for the night. At every other inn in the town we met with the same answer; and finally we decided to ask permission to go on as far as Epernay, about twelve miles off. At Head-quarters we were told that our request could not be granted. No motors are allowed to circulate after night-fall in the zone of war, and the officer charged with the distribution of motor-permits pointed out that, even if an exception were made in our favour, we should probably be turned back by the first sentinel we met, only to find ourselves unable to re-enter Chalons without another permit! This alternative was so alarming that we began to think ourselves relatively lucky to be on the right side of the gates; and we went back to the Haute Mere-Dieu to squeeze into a crowded corner of the restaurant for dinner. The hope that some one might have suddenly left the hotel in the interval was not realized; but after dinner we learned from the landlady that she had certain rooms permanently reserved for the use of the Staff, and that, as these rooms had not yet been called for that evening, we might possibly be allowed to occupy them for the night.

At Chalons the Head-quarters are in the Prefecture, a coldly handsome building of the eighteenth century, and there, in a majestic stone vestibule, beneath the gilded ramp of a great festal staircase, we waited in anxious suspense, among the orderlies and estafettes, while our unusual request was considered. The result of the deliberation, was an expression of regret: nothing could be done for us, as officers might at any moment arrive from the General Head-quarters and require the rooms. It was then past nine o'clock, and bitterly cold—and we began to wonder. Finally the polite officer who had been charged to dismiss us, moved to compassion at our plight, offered to give us a laissez-passer back to Paris. But Paris was about a hundred and twenty-five miles off, the night was dark, the cold was piercing—and at every cross-road and railway crossing a sentinel would have to be convinced of our right to go farther. We remembered the warning given us earlier in the evening, and, declining the offer, went out again into the cold. And just then chance took pity on us. In the restaurant we had run across a friend attached to the Staff, and now, meeting him again in the depth of our difficulty, we were told of lodgings to be found near by. He could not take us there, for it was past the hour when he had a right to be out, or we either, for that matter, since curfew sounds at nine at Chalons. But he told us how to find our way through the maze of little unlit streets about the Cathedral; standing there beside the motor, in the icy darkness of the deserted square, and whispering hastily, as he turned to leave us: "You ought not to be out so late; but the word tonight is Jena. When you give it to the chauffeur, be sure no sentinel overhears you." With that he was up the wide steps, the glass doors had closed on him, and I stood there in the pitch-black night, suddenly unable to believe that I was I, or Chalons Chalons, or that a young man who in Paris drops in to dine with me and talk over new books and plays, had been whispering a password in my ear to carry me unchallenged to a house a few streets away! The sense of unreality produced by that one word was so overwhelming that for a blissful moment the whole fabric of what I had been experiencing, the whole huge and oppressive and unescapable fact of the war, slipped away like a torn cobweb, and I seemed to see behind it the reassuring face of things as they used to be.

The next morning dispelled that vision. We woke to a noise of guns closer and more incessant than even the first night's cannonade at Verdun; and when we went out into the streets it seemed as if, overnight, a new army had sprung out of the ground. Waylaid at one corner after another by the long tide of troops streaming out through the town to the northern suburbs, we saw in turn all the various divisions of the unfolding frieze: first the infantry and artillery, the sappers and miners, the endless trains of guns and ammunition, then the long line of grey supply-waggons, and finally the stretcher-bearers following the Red Cross ambulances. All the story of a day's warfare was written in the spectacle of that endless silent flow to the front: and we were to read it again, a few days later, in the terse announcement of "renewed activity" about Suippes, and of the bloody strip of ground gained between Perthes and Beausejour.

IN LORRAINE AND THE VOSGES

NANCY, May 13th, 1915

Beside me, on my writing-table, stands a bunch of peonies, the jolly round-faced pink peonies of the village garden. They were picked this afternoon in the garden of a ruined house at Gerbeviller—a house so calcined and convulsed that, for epithets dire enough to fit it, one would have to borrow from a Hebrew prophet gloating over the fall of a city of idolaters.

Since leaving Paris yesterday we have passed through streets and streets of such murdered houses, through town after town spread out in its last writhings; and before the black holes that were homes, along the edge of the chasms that were streets, everywhere we have seen flowers and vegetables springing up in freshly raked and watered gardens. My pink peonies were not introduced to point the stale allegory of unconscious Nature veiling Man's havoc: they are put on my first page as a symbol of conscious human energy coming back to replant and rebuild the wilderness...

Last March, in the Argonne, the towns we passed through seemed quite dead; but yesterday new life was budding everywhere. We were following another track of the invasion, one of the huge tiger-scratches that the Beast flung over the land last September, between Vitry-le-Francois and Bar-le-Duc. Etrepy, Pargny, Sermaize-les-Bains, Andernay, are the names of this group of victims: Sermaize a pretty watering-place along wooded slopes, the others large villages fringed with farms, and all now mere scrofulous blotches on the soft spring scene. But in many we heard the sound of hammers, and saw brick-layers and masons at work. Even in the most mortally stricken there were signs of returning life: children playing among the stone heaps, and now and then a cautious older face peering out of a shed propped against the ruins. In one place an ancient tram-car had been converted into a cafe and labelled: "Au Restaurant des Ruines"; and everywhere between the calcined walls the carefully combed gardens aligned their radishes and lettuce-tops.

From Bar-le-Duc we turned northeast, and as we entered the forest of Commercy we began to hear again the Voice of the Front. It was the warmest and stillest of May days, and in the clearing where we stopped for luncheon the familiar boom broke with a magnified loudness on the noonday hush. In the intervals between the crashes there was not a sound but the gnats' hum in the moist sunshine and the dryad-call of the cuckoo from greener depths. At the end of the lane a few cavalrymen rode by in shabby blue, their horses' flanks glinting like ripe chestnuts. They stopped to chat and accept some cigarettes, and when they had trotted off again the gnat, the cuckoo and the cannon took up their trio...

The town of Commercy looked so undisturbed that the cannonade rocking it might have been some unheeded echo of the hills. These frontier towns inured to the clash of war go about their business with what one might call stolidity if there were not finer, and truer, names for it. In Commercy, to be sure, there is little business to go about just now save that connected with the military occupation; but the peaceful look of the sunny sleepy streets made one doubt if the fighting line was really less than five miles away... Yet the French, with an odd perversion of race-vanity, still persist in speaking of themselves as a "nervous and impressionable" people!

This afternoon, on the road to Gerbeviller, we were again in the track of the September invasion. Over all the slopes now cool with spring foliage the battle rocked backward and forward during those burning autumn days; and every mile of the struggle has left its ghastly traces. The fields are full of wooden crosses which the ploughshare makes a circuit to avoid; many of the villages have been partly wrecked, and here and there an isolated ruin marks the nucleus of a fiercer struggle. But the landscape, in its first sweet leafiness, is so alive with ploughing and sowing and all the natural tasks of spring, that the war scars seem like traces of a long-past woe; and it was not till a bend of the road brought us in sight of Gerbeviller that we breathed again the choking air of present horror.

Gerbeviller, stretched out at ease on its slopes above the Meurthe, must have been a happy place to live in. The streets slanted up between scattered houses in gardens to the great Louis XIV chateau above the town and the church that balanced it. So much one can reconstruct from the first glimpse across the valley; but when one enters the town all perspective is lost in chaos. Gerbeviller has taken to herself the title of "the martyr town"; an honour to which many sister victims might dispute her claim! But as a sensational image of havoc it seems improbable that any can surpass her. Her ruins seem to have been simultaneously vomited up from the depths and hurled down from the skies, as though she had perished in some monstrous clash of earthquake and tornado; and it fills one with a cold despair to know that this double destruction was no accident of nature but a piously planned and methodically executed human deed. From the opposite heights the poor little garden-girt town was shelled like a steel fortress; then, when the Germans entered, a fire was built in every house, and at the nicely-timed right moment one of the explosive tabloids which the fearless Teuton carries about for his land-Lusitanias was tossed on each hearth. It was all so well done that one wonders— almost apologetically for German thoroughness—that any of the human rats escaped from their holes; but some did, and were neatly spitted on lurking bayonets.

One old woman, hearing her son's deathcry, rashly looked out of her door. A bullet instantly laid her low among her phloxes and lilies; and there, in her little garden, her dead body was dishonoured. It seemed singularly appropriate, in such a scene, to read above a blackened doorway the sign: "Monuments Funebres," and to observe that the house the doorway once belonged to had formed the angle of a lane called "La Ruelle des Orphelines."

At one end of the main street of Gerbeviller there once stood a charming house, of the sober old Lorraine pattern, with low door, deep roof and ample gables: it was in the garden of this house that my pink peonies were picked for me by its owner, Mr. Liegeay, a former Mayor of Gerbeviller, who witnessed all the horrors of the invasion.

Mr. Liegeay is now living in a neighbour's cellar, his own being fully occupied by the debris of his charming house. He told us the story of the three days of the German occupation; how he and his wife and niece, and the niece's babies, took to their cellar while the Germans set the house on fire, and how, peering through a door into the stable-yard, they saw that the soldiers suspected they were within and were trying to get at them. Luckily the incendiaries had heaped wood and straw all round the outside of the house, and the blaze was so hot that they could not reach the door. Between the arch of the doorway and the door itself was a half-moon opening; and Mr. Liegeay and his family, during three days and three nights, broke up all the barrels in the cellar and threw the bits out through the opening to feed the fire in the yard.

Finally, on the third day, when they began to be afraid that the ruins of the house would fall in on them, they made a dash for safety. The house was on the edge of the town, and the women and children managed to get away into the country; but Mr. Liegeay was surprised in his garden by a German soldier. He made a rush for the high wall of the adjoining cemetery, and scrambling over it slipped down between the wall and a big granite cross. The cross was covered with the hideous wire and glass wreaths dear to French mourners; and with these opportune mementoes Mr. Liegeay roofed himself in, lying wedged in his narrow hiding-place from three in the afternoon till night, and listening to the voices of the soldiers who were hunting for him among the grave-stones. Luckily it was their last day at Gerbeviller, and the German retreat saved his life.

Even in Gerbeviller we saw no worse scene of destruction than the particular spot in which the ex-mayor stood while he told his story. He looked about him at the heaps of blackened brick and contorted iron. "This was my dining-room," he said. "There were some good old paneling on the walls, and some fine prints that had been a wedding-present to my grand-father." He led us into another black pit. "This was our sitting-room: you see what a view we had." He sighed, and added philosophically: "I suppose we were too well off. I even had an electric light out there on the terrace, to read my paper by on summer evenings. Yes, we were too well off..." That was all.

Meanwhile all the town had been red with horror—flame and shot and tortures unnameable; and at the other end of the long street, a woman, a Sister of Charity, had held her own like Soeur Gabrielle at Clermont-en-Argonne, gathering her flock of old men and children about her and interposing her short stout figure between them and the fury of the Germans. We found her in her Hospice, a ruddy, indomitable woman who related with a quiet indignation more thrilling than invective the hideous details of the bloody three days; but that already belongs to the past, and at present she is much more concerned with the task of clothing and feeding Gerbeviller. For two thirds of the population have already "come home"—that is what they call the return to this desert! "You see," Soeur Julie explained, "there are the crops to sow, the gardens to tend. They had to come back. The government is building wooden shelters for them; and people will surely send us beds and linen." (Of course they would, one felt as one listened!) "Heavy boots, too—boots for field-labourers. We want them for women as well as men—like these." Soeur Julie, smiling, turned up a hob-nailed sole. "I have directed all the work on our Hospice farm myself. All the women are working in the fields—we must take the place of the men." And I seemed to see my pink peonies flowering in the very prints of her sturdy boots!

May 14th.

Nancy, the most beautiful town in France, has never been as beautiful as now. Coming back to it last evening from a round of ruins one felt as if the humbler Sisters sacrificed to spare it were pleading with one not to forget them in the contemplation of its dearly-bought perfection.

The last time I looked out on the great architectural setting of the Place Stanislas was on a hot July evening, the evening of the National Fete. The square and the avenues leading to it swarmed with people, and as darkness fell the balanced lines of arches and palaces sprang out in many coloured light. Garlands of lamps looped the arcades leading into the Place de la Carriere, peacock-coloured fires flared from the Arch of Triumph, long curves of radiance beat like wings over the thickets of the park, the sculptures of the fountains, the brown-and-gold foliation of Jean Damour's great gates; and under this roofing of light was the murmur of a happy crowd carelessly celebrating the tradition of half-forgotten victories.

Now, at sunset, all life ceases in Nancy and veil after veil of silence comes down on the deserted Place and its empty perspectives. Last night by nine the few lingering lights in the streets had been put out, every window was blind, and the moonless night lay over the city like a canopy of velvet. Then, from some remote point, the arc of a search-light swept the sky, laid a fugitive pallor on darkened palace-fronts, a gleam of gold on invisible gates, trembled across the black vault and vanished, leaving it still blacker. When we came out of the darkened restaurant on the corner of the square, and the iron curtain of the entrance had been hastily dropped on us, we stood in such complete night that it took a waiter's friendly hand to guide us to the curbstone. Then, as we grew used to the darkness, we saw it lying still more densely under the colonnade of the Place de la Carriere and the clipped trees beyond. The ordered masses of architecture became august, the spaces between them immense, and the black sky faintly strewn with stars seemed to overarch an enchanted city. Not a footstep sounded, not a leaf rustled, not a breath of air drew under the arches. And suddenly, through the dumb night, the sound of the cannon began.

Luncheon with the General Staff in an old bourgeois house of a little town as sleepy as "Cranford." In the warm walled gardens everything was blooming at once: laburnums, lilacs, red hawthorn, Banksia roses and all the pleasant border plants that go with box and lavender. Never before did the flowers answer the spring roll-call with such a rush! Upstairs, in the Empire bedroom which the General has turned into his study, it was amusingly incongruous to see the sturdy provincial furniture littered with war-maps, trench-plans, aeroplane photographs and all the documentation of modern war. Through the windows bees hummed, the garden rustled, and one felt, close by, behind the walls of other gardens, the untroubled continuance of a placid and orderly bourgeois life.

We started early for Mousson on the Moselle, the ruined hill-fortress that gives its name to the better-known town at its foot. Our road ran below the long range of the "Grand Couronne," the line of hills curving southeast from Pont-a-Mousson to St. Nicolas du Port. All through this pleasant broken country the battle shook and swayed last autumn; but few signs of those days are left except the wooden crosses in the fields. No troops are visible, and the pictures of war that made the

Argonne so tragic last March are replaced by peaceful rustic scenes. On the way to Mousson the road is overhung by an Italian-looking village clustered about a hill-top. It marks the exact spot at which, last August, the German invasion was finally checked and flung back; and the Muse of History points out that on this very hill has long stood a memorial shaft inscribed: Here, in the year 362, Jovinus defeated the Teutonic hordes.

A little way up the ascent to Mousson we left the motor behind a bit of rising ground. The road is raked by the German lines, and stray pedestrians (unless in a group) are less liable than a motor to have a shell spent on them. We climbed under a driving grey sky which swept gusts of rain across our road. In the lee of the castle we stopped to look down at the valley of the Moselle, the slate roofs of Pont-a-Mousson and the broken bridge which once linked together the two sides of the town. Nothing but the wreck of the bridge showed that we were on the edge of war. The wind was too high for firing, and we saw no reason for believing that the wood just behind the Hospice roof at our feet was seamed with German trenches and bristling with guns, or that from every slope across the valley the eye of the cannon sleeplessly glared. But there the Germans were, drawing an iron ring about three sides of the watch-tower; and as one peered through an embrasure of the ancient walls one gradually found one's self re-living the sensations of the little mediaeval burgh as it looked out on some earlier circle of besiegers. The longer one looked, the more oppressive and menacing the invisibility of the foe became. "There they are—and there—and there." We strained our eyes obediently, but saw only calm hillsides, dozing farms. It was as if the earth itself were the enemy, as if the hordes of evil were in the clods and grass-blades. Only one conical hill close by showed an odd artificial patterning, like the work of huge ants who had scarred it with criss-cross ridges. We were told that these were French trenches, but they looked much more like the harmless traces of a prehistoric camp.

Suddenly an officer, pointing to the west of the trenched hill said: "Do you see that farm?" It lay just below, near the river, and so close that good eyes could easily have discerned people or animals in the farm-yard, if there had been any; but the whole place seemed to be sleeping the sleep of bucolic peace. "They are there," the officer said; and the innocent vignette framed by my field-glass suddenly glared back at me like a human mask of hate. The loudest cannonade had not made "them" seem as real as that!...

At this point the military lines and the old political frontier everywhere overlap, and in a cleft of the wooded hills that conceal the German batteries we saw a dark grey blur on the grey horizon. It was Metz, the Promised City, lying there with its fair steeples and towers, like the mystic banner that Constantine saw upon the sky...

Through wet vineyards and orchards we scrambled down the hill to the river and entered Pont-a-Mousson. It was by mere meteorological good luck that we got there, for if the winds had been asleep the guns would have been awake, and when they wake poor Pont-a-Mousson is not at home to visitors. One understood why as one stood in the riverside garden of the great Premonstratensian Monastery which is now the hospital and the general asylum of the town. Between the clipped limes and formal borders the German shells had scooped out three or four "dreadful hollows," in one of which, only last week, a little girl found her death; and the facade of the building is pock-marked by shot and disfigured with gaping holes. Yet in this precarious shelter Sister Theresia, of the same indomitable breed as the Sisters of Clermont and Gerbeviller, has gathered a miscellaneous flock of soldiers wounded in the trenches, civilians shattered by the bombardment, eclopes, old women and children: all the human wreckage of this storm-beaten point of the front. Sister Theresia seems in no wise disconcerted by the fact that the shells continually play over her roof. The building is immense and spreading, and when one wing is damaged she picks up her proteges and trots them off, bed and baggage, to another. "Je promene mes malades," she said calmly, as if boasting of the varied accommodation of an ultra-modern hospital, as she led us through vaulted and stuccoed galleries where caryatid-saints look down in plaster pomp on the rows of brown-blanketed pallets and the long tables at which haggard eclopes were enjoying their evening soup.

I have seen the happiest being on earth: a man who has found his job.

This afternoon we motored southwest of Nancy to a little place called Menil-sur-Belvitte. The name is not yet intimately known to history, but there are reasons why it deserves to be, and in one man's mind it already is. Menil-sur-Belvitte is a village on the edge of the Vosges. It is badly battered, for awful fighting took place there in the first month of the war. The houses lie in a hollow, and just beyond it the ground rises and spreads into a plateau waving with wheat and backed by wooded slopes—the ideal "battleground" of the history-books. And here a real above-ground battle of the old obsolete kind took place, and the French, driving the Germans back victoriously, fell by thousands in the trampled wheat.

The church of Menil is a ruin, but the parsonage still stands—a plain little house at the end of the street; and here the cure received us, and led us into a room which he has turned into a chapel. The chapel is also a war museum, and everything in it has something to do with the battle that took place among the wheat-fields. The candelabra on the altar are made of "Seventy-five" shells, the Virgin's halo is composed of radiating bayonets, the walls are intricately adorned with German trophies and French relics, and on the ceiling the cure has had painted a kind of zodiacal chart of the whole region, in which Menil-sur-Belvitte's handful of houses figures as the central orb of the system, and Verdun, Nancy, Metz, and Belfort as its humble satellites. But the chapel-museum is only a surplus expression of the cure's impassioned dedication to the dead. His real work has been done on the battle-field, where row after row of graves, marked and listed as soon as the struggle was over, have been fenced about, symmetrically disposed, planted with flowers and young firs, and marked by the names and death-dates of the fallen. As he led us from one of these enclosures to another his face was lit with the flame of a gratified vocation. This particular man was made to do this particular thing: he is a born collector, classifier, and hero-worshipper. In the hall of the "presbytere" hangs a case of carefully-mounted butterflies, the result, no doubt, of an earlier passion for collecting. His "specimens" have changed, that is all: he has passed from butterflies to men, from the actual to the visionary Psyche.

On the way to Menil we stopped at the village of Crevic. The Germans were there in August, but the place is untouched—except for one house. That house, a large one, standing in a park at one end of the village, was the birth-place and home of General Lyautey, one of France's best soldiers, and Germany's worst enemy in Africa. It is no exaggeration to say that last August General Lyautey, by his promptness and audacity, saved Morocco for France. The Germans know it, and hate him; and as soon as the first soldiers reached Crevic—so obscure and imperceptible a spot that even German omniscience might have missed it—the officer in command asked for General Lyautey's house, went straight to it, had all the papers, portraits, furniture and family relics piled in a bonfire in the court, and then burnt down the house. As we sat in the neglected park with the plaintive ruin before us we heard from the gardener this typical tale of German thoroughness and German chivalry. It is corroborated by the fact that not another house in Crevic was destroyed.

May 16th.

About two miles from the German frontier (frontier just here as well as front) an isolated hill rises out of the Lorraine meadows. East of it, a ribbon of river winds among poplars, and that ribbon is the boundary between Empire and Republic. On such a clear day as this the view from the hill is extraordinarily interesting. From its grassy top a little aeroplane cannon stares to heaven, watching the east for the danger speck; and the circumference of the hill is furrowed by a deep trench—a "bowel," rather—winding invisibly from one subterranean observation post to another. In each of these earthly warrens (ingeniously wattled, roofed and iron-sheeted) stand two or three artillery officers with keen quiet faces, directing by telephone the fire of batteries nestling somewhere in the woods four or five miles away. Interesting as the place was, the men who lived there interested me far more. They obviously belonged to different classes, and had received a different social education; but their mental and moral fraternity was complete. They were all fairly young, and their faces had the look that war has given to French faces: a look of sharpened intelligence, strengthened will and sobered judgment, as if every faculty, trebly vivified, were so bent on the one end that personal problems had been pushed back to the vanishing point of the great perspective.

From this vigilant height—one of the intentest eyes open on the frontier—we went a short distance down the hillside to a village out of range of the guns, where the commanding officer gave us tea in a charming old house with a terraced garden full of flowers and puppies. Below the terrace, lost Lorraine stretched away to her blue heights, a vision of summer peace: and just above us the unsleeping hill kept watch, its signal-wires trembling night and day. It was one of the intervals of rest and sweetness when the whole horrible black business seems to press most intolerably on the nerves.

Below the village the road wound down to a forest that had formed a dark blur in our bird's-eye view of the plain. We passed into the forest and halted on the edge of a colony of queer exotic huts. On all sides they peeped through the branches, themselves so branched and sodded and leafy that they seemed like some transition form between tree and house. We were in one of the so-called "villages negres" of the second-line trenches, the jolly little settlements to which the troops retire after doing their shift under fire. This particular colony has been developed to an extreme degree of comfort and safety. The houses are partly underground, connected by deep winding "bowels" over which light rustic bridges have been thrown, and so profoundly roofed with sods that as much of them as shows above ground is shell-proof. Yet they are real houses, with real doors and windows under their grass-eaves, real furniture inside, and real beds of daisies and pansies at their doors. In the Colonel's bungalow a big bunch of spring flowers bloomed on the table, and everywhere we saw the same neatness and order, the same amused pride in the look of things. The men were dining at long trestle-tables under the trees; tired, unshaven men in shabby uniforms of all cuts and almost every colour. They were off duty, relaxed, in a good humour; but every face had the look of the faces watching on the hill-top. Wherever I go among these men of the front I have the same impression: the impression that the absorbing undivided thought of the Defense of France lives in the heart and brain of each soldier as intensely as in the heart and brain of their chief.

We walked a dozen yards down the road and came to the edge of the forest. A wattled palisade bounded it, and through a gap in the palisade we looked out across a field to the roofs of a quiet village a mile away. I went out a few steps into the field and was abruptly pulled back. "Take care— those are the trenches!" What looked like a ridge thrown up by a plough was the enemy's line; and in the quiet village French cannon watched. Suddenly, as we stood there, they woke, and at the same moment we heard the unmistakable Gr-r-r of an aeroplane and saw a Bird of Evil high up against the blue. Snap, snap, snap barked the mitrailleuse on the hill, the soldiers jumped from their wine and strained their eyes through the trees, and the Taube, finding itself the centre of so much attention, turned grey tail and swished away to the concealing clouds.

Today we started with an intenser sense of adventure. Hitherto we had always been told beforehand where we were going and how much we were to be allowed to see; but now we were being launched into the unknown. Beyond a certain point all was conjecture—we knew only that what happened after that would depend on the good-will of a Colonel of Chasseurs-a-pied whom we were to go a long way to find, up into the folds of the mountains on our southeast horizon.

We picked up a staff-officer at Head-quarters and flew on to a battered town on the edge of the hills. From there we wound up through a narrowing valley, under wooded cliffs, to a little settlement where the Colonel of the Brigade was to be found. There was a short conference between the Colonel and our staff-officer, and then we annexed a Captain of Chasseurs and spun away again. Our road lay through a town so exposed that our companion from Head-quarters suggested the advisability of avoiding it; but our guide hadn't the heart to inflict such a disappointment on his new acquaintances. "Oh, we won't stop the motor—we'll just dash through," he said indulgently; and in the excess of his indulgence he even permitted us to dash slowly.

Oh, that poor town—when we reached it, along a road ploughed with fresh obus-holes, I didn't want to stop the motor; I wanted to hurry on and blot the picture from my memory! It was doubly sad to look at because of the fact that it wasn't quite dead; faint spasms of life still quivered through it. A few children played in the ravaged streets; a few pale mothers watched them from cellar doorways. "They oughtn't to be here," our guide explained; "but about a hundred and fifty begged so hard to stay that the General gave them leave. The officer in command has an eye on them, and whenever he gives the signal they dive down into their burrows. He says they are perfectly obedient. It was he who asked that they might stay..."

Up and up into the hills. The vision of human pain and ruin was lost in beauty. We were among the firs, and the air was full of balm. The mossy banks gave out a scent of rain, and little water-falls from the heights set the branches trembling over secret pools. At each turn of the road, forest, and always more forest, climbing with us as we climbed, and dropped away from us to narrow valleys that converged on slate-blue distances. At one of these turns we overtook a company of soldiers, spade on shoulder and bags of tools across their backs—"trench-workers" swinging up to the heights to which we were bound. Life must be a better thing in this crystal air than in the mud-welter of the Argonne and the fogs of the North; and these men's faces were fresh with wind and weather.

Higher still ... and presently a halt on a ridge, in another "black village," this time almost a town! The soldiers gathered round us as the motor stopped—throngs of chasseurs-a-pied in faded, trench-stained uniforms—for few visitors climb to this point, and their pleasure at the sight of new faces was presently expressed in a large "Vive l'Amerique!" scrawled on the door of the car. L'Amerique was glad and proud to be there, and instantly conscious of breathing an air saturated with courage and the dogged determination to endure. The men were all reservists: that is to say, mostly married, and all beyond the first fighting age. For many months there has not been much active work along this front, no great adventure to rouse the blood and wing the imagination: it has just been month after month of monotonous watching and holding on. And the soldiers' faces showed it: there was no light of heady enterprise in their eyes, but the look of men who knew their job, had thought it over, and were there to hold their bit of France till the day of victory or extermination.

Meanwhile, they had made the best of the situation and turned their quarters into a forest colony that would enchant any normal boy. Their village architecture was more elaborate than any we had yet seen. In the Colonel's "dugout" a long table decked with lilacs and tulips was spread for tea. In other cheery catacombs we found neat rows of bunks, mess-tables, sizzling sauce-pans over kitchen-fires. Everywhere were endless ingenuities in the way of camp-furniture and household decoration. Farther down the road a path between fir-boughs led to a hidden hospital, a marvel of underground compactness. While we chatted with the surgeon a soldier came in from the trenches: an elderly, bearded man, with a good average civilian face—the kind that one runs against by hundreds in any French crowd. He had a scalp-wound which had just been dressed, and was very pale. The Colonel stopped to ask a few questions, and then, turning to him, said: "Feeling rather better now?"

"Yes, sir."

"Good. In a day or two you'll be thinking about going back to the trenches, eh?"

"I'm going now, sir." It was said quite simply, and received in the same way. "Oh, all right," the Colonel merely rejoined; but he laid his hand on the man's shoulder as we went out.

Our next visit was to a sod-thatched hut, "At the sign of the Ambulant Artisans," where two or three soldiers were modelling and chiselling all kinds of trinkets from the aluminum of enemy shells. One of the ambulant artisans was just finishing a ring with beautifully modelled fauns' heads, another offered me a "Pickelhaube" small enough for Mustard-seed's wear, but complete in every detail, and inlaid with the bronze eagle from an Imperial pfennig. There are many such ringsmiths among the privates at the front, and the severe, somewhat archaic design of their rings is a proof of the sureness of French taste; but the two we visited happened to be Paris jewellers, for whom "artisan" was really too modest a pseudonym. Officers and men were evidently proud of their work, and as they stood hammering away in their cramped smithy, a red gleam lighting up the intentness of their faces, they seemed to be beating out the cheerful rhythm of "I too will something make, and joy in the making."...

Up the hillside, in deeper shadow, was another little structure; a wooden shed with an open gable sheltering an altar with candles and flowers. Here mass is said by one of the conscript priests of the regiment, while his congregation kneel between the fir-trunks, giving life to the old metaphor of the cathedral-forest. Near by was the grave-yard, where day by day these quiet elderly men lay their comrades, the peres de famille who don't go back. The care of this woodland cemetery is left entirely to the soldiers, and they have spent treasures of piety on the inscriptions and decorations of the graves. Fresh flowers are brought up from the valleys to cover them, and when some favourite comrade goes, the men scorning ephemeral tributes, club together to buy a monstrous indestructible wreath with emblazoned streamers. It was near the end of the afternoon, and many soldiers were strolling along the paths between the graves. "It's their favourite walk at this hour," the Colonel said. He stopped to look down on a grave smothered in beady tokens, the grave of the last pal to fall. "He was mentioned in the Order of the Day," the Colonel explained; and the group of soldiers standing near looked at us proudly, as if sharing their comrade's honour, and wanting to be sure that we understood the reason of their pride...

"And now," said our Captain of Chasseurs, "that you've seen the second-line trenches, what do you say to taking a look at the first?"

We followed him to a point higher up the hill, where we plunged into a deep ditch of red earth—the "bowel" leading to the first lines. It climbed still higher, under the wet firs, and then, turning, dipped over the edge and began to wind in sharp loops down the other side of the ridge. Down we scrambled, single file, our chins on a level with the top of the passage, the close green covert above us. The "bowel" went twisting down more and more sharply into a deep ravine; and presently, at a bend, we came to a fir-thatched outlook, where a soldier stood with his back to us, his eye glued to a peep-hole in the wattled wall. Another turn, and another outlook; but here it was the iron-rimmed eye of the mitrailleuse that stared across the ravine. By this time we were within a hundred yards or so of the German lines, hidden, like ours, on the other side of the narrowing hollow; and as we stole down and down, the hush and secrecy of the scene, and the sense of that imminent lurking hatred only a few branch-lengths away, seemed to fill the silence with mysterious pulsations. Suddenly a sharp noise broke on them: the rap of a rifle-shot against a tree-trunk a few yards ahead.

"Ah, the sharp-shooter," said our guide. "No more talking, please—he's over there, in a tree somewhere, and whenever he hears voices he fires. Some day we shall spot his tree."

We went on in silence to a point where a few soldiers were sitting on a ledge of rock in a widening of the "bowel." They looked as quiet as if they had been waiting for their bocks before a Boulevard cafe.

"Not beyond, please," said the officer, holding me back; and I stopped.

Here we were, then, actually and literally in the first lines! The knowledge made one's heart tick a little; but, except for another shot or two from our arboreal listener, and the motionless intentness of the soldier's back at the peep-hole, there was nothing to show that we were not a dozen miles away.

Perhaps the thought occurred to our Captain of Chasseurs; for just as I was turning back he said with his friendliest twinkle: "Do you want awfully to go a little farther? Well, then, come on."

We went past the soldiers sitting on the ledge and stole down and down, to where the trees ended at the bottom of the ravine. The sharp-shooter had stopped firing, and nothing disturbed the leafy silence but an intermittent drip of rain. We were at the end of the burrow, and the Captain signed to me that I might take a cautious peep round its corner. I looked out and saw a strip of intensely green meadow just under me, and a wooded cliff rising abruptly on its other side. That was all. The wooded cliff swarmed with "them," and a few steps would have carried us across the interval; yet all about us was silence, and the peace of the forest. Again, for a minute, I had the sense of an all-pervading, invisible power of evil, a saturation of the whole landscape with some hidden vitriol of hate. Then the reaction of the unbelief set in, and I felt myself in a harmless ordinary glen, like a million others on an untroubled earth. We turned and began to climb again, loop by loop, up the "bowel"—we passed the lolling soldiers, the silent mitrailleuse, we came again to the watcher at his peep-hole. He heard us, let the officer pass, and turned his head with a little sign of understanding.

"Do you want to look down?"

He moved a step away from his window. The look-out projected over the ravine, raking its depths; and here, with one's eye to the leaf-lashed hole, one saw at last ... saw, at the bottom of the harmless glen, half way between cliff and cliff, a grey uniform huddled in a dead heap. "He's been there for days: they can't fetch him away," said the watcher, regluing his eye to the hole; and it was almost a relief to find it was after all a tangible enemy hidden over there across the meadow...

The sun had set when we got back to our starting-point in the underground village. The chasseurs-a-pied were lounging along the roadside and standing in gossiping groups about the motor. It was long since they had seen faces from the other life, the life they had left nearly a year earlier and had not been allowed to go back to for a day; and under all their jokes and good-humour their farewell had a tinge of wistfulness. But one felt that this fugitive reminder of a world they had put behind them would pass like a dream, and their minds revert without effort to the one reality: the business of holding their bit of France.

It is hard to say why this sense of the French soldier's single-mindedness is so strong in all who have had even a glimpse of the front; perhaps it is gathered less from what the men say than from the look in their eyes. Even while they are accepting cigarettes and exchanging trench-jokes, the look is there; and when one comes on them unaware it is there also. In the dusk of the forest that look followed us down the mountain; and as we skirted the edge of the ravine between the armies, we felt that on the far side of that dividing line were the men who had made the war, and on the near side the men who had been made by it.

IN THE NORTH

June 19th, 1915.

On the way from Doullens to Montreuil-sur-Mer, on a shining summer afternoon. A road between dusty hedges, choked, literally strangled, by a torrent of westward-streaming troops of all arms. Every few minutes there would come a break in the flow, and our motor would wriggle through, advance a few yards, and be stopped again by a widening of the torrent that jammed us into the ditch and splashed a dazzle of dust into our eyes. The dust was stifling—but through it, what a sight!

Standing up in the car and looking back, we watched the river of war wind toward us. Cavalry, artillery, lancers, infantry, sappers and miners, trench-diggers, road-makers, stretcher-bearers, they swept on as smoothly as if in holiday order. Through the dust, the sun picked out the flash of lances and the gloss of chargers' flanks, flushed rows and rows of determined faces, found the least touch of gold on faded uniforms, silvered the sad grey of mitrailleuses and munition waggons. Close as the men were, they seemed allegorically splendid: as if, under the arch of the sunset, we had been watching the whole French army ride straight into glory...

Finally we left the last detachment behind, and had the country to ourselves. The disfigurement of war has not touched the fields of Artois. The thatched farmhouses dozed in gardens full of roses and hollyhocks, and the hedges above the duck-ponds were weighed down with layers of elder-blossom. On all sides wheat-fields skirted with woodland went billowing away under the breezy light that seemed to carry a breath of the Atlantic on its beams. The road ran up and down as if our motor were a ship on a deep-sea swell; and such a sense of space and light was in the distances, such a veil of beauty over the whole world, that the vision of that army on the move grew more and more fabulous and epic.

The sun had set and the sea-twilight was rolling in when we dipped down from the town of Montreuil to the valley below, where the towers of an ancient abbey-church rise above terraced orchards. The gates at the end of the avenue were thrown open, and the motor drove into a monastery court full of box and roses. Everything was sweet and secluded in this mediaeval place; and from the shadow of cloisters and arched passages groups of nuns fluttered out, nuns all black or all white, gliding, peering and standing at gaze. It was as if we had plunged back into a century to which motors were unknown and our car had been some monster cast up from a Barbary shipwreck;

and the startled attitudes of these holy women did credit to their sense of the picturesque; for the Abbey of Neuville is now a great Belgian hospital, and such monsters must frequently intrude on its seclusion...

Sunset, and summer dusk, and the moon. Under the monastery windows a walled garden with stone pavilions at the angles and the drip of a fountain. Below it, tiers of orchard-terraces fading into a great moon-confused plain that might be either fields or sea...

June 20th.

Today our way ran northeast, through a landscape so English that there was no incongruity in the sprinkling of khaki along the road. Even the villages look English: the same plum-red brick of tidy self-respecting houses, neat, demure and freshly painted, the gardens all bursting with flowers, the landscape hedgerowed and willowed and fed with water-courses, the people's faces square and pink and honest, and the signs over the shops in a language half way between English and German. Only the architecture of the towns is French, of a reserved and robust northern type, but unmistakably in the same great tradition.

War still seemed so far off that one had time for these digressions as the motor flew on over the undulating miles. But presently we came on an aviation camp spreading its sheds over a wide plateau. Here the khaki throng was thicker and the familiar military stir enlivened the landscape. A few miles farther, and we found ourselves in what was seemingly a big English town oddly grouped about a nucleus of French churches. This was St. Omer, grey, spacious, coldly clean in its Sunday emptiness. At the street crossings English sentries stood mechanically directing the absent traffic with gestures familiar to Piccadilly; and the signs of the British Red Cross and St. John's Ambulance hung on club-like facades that might almost have claimed a home in Pall Mall.

The Englishness of things was emphasized, as we passed out through the suburbs, by the look of the crowd on the canal bridges and along the roads. Every nation has its own way of loitering, and there is nothing so unlike the French way as the English. Even if all these tall youths had not been in khaki, and the girls with them so pink and countrified, one would instantly have recognized the passive northern way of letting a holiday soak in instead of squeezing out its juices with feverish fingers.

When we turned westward from St. Omer, across the same pastures and watercourses, we were faced by two hills standing up abruptly out of the plain; and on the top of one rose the walls and towers of a compact little mediaeval town. As we took the windings that led up to it a sense of Italy began to penetrate the persistent impression of being somewhere near the English Channel. The town we were approaching might have been a queer dream-blend of Winchelsea and San Gimignano; but when we entered the gates of Cassel we were in a place so intensely itself that all analogies dropped out of mind.

It was not surprising to learn from the guide-book that Cassel has the most extensive view of any town in Europe: one felt at once that it differed in all sorts of marked and self-assertive ways from every other town, and would be almost sure to have the best things going in every line. And the line of an illimitable horizon is exactly the best to set off its own quaint compactness.

We found our hotel in the most perfect of little market squares, with a Renaissance town-hall on one side, and on the other a miniature Spanish palace with a front of rosy brick adorned by grey carvings. The square was crowded with English army motors and beautiful prancing chargers; and the restaurant of the inn (which has the luck to face the pink and grey palace) swarmed with khaki tea-drinkers turning indifferent shoulders to the widest view in Europe. It is one of the most detestable things about war that everything connected with it, except the death and ruin that result, is such a heightening of life, so visually stimulating and absorbing. "It was gay and terrible," is the phrase forever recurring in "War and Peace"; and the gaiety of war was everywhere in Cassel, transforming the lifeless little town into a romantic stage-setting full of the flash of arms and the virile animation of young faces.

From the park on top of the hill we looked down on another picture. All about us was the plain, its distant rim merged in northern sea-mist; and through the mist, in the glitter of the afternoon sun, far-off towns and shadowy towers lay steeped, as it seemed, in summer quiet. For a moment, while we looked, the vision of war shrivelled up like a painted veil; then we caught the names pronounced by a group of English soldiers leaning over the parapet at our side. "That's Dunkerque"—one of them pointed it out with his pipe—"and there's Poperinghe, just under us; that's Furnes beyond, and Ypres and Dixmude, and Nieuport... "And at the mention of those names the scene grew dark again, and we felt the passing of the Angel to whom was given the Key of the Bottomless Pit.

That night we went up once more to the rock of Cassel. The moon was full, and as civilians are not allowed out alone after dark a staff-officer went with us to show us the view from the roof of the disused Casino on top of the rock. It was the queerest of sensations to push open a glazed door and find ourselves in a spectral painted room with soldiers dozing in the moonlight on polished floors, their kits stacked on the gaming tables. We passed through a big vestibule among more soldiers lounging in the half-light, and up a long staircase to the roof where a watcher challenged us and then let us go to the edge of the parapet. Directly below lay the unlit mass of the town. To the northwest a single sharp hill, the "Mont des Cats," stood out against the sky; the rest of the horizon was unbroken, and floating in misty moonlight. The outline of the ruined towns had vanished and peace seemed to have won back the world. But as we stood there a red flash started out of the mist far off to the northwest; then another and another flickered up at different points of the long curve. "Luminous bombs thrown up along the lines," our guide explained; and just then, at still another point a white light opened like a tropical flower, spread to full bloom and drew itself back into the night. "A flare," we were told; and another white flower bloomed out farther down. Below us, the roofs of Cassel slept their provincial sleep, the moonlight picking out every leaf in the gardens; while beyond, those infernal flowers continued to open and shut along the curve of death.

June 21st.

On the road from Cassel to Poperinghe. Heat, dust, crowds, confusion, all the sordid shabby rear-view of war. The road running across the plain between white-powdered hedges was ploughed up by numberless motor-vans, supply-waggons and Red Cross ambulances. Labouring through between them came detachments of British artillery, clattering gun-carriages, straight young figures on glossy horses, long Phidian lines of youths so ingenuously fair that one wondered how they could have looked on the Medusa face of war and lived. Men and beasts, in spite of the dust, were as fresh and sleek as if they had come from a bath; and everywhere along the wayside were improvised camps, with tents made of waggon-covers, where the ceaseless indomitable work of cleaning was being carried out in all its searching details. Shirts were drying on elder-bushes, kettles boiling over gypsy fires, men shaving, blacking their boots, cleaning their guns, rubbing down their horses, greasing their saddles, polishing their stirrups and bits: on all sides a general cheery struggle against the prevailing dust, discomfort and disorder. Here and there a young soldier leaned against a garden paling to talk to a girl among the hollyhocks, or an older soldier initiated a group of children into some mystery of military housekeeping; and everywhere were the same signs of friendly inarticulate understanding with the owners of the fields and gardens.

From the thronged high-road we passed into the emptiness of deserted Poperinghe, and out again on the way to Ypres. Beyond the flats and wind-mills to our left were the invisible German lines, and the staff-officer who was with us leaned forward to caution our chauffeur: "No tooting between here and Ypres." There was still a good deal of movement on the road, though it was less crowded with troops than near Poperinghe; but as we passed through the last village and approached the low line of houses ahead, the silence and emptiness widened about us. That low line was Ypres; every monument that marked it, that gave it an individual outline, is gone. It is a town without a profile.

The motor slipped through a suburb of small brick houses and stopped under cover of some slightly taller buildings. Another military motor waited there, the chauffeur relic-hunting in the gutted houses.

We got out and walked toward the centre of the Cloth Market. We had seen evacuated towns— Verdun, Badonviller, Raon-l'Etape—but we had seen no emptiness like this. Not a human being was in the streets. Endless lines of houses looked down on us from vacant windows. Our footsteps echoed like the tramp of a crowd, our lowered voices seemed to shout. In one street we came on three English soldiers who were carrying a piano out of a house and lifting it onto a hand-cart. They stopped to stare at us, and we stared back. It seemed an age since we had seen a living being! One of the soldiers scrambled into the cart and tapped out a tune on the cracked key-board, and we all laughed with relief at the foolish noise... Then we walked on and were alone again.

We had seen other ruined towns, but none like this. The towns of Lorraine were blown up, burnt down, deliberately erased from the earth. At worst they are like stone-yards, at best like Pompeii. But Ypres has been bombarded to death, and the outer walls of its houses are still standing, so that it presents the distant semblance of a living city, while near by it is seen to be a disembowelled corpse. Every window-pane is smashed, nearly every building unroofed, and some house-fronts are sliced clean off, with the different stories exposed, as if for the stage-setting of a farce. In these exposed interiors the poor little household gods shiver and blink like owls surprised in a hollow tree. A hundred signs of intimate and humble tastes, of humdrum pursuits, of family association, cling to the unmasked walls. Whiskered photographs fade on morning-glory wallpapers, plaster saints pine under glass bells, antimacassars droop from plush sofas, yellowing diplomas display their seals on office walls. It was all so still and familiar that it seemed as if the people for whom these things had a meaning might at any moment come back and take up their daily business. And then—crash! the guns began, slamming out volley after volley all along the English lines, and the poor frail web of things that had made up the lives of a vanished city-full hung dangling before us in that deathly blast.

We had just reached the square before the Cathedral when the cannonade began, and its roar seemed to build a roof of iron over the glorious ruins of Ypres. The singular distinction of the city is that it is destroyed but not abased. The walls of the Cathedral, the long bulk of the Cloth Market, still lift themselves above the market place with a majesty that seems to silence compassion. The sight of those facades, so proud in death, recalled a phrase used soon after the fall of Liege by Belgium's Foreign Minister—"La Belgique ne regrette rien "—which ought some day to serve as the motto of the renovated city.

We were turning to go when we heard a whirr overhead, followed by a volley of mitrailleuse. High up in the blue, over the centre of the dead city, flew a German aeroplane; and all about it hundreds of white shrapnel tufts burst out in the summer sky like the miraculous snow-fall of Italian legend.

Up and up they flew, on the trail of the Taube, and on flew the Taube, faster still, till quarry and pack were lost in mist, and the barking of the mitrailleuse died out. So we left Ypres to the death-silence in which we had found her.

The afternoon carried us back to Poperinghe, where I was bound on a quest for lace-cushions of the special kind required by our Flemish refugees. The model is unobtainable in France, and I had been told—with few and vague indications—that I might find the cushions in a certain convent of the city. But in which?

Poperinghe, though little injured, is almost empty. In its tidy desolation it looks like a town on which a wicked enchanter has laid a spell. We roamed from quarter to quarter, hunting for some one to show us the way to the convent I was looking for, till at last a passer-by led us to a door which seemed the right one. At our knock the bars were drawn and a cloistered face looked out. No, there were no cushions there; and the nun had never heard of the order we named. But there were the Penitents, the Benedictines—we might try. Our guide offered to show us the way and we went on. From one or two windows, wondering heads looked out and vanished; but the streets were lifeless. At last we came to a convent where there were no nuns left, but where, the caretaker told us, there were cushions—a great many. He led us through pale blue passages, up cold stairs, through rooms that smelt of linen and lavender. We passed a chapel with plaster saints in white niches above paper flowers. Everything was cold and bare and blank: like a mind from which memory has gone. We came to a class room with lines of empty benches facing a blue-mantled Virgin; and here, on the floor, lay rows and rows of lace-cushions. On each a bit of lace had been begun—and there they had been dropped when nuns and pupils fled. They had not been left in disorder: the rows had been laid out evenly, a handkerchief thrown over each cushion. And that orderly arrest of life seemed sadder than any scene of disarray. It symbolized the senseless paralysis of a whole nation's activities. Here were a houseful of women and children, yesterday engaged in a useful task and now aimlessly astray over the earth. And in hundreds of such houses, in dozens, in hundreds of open towns, the hand of time had been stopped, the heart of life had ceased to beat, all the currents of hope and happiness and industry been choked—not that some great military end might be gained, or the length of the war curtailed, but that, wherever the shadow of Germany falls, all things should wither at the root.

The same sight met us everywhere that afternoon. Over Furnes and Bergues, and all the little intermediate villages, the evil shadow lay. Germany had willed that these places should die, and wherever her bombs could not reach her malediction had carried. Only Biblical lamentation can convey a vision of this life-drained land. "Your country is desolate; your cities are burned with fire; your land, strangers devour it in your presence, and it is desolate, as overthrown by strangers."

Late in the afternoon we came to Dunkerque, lying peacefully between its harbour and canals. The bombardment of the previous month had emptied it, and though no signs of damage were visible the same spellbound air lay over everything. As we sat alone at tea in the hall of the hotel on the Place Jean Bart, and looked out on the silent square and its lifeless shops and cafes, some one suggested that the hotel would be a convenient centre for the excursions we had planned, and we decided to return there the next evening. Then we motored back to Cassel.

June 22nd.

My first waking thought was: "How time flies! It must be the Fourteenth of July!" I knew it could not be the Fourth of that specially commemorative month, because I was just awake enough to be sure I was not in America; and the only other event to justify such a terrific clatter was the French national anniversary. I sat up and listened to the popping of guns till a completed sense of reality stole over me, and I realized that I was in the inn of the Wild Man at Cassel, and that it was not the fourteenth of July but the twenty-second of June.

Then, what—? A Taube, of course! And all the guns in the place were cracking at it! By the time this mental process was complete, I had scrambled up and hurried downstairs and, unbolting the heavy doors, had rushed out into the square. It was about four in the morning, the heavenliest moment of a summer dawn, and in spite of the tumult Cassel still apparently slept. Only a few soldiers stood in the square, looking up at a drift of white cloud behind which—they averred—a Taube had just slipped out of sight. Cassel was evidently used to Taubes, and I had the sense of having overdone my excitement and not being exactly in tune; so after gazing a moment at the white cloud I slunk back into the hotel, barred the door and mounted to my room. At a window on the stairs I paused to look out over the sloping roofs of the town, the gardens, the plain; and suddenly there was another crash and a drift of white smoke blew up from the fruit-trees just under the window. It was a last shot at the fugitive, from a gun hidden in one of those quiet provincial gardens between the houses; and its secret presence there was more startling than all the clatter of mitrailleuses from the rock.

Silence and sleep came down again on Cassel; but an hour or two later the hush was broken by a roar like the last trump. This time it was no question of mitrailleuses. The Wild Man rocked on its base, and every pane in my windows beat a tattoo. What was that incredible unimagined sound? Why, it could be nothing, of course, but the voice of the big siege-gun of Dixmude! Five times, while I was dressing, the thunder shook my windows, and the air was filled with a noise that may be compared—if the human imagination can stand the strain—to the simultaneous closing of all the iron shop-shutters in the world. The odd part was that, as far as the Wild Man and its inhabitants were concerned, no visible effects resulted, and dressing, packing and coffee-drinking went on comfortably in the strange parentheses between the roars.

We set off early for a neighbouring Head-quarters, and it was not till we turned out of the gates of Cassel that we came on signs of the bombardment: the smashing of a gas-house and the converting of a cabbage-field into a crater which, for some time to come, will spare photographers the trouble of climbing Vesuvius. There was a certain consolation in the discrepancy between the noise and the damage done.

At Head-quarters we learned more of the morning's incidents. Dunkerque, it appeared, had first been visited by the Taube which afterward came to take the range of Cassel; and the big gun of Dixmude had then turned all its fury on the French sea-port. The bombardment of Dunkuerque was still going on; and we were asked, and in fact bidden, to give up our plan of going there for the night.

After luncheon we turned north, toward the dunes. The villages we drove through were all evacuated, some quite lifeless, others occupied by troops. Presently we came to a group of military motors drawn up by the roadside, and a field black with wheeling troops. "Admiral Ronarc'h!" our companion from Head-quarters exclaimed; and we understood that we had had the good luck to come on the hero of Dixmude in the act of reviewing the marine fusiliers and territorials whose magnificent defense of last October gave that much-besieged town another lease of glory.

We stopped the motor and climbed to a ridge above the field. A high wind was blowing, bringing with it the booming of the guns along the front. A sun half-veiled in sand-dust shone on pale meadows, sandy flats, grey wind-mills. The scene was deserted, except for the handful of troops deploying before the officers on the edge of the field. Admiral Ronarc'h, white-gloved and in full-dress uniform, stood a little in advance, a young naval officer at his side. He had just been distributing decorations to his fusiliers and territorials, and they were marching past him, flags flying and bugles playing. Every one of those men had a record of heroism, and every face in those ranks had looked on horrors unnameable. They had lost Dixmude—for a while—but they had gained great glory, and the inspiration of their epic resistance had come from the quiet officer who stood there, straight and grave, in his white gloves and gala uniform.

One must have been in the North to know something of the tie that exists, in this region of bitter and continuous fighting, between officers and soldiers. The feeling of the chiefs is almost one of veneration for their men; that of the soldiers, a kind of half-humorous tenderness for the officers who have faced such odds with them. This mutual regard reveals itself in a hundred undefinable ways; but its fullest expression is in the tone with which the commanding officers speak the two words oftenest on their lips: "My men."

The little review over, we went on to Admiral Ronarc'h's quarters in the dunes, and thence, after a brief visit, to another brigade Head-quarters. We were in a region of sandy hillocks feathered by tamarisk, and interspersed with poplar groves slanting like wheat in the wind. Between these meagre thickets the roofs of seaside bungalows showed above the dunes; and before one of these we stopped, and were led into a sitting-room full of maps and aeroplane photographs. One of the officers of the brigade telephoned to ask if the way was clear to Nieuport; and the answer was that we might go on.

Our road ran through the "Bois Triangulaire," a bit of woodland exposed to constant shelling. Half the poor spindling trees were down, and patches of blackened undergrowth and ragged hollows marked the path of the shells. If the trees of a cannonaded wood are of strong inland growth their fallen trunks have the majesty of a ruined temple; but there was something humanly pitiful in the frail trunks of the Bois Triangulaire, lying there like slaughtered rows of immature troops.

A few miles more brought us to Nieuport, most lamentable of the victim towns. It is not empty as Ypres is empty: troops are quartered in the cellars, and at the approach of our motor knots of cheerful zouaves came swarming out of the ground like ants. But Ypres is majestic in death, poor Nieuport gruesomely comic. About its splendid nucleus of mediaeval architecture a modern town had grown up; and nothing stranger can be pictured than the contrast between the streets of flimsy houses, twisted like curl-papers, and the ruins of the Gothic Cathedral and the Cloth Market. It is like passing from a smashed toy to the survival of a prehistoric cataclysm.

Modern Nieuport seems to have died in a colic. No less homely image expresses the contractions and contortions of the houses reaching out the appeal of their desperate chimney-pots and agonized girders. There is one view along the exterior of the town like nothing else on the warfront. On the left, a line of palsied houses leads up like a string of crutch-propped beggars to the mighty ruin of the Templars' Tower; on the right the flats reach away to the almost imperceptible humps of masonry that were once the villages of St. Georges, Ramscappelle, Pervyse. And over it all the incessant crash of the guns stretches a sounding-board of steel.

In front of the cathedral a German shell has dug a crater thirty feet across, overhung by splintered tree-trunks, burnt shrubs, vague mounds of rubbish; and a few steps beyond lies the peacefullest spot in Nieuport, the grave-yard where the zouaves have buried their comrades. The dead are laid in rows under the flank of the cathedral, and on their carefully set grave-stones have been placed collections of pious images gathered from the ruined houses. Some of the most privileged are guarded by colonies of plaster saints and Virgins that cover the whole slab; and over the handsomest Virgins and the most gaily coloured saints the soldiers have placed the glass bells that once protected the parlour clocks and wedding-wreaths in the same houses.

From sad Nieuport we motored on to a little seaside colony where gaiety prevails. Here the big hotels and the adjoining villas along the beach are filled with troops just back from the trenches: it is one of the "rest cures" of the front. When we drove up, the regiment "au repos" was assembled in the wide sandy space between the principal hotels, and in the centre of the jolly crowd the band was playing. The Colonel and his officers stood listening to the music, and presently the soldiers broke into the wild "chanson des zouaves" of the —th zouaves. It was the strangest of sights to watch that throng of dusky merry faces under their red fezes against the background of sunless northern sea. When the music was over some one with a kodak suggested "a group": we struck a collective attitude on one of the hotel terraces, and just as the camera was being aimed at us the Colonel turned and drew into the foreground a little grinning pock-marked soldier. "He's just been decorated—he's got to be in the group." A general exclamation of assent from the other officers, and a protest from the hero: "Me? Why, my ugly mug will smash the plate!" But it didn't—

Reluctantly we turned from this interval in the day's sad round, and took the road to La Panne. Dust, dunes, deserted villages: my memory keeps no more definite vision of the run. But at sunset we came on a big seaside colony stretched out above the longest beach I ever saw: along the sea-front, an esplanade bordered by the usual foolish villas, and behind it a single street filled with hotels and shops. All the life of the desert region we had traversed seemed to have taken refuge at La Panne. The long street was swarming with throngs of dark-uniformed Belgian soldiers, every shop seemed to be doing a thriving trade, and the hotels looked as full as beehives.

June 23rd LA PANNE.

The particular hive that has taken us in is at the extreme end of the esplanade, where asphalt and iron railings lapse abruptly into sand and sea-grass. When I looked out of my window this morning I saw only the endless stretch of brown sand against the grey roll of the Northern Ocean and, on a crest of the dunes, the figure of a solitary sentinel. But presently there was a sound of martial music, and long lines of troops came marching along the esplanade and down to the beach. The sands stretched away to east and west, a great "field of Mars" on which an army could have manoeuvred; and the morning exercises of cavalry and infantry began. Against the brown beach the regiments in their dark uniforms looked as black as silhouettes; and the cavalry galloping by in single file suggested a black frieze of warriors encircling the dun-coloured flanks of an Etruscan vase. For hours these long-drawn-out movements of troops went on, to the wail of bugles, and under the eye of the lonely sentinel on the sand-crest; then the soldiers poured back into the town, and La Panne was once more a busy common-place bain-de-mer. The common-placeness, however, was only on the surface; for as one walked along the esplanade one discovered that the town had become a citadel, and that all the doll's-house villas with their silly gables and sillier names—"Seaweed," "The Sea-gull," "Mon Repos," and the rest—were really a continuous line of barracks swarming with Belgian troops. In the main street there were hundreds of soldiers, pottering along in couples, chatting in groups, romping and wrestling like a crowd of school-boys, or bargaining in the shops for shell-work souvenirs and sets of post-cards; and between the dark-green and crimson uniforms was a frequent sprinkling of khaki, with the occasional pale blue of a French officer's tunic.

Before luncheon we motored over to Dunkerque. The road runs along the canal, between grass-flats and prosperous villages. No signs of war were noticeable except on the road, which was crowded with motor vans, ambulances and troops. The walls and gates of Dunkerque rose before us as calm and undisturbed as when we entered the town the day before yesterday. But within the gates we were in a desert. The bombardment had ceased the previous evening, but a death-hush lay on the town, Every house was shuttered and the streets were empty. We drove to the Place Jean Bart, where two days ago we sat at tea in the hall of the hotel. Now there was not a whole pane of glass in the windows of the square, the doors of the hotel were closed, and every now and then some one came out carrying a basketful of plaster from fallen ceilings. The whole surface of the square was literally paved with bits of glass from the hundreds of broken windows, and at the foot of David's statue of Jean Bart, just where our motor had stood while we had tea, the siege-gun of Dixmude had scooped out a hollow as big as the crater at Nieuport.

Though not a house on the square was touched, the scene was one of unmitigated desolation. It was the first time we had seen the raw wounds of a bombardment, and the freshness of the havoc seemed to accentuate its cruelty. We wandered down the street behind the hotel to the graceful Gothic church of St. Eloi, of which one aisle had been shattered; then, turning another corner, we came on a poor bourgeois house that had had its whole front torn away. The squalid revelation of caved-in floors, smashed wardrobes, dangling bedsteads, heaped-up blankets, topsy-turvy chairs and stoves and wash-stands was far more painful than the sight of the wounded church. St. Eloi was draped in the dignity of martyrdom, but the poor little house reminded one of some shy humdrum person suddenly exposed in the glare of a great misfortune.

A few people stood in clusters looking up at the ruins, or strayed aimlessly about the streets. Not a loud word was heard. The air seemed heavy with the suspended breath of a great city's activities: the mournful hush of Dunkerque was even more oppressive than the death-silence of Ypres. But when we came back to the Place Jean Bart the unbreakable human spirit had begun to reassert itself. A handful of children were playing in the bottom of the crater, collecting "specimens" of glass and splintered brick; and about its rim the market-people, quietly and as a matter of course, were setting up their wooden stalls. In a few minutes the signs of German havoc would be hidden behind stacks of crockery and household utensils, and some of the pale women we had left in mournful contemplation of the ruins would be bargaining as sharply as ever for a sauce-pan or a butter-tub. Not once but a hundred times has the attitude of the average French civilian near the front reminded me of the gallant cry of Calanthea in The Broken Heart: "Let me die smiling!" I should have liked to stop and spend all I had in the market of Dunkerque...

All the afternoon we wandered about La Panne. The exercises of the troops had begun again, and the deploying of those endless black lines along the beach was a sight of the strangest beauty. The sun was veiled, and heavy surges rolled in under a northerly gale. Toward evening the sea turned to cold tints of jade and pearl and tarnished silver. Far down the beach a mysterious fleet of fishing boats was drawn up on the sand, with black sails bellying in the wind; and the black riders galloping by might have landed from them, and been riding into the sunset out of some wild northern legend. Presently a knot of buglers took up their stand on the edge of the sea, facing inward, their feet in the surf, and began to play; and their call was like the call of Roland's horn, when he blew it down the pass against the heathen. On the sandcrest below my window the lonely sentinel still watched...

June 24th.

It is like coming down from the mountains to leave the front. I never had the feeling more strongly than when we passed out of Belgium this afternoon. I had it most strongly as we drove by a cluster of villas standing apart in a sterile region of sea-grass and sand. In one of those villas for nearly a year, two hearts at the highest pitch of human constancy have held up a light to the world. It is impossible to pass that house without a sense of awe. Because of the light that comes from it, dead faiths have come to life, weak convictions have grown strong, fiery impulses have turned to long endurance, and long endurance has kept the fire of impulse. In the harbour of New York there is a pompous statue of a goddess with a torch, designated as "Liberty enlightening the World." It seems as though the title on her pedestal might well, for the time, be transferred to the lintel of that villa in the dunes.

On leaving St. Omer we took a short cut southward across rolling country. It was a happy accident that caused us to leave the main road, for presently, over the crest of a hill, we saw surging toward us a mighty movement of British and Indian troops. A great bath of silver sunlight lay on the wheat-fields, the clumps of woodland and the hilly blue horizon, and in that slanting radiance the cavalry rode toward us, regiment after regiment of slim turbaned Indians, with delicate proud faces like the faces of Princes in Persian miniatures. Then came a long train of artillery; splendid horses, clattering gun-carriages, clear-faced English youths galloping by all aglow in the sunset. The stream of them seemed never-ending. Now and then it was checked by a train of ambulances and supply-waggons, or caught and congested in the crooked streets of a village where children and girls had come out with bunches of flowers, and bakers were selling hot loaves to the sutlers; and when we had extricated our motor from the crowd, and climbed another hill, we came on another cavalcade surging toward us through the wheat-fields. For over an hour the procession poured by, so like and yet so unlike the French division we had met on the move as we went north a few days ago; so that we seemed to have passed to the northern front, and away from it again, through a great flashing gateway in the long wall of armies guarding the civilized world from the North Sea to the Vosges.

IN ALSACE

August 13th, 1915.

My trip to the east began by a dash toward the north. Near Rheims is a little town—hardly more than a village, but in English we have no intermediate terms such as "bourg" and "petit bourg"—where one of the new Red Cross sanitary motor units was to be seen "in action." The inspection over, we climbed to a vineyard above the town and looked down at a river valley traversed by a double line of trees. The first line marked the canal, which is held by the French, who have gun-boats on it. Behind this ran the high-road, with the first-line French trenches, and just above, on the opposite slope, were the German lines. The soil being chalky, the German positions were clearly marked by two parallel white scorings across the brown hill-front; and while we watched we heard desultory firing, and saw, here and there along the ridge, the smoke-puff of an exploding shell. It was incredibly strange to stand there, among the vines humming with summer insects, and to look out over a peaceful country heavy with the coming vintage, knowing that the trees at our feet hid a line of gun-boats that were crashing death into those two white scorings on the hill.

Rheims itself brings one nearer to the war by its look of deathlike desolation. The paralysis of the bombarded towns is one of the most tragic results of the invasion. One's soul revolts at this senseless disorganizing of innumerable useful activities. Compared with the towns of the north, Rheims is relatively unharmed; but for that very reason the arrest of life seems the more futile and cruel. The Cathedral square was deserted, all the houses around it were closed. And there, before us, rose the Cathedral—a cathedral, rather, for it was not the one we had always known. It was, in fact, not like any cathedral on earth. When the German bombardment began, the west front of Rheims was covered with scaffolding: the shells set it on fire, and the whole church was wrapped in flames. Now the scaffolding is gone, and in the dull provincial square there stands a structure so strange and beautiful that one must search the Inferno, or some tale of Eastern magic, for words to picture the luminous unearthly vision. The lower part of the front has been warmed to deep tints of umber and burnt siena. This rich burnishing passes, higher up, through yellowish-pink and carmine, to a sulphur whitening to ivory; and the recesses of the portals and the hollows behind the statues are lined with a black denser and more velvety than any effect of shadow to be obtained by sculptured relief. The interweaving of colour over the whole blunted bruised surface recalls the metallic tints, the peacock-and-pigeon iridescences, the incredible mingling of red, blue, umber and yellow of the rocks along the Gulf of AEgina. And the wonder of the impression is increased by the sense of its evanescence; the knowledge that this is the beauty of disease and death, that every one of the transfigured statues must crumble under the autumn rains, that every one of the pink or golden stones is already eaten away to the core, that the Cathedral of Rheims is glowing and dying before us like a sunset...

August 14th.

A stone and brick chateau in a flat park with a stream running through it. Pampas-grass, geraniums, rustic bridges, winding paths: how bourgeois and sleepy it would all seem but for the sentinel challenging our motor at the gate!

Before the door a collie dozing in the sun, and a group of staff-officers waiting for luncheon. Indoors, a room with handsome tapestries, some good furniture and a table spread with the usual military maps and aeroplane-photographs. At luncheon, the General, the chiefs of the staff—a dozen in all—an officer from the General Head-quarters. The usual atmosphere of camaraderie, confidence, good-humour, and a kind of cheerful seriousness that I have come to regard as characteristic of the men immersed in the actual facts of the war. I set down this impression as typical of many such luncheon hours along the front...

August 15th.

This morning we set out for reconquered Alsace. For reasons unexplained to the civilian this corner of old-new France has hitherto been inaccessible, even to highly placed French officials; and there was a special sense of excitement in taking the road that led to it.

We slipped through a valley or two, passed some placid villages with vine-covered gables, and noticed that most of the signs over the shops were German. We had crossed the old frontier unawares, and were presently in the charming town of Massevaux. It was the Feast of the Assumption, and mass was just over when we reached the square before the church. The streets were full of holiday people, well-dressed, smiling, seemingly unconscious of the war. Down the church-steps, guided by fond mammas, came little girls in white dresses, with white wreaths in their hair, and carrying, in baskets slung over their shoulders, woolly lambs or blue and white Virgins. Groups of cavalry officers stood chatting with civilians in their Sunday best, and through the windows of the Golden Eagle we saw active preparations for a crowded mid-day dinner. It was all as happy and parochial as a "Hansi" picture, and the fine old gabled houses and clean cobblestone streets made the traditional setting for an Alsacian holiday.

At the Golden Eagle we laid in a store of provisions, and started out across the mountains in the direction of Thann. The Vosges, at this season, are in their short midsummer beauty, rustling with streams, dripping with showers, balmy with the smell of firs and braken, and of purple thyme on hot banks. We reached the top of a ridge, and, hiding the motor behind a skirt of trees, went out into the open to lunch on a sunny slope. Facing us across the valley was a tall conical hill clothed with forest. That hill was Hartmannswillerkopf, the centre of a long contest in which the French have lately been victorious; and all about us stood other crests and ridges from which German guns still look down on the valley of Thann.

Thann itself is at the valley-head, in a neck between hills; a handsome old town, with the air of prosperous stability so oddly characteristic of this tormented region. As we drove through the main street the pall of war-sadness fell on us again, darkening the light and chilling the summer air. Thann is raked by the German lines, and its windows are mostly shuttered and its streets deserted. One or two houses in the Cathedral square have been gutted, but the somewhat over-pinnacled and statued cathedral which is the pride of Thann is almost untouched, and when we entered it vespers were being sung, and a few people—mostly in black—knelt in the nave.

No greater contrast could be imagined to the happy feast-day scene we had left, a few miles off, at Massevaux; but Thann, in spite of its empty streets, is not a deserted city. A vigorous life beats in it, ready to break forth as soon as the German guns are silenced. The French administration, working on the best of terms with the population, are keeping up the civil activities of the town as the Canons of the Cathedral are continuing the rites of the Church. Many inhabitants still remain behind their closed shutters and dive down into their cellars when the shells begin to crash; and the schools, transferred to a neighbouring village, number over two thousand pupils. We walked through the town, visited a vast catacomb of a wine-cellar fitted up partly as an ambulance and partly as a shelter for the cellarless, and saw the lamentable remains of the industrial quarter along the river, which has been the special target of the German guns. Thann has been industrially ruined, all its mills are wrecked; but unlike the towns of the north it has had the good fortune to preserve its outline, its civic personality, a face that its children, when they come back, can recognize and take comfort in.

After our visit to the ruins, a diversion was suggested by the amiable administrators of Thann who had guided our sight-seeing. They were just off for a military tournament which the —th dragoons were giving that afternoon in a neighboring valley, and we were invited to go with them.

The scene of the entertainment was a meadow enclosed in an amphitheatre of rocks, with grassy ledges projecting from the cliff like tiers of opera-boxes. These points of vantage were partly occupied by interested spectators and partly by ruminating cattle; on the lowest slope, the rank and fashion of the neighbourhood was ranged on a semi-circle of chairs, and below, in the meadow, a lively steeple-chase was going on. The riding was extremely pretty, as French military riding always is. Few of the mounts were thoroughbreds—the greater number, in fact, being local cart-horses barely broken to the saddle—but their agility and dash did the greater credit to their riders. The lancers, in particular, executed an effective "musical ride" about a central pennon, to the immense satisfaction of the fashionable public in the foreground and of the gallery on the rocks.

The audience was even more interesting than the artists. Chatting with the ladies in the front row were the General of division and his staff, groups of officers invited from the adjoining Head-quarters, and most of the civil and military administrators of the restored "Departement du Haut Rhin." All classes had turned out in honour of the fete, and every one was in a holiday mood. The people among whom we sat were mostly Alsatian property-owners, many of them industrials of Thann. Some had been driven from their homes, others had seen their mills destroyed, all had been living for a year on the perilous edge of war, under the menace of reprisals too hideous to picture; yet the humour prevailing was that of any group of merry-makers in a peaceful garrison town. I have seen nothing, in my wanderings along the front, more indicative of the good-breeding of the French than the spirit of the ladies and gentlemen who sat chatting with the officers on that grassy slope of Alsace.

The display of haute ecole was to be followed by an exhibition of "transportation throughout the ages," headed by a Gaulish chariot driven by a trooper with a long horsehair moustache and mistletoe wreath, and ending in a motor of which the engine had been taken out and replaced by a large placid white horse. Unluckily a heavy rain began while this instructive "number" awaited its turn, and we had to leave before Vercingetorix had led his warriors into the ring...

August 16th.

Up and up into the mountains. We started early, taking our way along a narrow interminable valley that sloped up gradually toward the east. The road was encumbered with a stream of hooded supply vans drawn by mules, for we were on the way to one of the main positions in the Vosges, and this train of provisions is kept up day and night. Finally we reached a mountain village under fir-clad slopes, with a cold stream rushing down from the hills. On one side of the road was a rustic inn, on the other, among the firs, a chalet occupied by the brigade Head-quarters. Everywhere about us swarmed the little "chasseurs Alpins" in blue Tam o'Shanters and leather gaiters. For a year we had been reading of these heroes of the hills, and here we were among them, looking into their thin weather-beaten faces and meeting the twinkle of their friendly eyes. Very friendly they all were, and yet, for Frenchmen, inarticulate and shy. All over the world, no doubt, the mountain silences breed this kind of reserve, this shrinking from the glibness of the valleys. Yet one had fancied that French fluency must soar as high as Mont Blanc.

Mules were brought, and we started on a long ride up the mountain. The way led first over open ledges, with deep views into valleys blue with distance, then through miles of forest, first of beech and fir, and finally all of fir. Above the road the wooded slopes rose interminably and here and there we came on tiers of mules, three or four hundred together, stabled under the trees, in stalls dug out of different levels of the slope. Near by were shelters for the men, and perhaps at the next bend a village of "trappers' huts," as the officers call the log-cabins they build in this region. These colonies are always bustling with life: men busy cleaning their arms, hauling material for new cabins, washing or mending their clothes, or carrying down the mountain from the camp-kitchen the two-handled pails full of steaming soup. The kitchen is always in the most protected quarter of the camp, and generally at some distance in the rear. Other soldiers, their job over, are lolling about in groups, smoking, gossiping or writing home, the "Soldiers' Letter-pad" propped on a patched blue knee, a scarred fist laboriously driving the fountain pen received in hospital. Some are leaning over the shoulder of a pal who has just received a Paris paper, others chuckling together at the jokes of their own French journal—the "Echo du Ravin," the "Journal des Poilus," or the "Diable Bleu": little papers ground out in purplish script on foolscap, and adorned with comic-sketches and a wealth of local humour.

Higher up, under a fir-belt, at the edge of a meadow, the officer who rode ahead signed to us to dismount and scramble after him. We plunged under the trees, into what seemed a thicker thicket, and found it to be a thatch of branches woven to screen the muzzles of a battery. The big guns were all about us, crouched in these sylvan lairs like wild beasts waiting to spring; and near each gun hovered its attendant gunner, proud, possessive, important as a bridegroom with his bride.

We climbed and climbed again, reaching at last a sun-and-wind-burnt common which forms the top of one of the highest mountains in the region. The forest was left below us and only a belt of dwarf firs ran along the edge of the great grassy shoulder. We dismounted, the mules were tethered among the trees, and our guide led us to an insignificant looking stone in the grass. On one face of the stone was cut the letter F., on the other was a D.; we stood on what, till a year ago, was the boundary line between Republic and Empire. Since then, in certain places, the line has been bent back a long way; but where we stood we were still under German guns, and we had to creep along in the shelter of the squat firs to reach the outlook on the edge of the plateau. From there, under a sky of racing clouds, we saw outstretched below us the Promised Land of Alsace. On one horizon, far off in the plain, gleamed the roofs and spires of Colmar, on the other rose the purplish heights beyond the Rhine. Near by stood a ring of bare hills, those closest to us scarred by ridges of upheaved earth, as if giant moles had been zigzagging over them; and just under us, in a little green valley, lay the roofs of a peaceful village. The earth-ridges and the peaceful village were still German; but the French positions went down the mountain, almost to the valley's edge; and one dark peak on the right was already French.

We stopped at a gap in the firs and walked to the brink of the plateau. Just under us lay a rock-rimmed lake. More zig-zag earthworks surmounted it on all sides, and on the nearest shore was the branched roofing of another great mule-shelter. We were looking down at the spot to which the night-caravans of the Chasseurs Alpins descend to distribute supplies to the fighting line.

"Who goes there? Attention! You're in sight of the lines!" a voice called out from the firs, and our companion signed to us to move back. We had been rather too conspicuously facing the German batteries on the opposite slope, and our presence might have drawn their fire on an artillery observation post installed near by. We retreated hurriedly and unpacked our luncheon-basket on the more sheltered side of the ridge. As we sat there in the grass, swept by a great mountain breeze full of the scent of thyme and myrtle, while the flutter of birds, the hum of insects, the still and busy life of the hills went on all about us in the sunshine, the pressure of the encircling line of death grew more intolerably real. It is not in the mud and jokes and every-day activities of the trenches that one most feels the damnable insanity of war; it is where it lurks like a mythical monster in scenes to which the mind has always turned for rest.

We had not yet made the whole tour of the mountain-top; and after luncheon we rode over to a point where a long narrow yoke connects it with a spur projecting directly above the German lines. We left our mules in hiding and walked along the yoke, a mere knife-edge of rock rimmed with dwarf vegetation. Suddenly we heard an explosion behind us: one of the batteries we had passed on the way up was giving tongue. The German lines roared back and for twenty minutes the exchange of invective thundered on. The firing was almost incessant; it seemed as if a great arch of steel were being built up above us in the crystal air. And we could follow each curve of sound from its incipience to its final crash in the trenches. There were four distinct phases: the sharp bang from the cannon, the long furious howl overhead, the dispersed and spreading noise of the shell's explosion, and then the roll of its reverberation from cliff to cliff. This is what we heard as we crouched in the lee of the firs: what we saw when we looked out between them was only an occasional burst of white smoke and red flame from one hillside, and on the opposite one, a minute later, a brown geyser of dust.

Presently a deluge of rain descended on us, driving us back to our mules, and down the nearest mountain-trail through rivers of mud. It rained all the way: rained in such floods and cataracts that the very rocks of the mountain seemed to dissolve and turn into mud. As we slid down through it we met strings of Chasseurs Alpins coming up, splashed to the waist with wet red clay, and leading pack-mules so coated with it that they looked like studio models from which the sculptor has just pulled off the dripping sheet. Lower down we came on more "trapper" settlements, so saturated and reeking with wet that they gave us a glimpse of what the winter months on the front must be. No more cheerful polishing of fire-arms, hauling of faggots, chatting and smoking in sociable groups: everybody had crept under the doubtful shelter of branches and tarpaulins; the whole army was back in its burrows.

Sunshine again for our arrival at Belfort. The invincible city lies unpretentiously behind its green glacis and escutcheoned gates; but the guardian Lion under the Citadel—well, the Lion is figuratively as well as literally a la hauteur. With the sunset flush on him, as he crouched aloft in his red lair below the fort, he might almost have claimed kin with his mighty prototypes of the Assarbanipal frieze. One wondered a little, seeing whose work he was; but probably it is easier for an artist to symbolize an heroic town than the abstract and elusive divinity who sheds light on the world from New York harbour.

From Belfort back into reconquered Alsace the road runs through a gentle landscape of fields and orchards. We were bound for Dannemarie, one of the towns of the plain, and a centre of the new administration. It is the usual "gros bourg" of Alsace, with comfortable old houses in espaliered gardens: dull, well-to-do, contented; not in the least the kind of setting demanded by the patriotism which has to be fed on pictures of little girls singing the Marseillaise in Alsatian head-dresses and old men with operatic waistcoats tottering forward to kiss the flag. What we saw at Dannemarie was less conspicuous to the eye but much more nourishing to the imagination. The military and civil administrators had the kindness and patience to explain their work and show us something of its results; and the visit left one with the impression of a slow and quiet process of adaptation wisely planned and fruitfully carried out. We did, in fact, hear the school-girls of Dannemarie sing the Marseillaise—and the boys too—but, what was far more interesting, we saw them studying under the direction of the teachers who had always had them in charge, and found that everywhere it had been the aim of the French officials to let the routine of the village policy go on undisturbed. The German signs remain over the shop-fronts except where the shop-keepers have chosen to paint them out; as is happening more and more frequently. When a functionary has to be replaced he is chosen from the same town or the same district, and even the personnel of the civil and military administration is mainly composed of officers and civilians of Alsatian stock. The heads of both these departments, who accompanied us on our rounds, could talk to the children and old people in German as well as in their local dialect; and, as far as a passing observer could discern, it seemed as though everything had been done to reduce to a minimum the sense of strangeness and friction which is inevitable in the transition from one rule to another. The interesting point was that this exercise of tact and tolerance seemed to proceed not from any pressure of expediency but from a sympathetic understanding of the point of view of this people of the border. I heard in Dannemarie not a syllable of lyrical patriotism or post-card sentimentality, but only a kindly and impartial estimate of facts as they were and must be dealt with.

Today again we started early for the mountains. Our road ran more to the westward, through the heart of the Vosges, and up to a fold of the hills near the borders of Lorraine. We stopped at a Head-quarters where a young officer of dragoons was to join us, and learned from him that we were to be allowed to visit some of the first-line trenches which we had looked out on from a high-perched observation post on our former visit to the Vosges. Violent fighting was going on in that particular region, and after a climb of an hour or two we had to leave the motor at a sheltered angle of the road and strike across the hills on foot. Our path lay through the forest, and every now and then we caught a glimpse of the high-road running below us in full view of the German batteries. Presently we reached a point where the road was screened by a thick growth of trees behind which an observation post had been set up. We scrambled down and looked through the peephole. Just below us lay a valley with a village in its centre, and to the left and right of the village were two hills, the one scored with French, the other with German trenches. The village, at first sight, looked as normal as those through which we had been passing; but a closer inspection showed that its steeple was shattered and that some of its houses were unroofed. Part of it was held by German, part by French troops. The cemetery adjoining the church, and a quarry just under it, belonged to the Germans; but a line of French trenches ran from the farther side of the church up to the French batteries on the right hand hill. Parallel with this line, but starting from the other side of the village, was a hollow lane leading up to a single tree. This lane was a German trench, protected by the guns of the left hand hill; and between the two lay perhaps fifty yards of ground. All this was close under us; and closer still was a slope of open ground leading up to the village and traversed by a rough cart-track. Along this track in the hot sunshine little French soldiers, the size of tin toys, were scrambling up with bags and loads of faggots, their ant-like activity as orderly and untroubled as if the two armies had not lain trench to trench a few yards away. It was one of those strange and contradictory scenes of war that bring home to the bewildered looker-on the utter impossibility of picturing how the thing really happens.

While we stood watching we heard the sudden scream of a battery close above us. The crest of the hill we were climbing was alive with "Seventy-fives," and the piercing noise seemed to burst out at our very backs. It was the most terrible war-shriek I had heard: a kind of wolfish baying that called up an image of all the dogs of war simultaneously tugging at their leashes. There is a dreadful majesty in the sound of a distant cannonade; but these yelps and hisses roused only thoughts of horror. And there, on the opposite slope, the black and brown geysers were beginning to spout up from the German trenches; and from the batteries above them came the puff and roar of retaliation. Below us, along the cart-track, the little French soldiers continued to scramble up peacefully to the dilapidated village; and presently a group of officers of dragoons, emerging from the wood, came down to welcome us to their Head-quarters.

We continued to climb through the forest, the cannonade still whistling overhead, till we reached the most elaborate trapper colony we had yet seen. Half underground, walled with logs, and deeply roofed by sods tufted with ferns and moss, the cabins were scattered under the trees and connected with each other by paths bordered with white stones. Before the Colonel's cabin the soldiers had made a banked-up flower-bed sown with annuals; and farther up the slope stood a log chapel, a mere gable with a wooden altar under it, all tapestried with ivy and holly. Near by was the chaplain's subterranean dwelling. It was reached by a deep cutting with ivy-covered sides, and ivy and fir-boughs masked the front. This sylvan retreat had just been completed, and the officers, the chaplain, and the soldiers loitering near by, were all equally eager to have it seen and hear it praised.

The commanding officer, having done the honours of the camp, led us about a quarter of a mile down the hillside to an open cutting which marked the beginning of the trenches. From the cutting we passed into a long tortuous burrow walled and roofed with carefully fitted logs. The earth floor was covered by a sort of wooden lattice. The only light entering this tunnel was a faint ray from an occasional narrow slit screened by branches; and beside each of these peep-holes hung a shield-shaped metal shutter to be pushed over it in case of emergency.

The passage wound down the hill, almost doubling on itself, in order to give a view of all the surrounding lines. Presently the roof became much higher, and we saw on one side a curtained niche about five feet above the floor. One of the officers pulled the curtain back, and there, on a narrow shelf, a gun between his knees, sat a dragoon, his eyes on a peep-hole. The curtain was hastily drawn again behind his motionless figure, lest the faint light at his back should betray him. We passed by several of these helmeted watchers, and now and then we came to a deeper recess in which a mitrailleuse squatted, its black nose thrust through a net of branches. Sometimes the roof of the tunnel was so low that we had to bend nearly double; and at intervals we came to heavy doors, made of logs and sheeted with iron, which shut off one section from another. It is hard to guess the distance one covers in creeping through an unlit passage with different levels and countless turnings; but we must have descended the hillside for at least a mile before we came out into a half-ruined farmhouse. This building, which had kept nothing but its outer walls and one or two partitions between the rooms, had been transformed into an observation post. In each of its corners a ladder led up to a little shelf on the level of what was once the second story, and on the shelf sat a dragoon at his peep-hole. Below, in the dilapidated rooms, the usual life of a camp was going on. Some of the soldiers were playing cards at a kitchen table, others mending their clothes, or writing letters or chuckling together (not too loud) over a comic newspaper. It might have been a scene anywhere along the second-line trenches but for the lowered voices, the suddenness with which I was drawn back from a slit in the wall through which I had incautiously peered, and the presence of these helmeted watchers overhead.

We plunged underground again and began to descend through another darker and narrower tunnel. In the upper one there had been one or two roofless stretches where one could straighten one's back and breathe; but here we were in pitch blackness, and saved from breaking our necks only by the gleam of the pocket-light which the young lieutenant who led the party shed on our path. As he whisked it up and down to warn us of sudden steps or sharp corners he remarked that at night even this faint glimmer was forbidden, and that it was a bad job going back and forth from the last outpost till one had learned the turnings.

The last outpost was a half-ruined farmhouse like the other. A telephone connected it with Head-quarters and more dumb dragoons sat motionless on their lofty shelves. The house was shut off from the tunnel by an armoured door, and the orders were that in case of attack that door should be barred from within and the access to the tunnel defended to the death by the men in the outpost. We were on the extreme verge of the defences, on a slope just above the village over which we had heard the artillery roaring a few hours earlier. The spot where we stood was raked on all sides by the enemy's lines, and the nearest trenches were only a few yards away. But of all this nothing was really perceptible or comprehensible to me. As far as my own observation went, we might have been a hundred miles from the valley we had looked down on, where the French soldiers were walking peacefully up the cart-track in the sunshine. I only knew that we had come out of a black labyrinth into a gutted house among fruit-trees, where soldiers were lounging and smoking, and people whispered as they do about a death-bed. Over a break in the walls I saw another gutted farmhouse close by in another orchard: it was an enemy outpost, and silent watchers in helmets of another shape sat there watching on the same high shelves. But all this was infinitely less real and terrible than the cannonade above the disputed village. The artillery had ceased and the air was full of summer murmurs. Close by on a sheltered ledge I saw a patch of vineyard with dewy cobwebs hanging to the vines. I could not understand where we were, or what it was all about, or why a shell from the enemy outpost did not suddenly annihilate us. And then, little by little, there came over me the sense of that mute reciprocal watching from trench to trench: the interlocked stare of innumerable pairs of eyes, stretching on, mile after mile, along the whole sleepless line from Dunkerque to Belfort.

My last vision of the French front which I had traveled from end to end was this picture of a shelled house where a few men, who sat smoking and playing cards in the sunshine, had orders to hold out to the death rather than let their fraction of that front be broken.

Nobody now asks the question that so often, at the beginning of the war, came to me from the other side of the world: "What is France like?" Everyone knows what France has proved to be like: from being a difficult problem she has long since become a luminous instance.

Nevertheless, to those on whom that illumination has shone only from far off, there may still be something to learn about its component elements; for it has come to consist of many separate rays, and the weary strain of the last year has been the spectroscope to decompose them. From the very beginning, when one felt the effulgence as the mere pale brightness before dawn, the attempt to define it was irresistible. "There is a tone—" the tingling sense of it was in the air from the first days, the first hours—"but what does it consist in? And just how is one aware of it?" In those days the answer was comparatively easy. The tone of France after the declaration of war was the white glow of dedication: a great nation's collective impulse (since there is no English equivalent for that winged word, elan) to resist destruction. But at that time no one knew what the resistance was to cost, how long it would have to last, what sacrifices, material and moral, it would necessitate. And for the moment baser sentiments were silenced: greed, self-interest, pusillanimity seemed to have been purged from the race. The great sitting of the Chamber, that almost religious celebration of defensive union, really expressed the opinion of the whole people. It is fairly easy to soar to the empyrean when one is carried on the wings of such an impulse, and when one does not know how long one is to be kept suspended at the breathing-limit.

But there is a term to the flight of the most soaring elan. It is likely, after a while, to come back broken-winged and resign itself to barn-yard bounds. National judgments cannot remain for long above individual feelings; and you cannot get a national "tone" out of anything less than a whole nation. The really interesting thing, therefore, was to see, as the war went on, and grew into a calamity unheard of in human annals, how the French spirit would meet it, and what virtues extract from it.

The war has been a calamity unheard of; but France has never been afraid of the unheard of. No race has ever yet so audaciously dispensed with old precedents; as none has ever so revered their relics. It is a great strength to be able to walk without the support of analogies; and France has always shown that strength in times of crisis. The absorbing question, as the war went on, was to discover how far down into the people this intellectual audacity penetrated, how instinctive it had become, and how it would endure the strain of prolonged inaction.

There was never much doubt about the army. When a warlike race has an invader on its soil, the men holding back the invader can never be said to be inactive. But behind the army were the waiting millions to whom that long motionless line in the trenches might gradually have become a mere condition of thought, an accepted limitation to all sorts of activities and pleasures. The danger was that such a war—static, dogged, uneventful—might gradually cramp instead of enlarging the mood of the lookers-on. Conscription, of course, was there to minimize this danger. Every one was sharing alike in the glory and the woe. But the glory was not of a kind to penetrate or dazzle. It requires more imagination to see the halo around tenacity than around dash; and the French still cling to the view that they are, so to speak, the patentees and proprietors of dash, and much less at home with his dull drudge of a partner. So there was reason to fear, in the long run, a gradual but irresistible disintegration, not of public opinion, but of something subtler and more fundamental: public sentiment. It was possible that civilian France, while collectively seeming to remain at the same height, might individually deteriorate and diminish in its attitude toward the war.

The French would not be human, and therefore would not be interesting, if one had not perceived in them occasional symptoms of such a peril. There has not been a Frenchman or a Frenchwoman—save a few harmless and perhaps nervous theorizers—who has wavered about the military policy of the country; but there have naturally been some who have found it less easy than they could have foreseen to live up to the sacrifices it has necessitated. Of course there have been such people: one would have had to postulate them if they had not come within one's experience. There have been some to whom it was harder than they imagined to give up a certain way of living, or a certain kind of breakfast-roll; though the French, being fundamentally temperate, are far less the slaves of the luxuries they have invented than are the other races who have adopted these luxuries.

There have been many more who found the sacrifice of personal happiness—of all that made life livable, or one's country worth fighting for—infinitely harder than the most apprehensive imagination could have pictured. There have been mothers and widows for whom a single grave, or the appearance of one name on the missing list, has turned the whole conflict into an idiot's tale. There have been many such; but there have apparently not been enough to deflect by a hair's breadth the subtle current of public sentiment; unless it is truer, as it is infinitely more inspiring, to suppose that, of this company of blinded baffled sufferers, almost all have had the strength to hide their despair and to say of the great national effort which has lost most of its meaning to them: "Though it slay me, yet will I trust in it." That is probably the finest triumph of the tone of France: that its myriad fiery currents flow from so many hearts made insensible by suffering, that so many dead hands feed its undying lamp.

This does not in the least imply that resignation is the prevailing note in the tone of France. The attitude of the French people, after fourteen months of trial, is not one of submission to unparalleled calamity. It is one of exaltation, energy, the hot resolve to dominate the disaster. In all classes the feeling is the same: every word and every act is based on the resolute ignoring of any alternative to victory. The French people no more think of a compromise than people would think of facing a flood or an earthquake with a white flag.

Two questions are likely to be put to any observer of the struggle who risks such assertions. What, one may be asked, are the proofs of this national tone? And what conditions and qualities seem to minister to it?

The proofs, now that "the tumult and the shouting dies," and civilian life has dropped back into something like its usual routine, are naturally less definable than at the outset. One of the most evident is the spirit in which all kinds of privations are accepted. No one who has come in contact with the work-people and small shop-keepers of Paris in the last year can fail to be struck by the extreme dignity and grace with which doing without things is practised. The Frenchwoman leaning in the door of her empty boutique still wears the smile with which she used to calm the impatience of crowding shoppers. The seam-stress living on the meagre pay of a charity work-room gives her day's sewing as faithfully as if she were working for full wages in a fashionable atelier, and never tries, by the least hint of private difficulties, to extract additional help. The habitual cheerfulness of the Parisian workwoman rises, in moments of sorrow, to the finest fortitude. In a work-room where many women have been employed since the beginning of the war, a young girl of sixteen heard late one afternoon that her only brother had been killed. She had a moment of desperate distress; but there was a big family to be helped by her small earnings, and the next morning punctually she was back at work. In this same work-room the women have one half-holiday in the week, without reduction of pay; yet if an order has to be rushed through for a hospital they give up that one afternoon as gaily as if they were doing it for their pleasure. But if any one who has lived for the last year among the workers and small tradesmen of Paris should begin to cite instances of endurance, self-denial and secret charity, the list would have no end. The essential of it all is the spirit in which these acts are accomplished.

The second question: What are the conditions and qualities that have produced such results? is less easy to answer. The door is so largely open to conjecture that every explanation must depend largely on the answerer's personal bias. But one thing is certain. France has not achieved her present tone by the sacrifice of any of her national traits, but rather by their extreme keying up; therefore the surest way of finding a clue to that tone is to try to single out whatever distinctively "French" characteristics—or those that appear such to the envious alien—have a direct bearing on the present attitude of France. Which (one must ask) of all their multiple gifts most help the French today to be what they are in just the way they are?

Intelligence! is the first and instantaneous answer. Many French people seem unaware of this. They are sincerely persuaded that the curbing of their critical activity has been one of the most important and useful results of the war. One is told that, in a spirit of patriotism, this fault-finding people has learned not to find fault. Nothing could be more untrue. The French, when they have a grievance, do not air it in the Times: their forum is the cafe and not the newspaper. But in the cafe they are talking as freely as ever, discriminating as keenly and judging as passionately. The difference is that the very exercise of their intelligence on a problem larger and more difficult than any they have hitherto faced has freed them from the dominion of most of the prejudices, catch-words and conventions that directed opinion before the war. Then their intelligence ran in fixed channels; now it has overflowed its banks.

This release has produced an immediate readjusting of all the elements of national life. In great trials a race is tested by its values; and the war has shown the world what are the real values of France. Never for an instant has this people, so expert in the great art of living, imagined that life consisted in being alive. Enamoured of pleasure and beauty, dwelling freely and frankly in the present, they have yet kept their sense of larger meanings, have understood life to be made up of many things past and to come, of renunciation as well as satisfaction, of traditions as well as experiments, of dying as much as of living. Never have they considered life as a thing to be cherished in itself, apart from its reactions and its relations.

Intelligence first, then, has helped France to be what she is; and next, perhaps, one of its corollaries, expression. The French are the first to laugh at themselves for running to words: they seem to regard their gift for expression as a weakness, a possible deterrent to action. The last year has not confirmed that view. It has rather shown that eloquence is a supplementary weapon. By "eloquence" I naturally do not mean public speaking, nor yet the rhetorical writing too often associated with the word. Rhetoric is the dressing-up of conventional sentiment, eloquence the fearless expression of real emotion. And this gift of the fearless expression of emotion—fearless, that is, of ridicule, or of indifference in the hearer—has been an inestimable strength to France. It is a sign of the high average of French intelligence that feeling well-worded can stir and uplift it; that "words" are not half shamefacedly regarded as something separate from, and extraneous to, emotion, or even as a mere vent for it, but as actually animating and forming it. Every additional faculty for exteriorizing states of feeling, giving them a face and a language, is a moral as well as an artistic asset, and Goethe was never wiser than when he wrote:

"A god gave me the voice to speak my pain."

It is not too much to say that the French are at this moment drawing a part of their national strength from their language. The piety with which they have cherished and cultivated it has made it a precious instrument in their hands. It can say so beautifully what they feel that they find strength and renovation in using it; and the word once uttered is passed on, and carries the same help to others. Countless instances of such happy expression could be cited by any one who has lived the last year in France. On the bodies of young soldiers have been found letters of farewell to their parents that made one think of some heroic Elizabethan verse; and the mothers robbed of these sons have sent them an answering cry of courage.

"Thank you," such a mourner wrote me the other day, "for having understood the cruelty of our fate, and having pitied us. Thank you also for having exalted the pride that is mingled with our unutterable sorrow." Simply that, and no more; but she might have been speaking for all the mothers of France.

When the eloquent expression of feeling does not issue in action—or at least in a state of mind equivalent to action—it sinks to the level of rhetoric; but in France at this moment expression and conduct supplement and reflect each other. And this brings me to the other great attribute which goes to making up the tone of France: the quality of courage. It is not unintentionally that it comes last on my list. French courage is courage rationalized, courage thought out, and found necessary to some special end; it is, as much as any other quality of the French temperament, the result of French intelligence.

No people so sensitive to beauty, so penetrated with a passionate interest in life, so endowed with the power to express and immortalize that interest, can ever really enjoy destruction for its own sake. The French hate "militarism." It is stupid, inartistic, unimaginative and enslaving; there could not be four better French reasons for detesting it. Nor have the French ever enjoyed the savage forms of sport which stimulate the blood of more apathetic or more brutal races. Neither prize-fighting nor bull-fighting is of the soil in France, and Frenchmen do not settle their private differences impromptu with their fists: they do it, logically and with deliberation, on the duelling-ground. But when a national danger threatens, they instantly become what they proudly and justly call themselves—"a warlike nation"—and apply to the business in hand the ardour, the imagination, the perseverance that have made them for centuries the great creative force of civilization. Every French soldier knows why he is fighting, and why, at this moment, physical courage is the first quality demanded of him; every Frenchwoman knows why war is being waged, and why her moral courage is needed to supplement the soldier's contempt of death.

The women of France are supplying this moral courage in act as well as in word. Frenchwomen, as a rule, are perhaps less instinctively "courageous," in the elementary sense, than their Anglo-Saxon sisters. They are afraid of more things, and are less ashamed of showing their fear. The French mother coddles her children, the boys as well as the girls: when they tumble and bark their knees they are expected to cry, and not taught to control themselves as English and American children are. I have seen big French boys bawling over a cut or a bruise that an Anglo-Saxon girl of the same age would have felt compelled to bear without a tear. Frenchwomen are timid for themselves as well as for their children. They are afraid of the unexpected, the unknown, the experimental. It is not part of the Frenchwoman's training to pretend to have physical courage. She has not the advantage of our discipline in the hypocrisies of "good form" when she is called on to be brave, she must draw her courage from her brains. She must first be convinced of the necessity of heroism; after that she is fit to go bridle to bridle with Jeanne d'Arc.

The same display of reasoned courage is visible in the hasty adaptation of the Frenchwoman to all kinds of uncongenial jobs. Almost every kind of service she has been called to render since the war began has been fundamentally uncongenial. A French doctor once remarked to me that Frenchwomen never make really good sick-nurses except when they are nursing their own people. They are too personal, too emotional, and too much interested in more interesting things, to take to the fussy details of good nursing, except when it can help someone they care for. Even then, as a rule, they are not systematic or tidy; but they make up for these deficiencies by inexhaustible willingness and sympathy. And it has been easy for them to become good war-nurses, because every Frenchwoman who nurses a French soldier feels that she is caring for her kin. The French war-nurse sometimes mislays an instrument or forgets to sterilize a dressing; but she almost always finds the consoling word to say and the right tone to take with her wounded soldiers. That profound solidarity which is one of the results of conscription flowers, in war-time, in an exquisite and impartial devotion.

This, then, is what "France is like." The whole civilian part of the nation seems merged in one symbolic figure, carrying help and hope to the fighters or passionately bent above the wounded. The devotion, the self-denial, seem instinctive; but they are really based on a reasoned knowledge of the situation and on an unflinching estimate of values. All France knows today that real "life" consists in the things that make it worth living, and that these things, for France, depend on the free expression of her national genius. If France perishes as an intellectual light and as a moral force every Frenchman perishes with her; and the only death that Frenchmen fear is not death in the trenches but death by the extinction of their national ideal. It is against this death that the whole nation is fighting; and it is the reasoned recognition of their peril which, at this moment, is making the most intelligent people in the world the most sublime.

IN MOROCCO

TO GENERAL LYAUTEY
RESIDENT GENERAL OF FRANCE IN MOROCCO AND TO MADAME LYAUTEY
THANKS TO WHOSE KINDNESS THE JOURNEY I HAD SO LONG DREAMED OF SURPASSED
WHAT I HAD DREAMED

PREFACE

I

Having begun my book with the statement that Morocco still lacks a guide-book, I should have wished to take a first step toward remedying that deficiency.

But the conditions in which I travelled, though full of unexpected and picturesque opportunities, were not suited to leisurely study of the places visited. The time was limited by the approach of the rainy season, which puts an end to motoring over the treacherous trails of the Spanish zone. In 1918, owing to the watchfulness of German submarines in the Straits and along the northwest coast of Africa, the trip by sea from Marseilles to Casablanca, ordinarily so easy, was not to be made without much discomfort and loss of time. Once on board the steamer, passengers were often kept in port (without leave to land) for six or eight days; therefore for any one bound by a time-limit, as most war-workers were, it was necessary to travel across country, and to be back at Tangier before the November rains.

This left me only one month in which to visit Morocco from the Mediterranean to the High Atlas, and from the Atlantic to Fez, and even had there been a Djinn's carpet to carry me, the multiplicity of impressions received would have made precise observation difficult.

The next best thing to a Djinn's carpet, a military motor, was at my disposal every morning; but war conditions imposed restrictions, and the wish to use the minimum of petrol often stood in the way of the second visit which alone makes it possible to carry away a definite and detailed impression.

These drawbacks were more than offset by the advantage of making my quick trip at a moment unique in the history of the country; the brief moment of transition between its virtually complete subjection to European authority, and the fast approaching hour when it is thrown open to all the banalities and promiscuities of modern travel.

Morocco is too curious, too beautiful, too rich in landscape and architecture, and above all too much of a novelty, not to attract one of the main streams of spring travel as soon as Mediterranean passenger traffic is resumed. Now that the war is over, only a few months' work on roads and railways divide it from the great torrent of "tourism"; and once that deluge is let loose, no eye will ever again see Moulay Idriss and Fez and Marrakech as I saw them.

In spite of the incessant efforts of the present French administration to preserve the old monuments of Morocco from injury, and her native arts and industries from the corruption of European bad taste, the impression of mystery and remoteness which the country now produces must inevitably vanish with the approach of the "Circular Ticket." Within a few years far more will be known of the past of Morocco, but that past will be far less visible to the traveller than it is to-day. Excavations will reveal fresh traces of Roman and Phenician occupation; the remote affinities between Copts and Berbers, between Bagdad and Fez, between Byzantine art and the architecture of the Souss, will be explored and elucidated, but, while these successive discoveries are being made, the strange survival of mediaeval life, of a life contemporary with the crusaders, with Saladin, even with the great days of the Caliphate of Bagdad, which now greets the astonished traveller, will gradually disappear, till at last even the mysterious autocthones of the Atlas will have folded their tents and silently stolen away.

II

Authoritative utterances on Morocco are not wanting for those who can read them in French, but they are to be found mainly in large and often inaccessible books, like M. Doutte's "En Tribu," the Marquis de Segonzac's remarkable explorations in the Atlas, or Foucauld's classic (but unobtainable) "Reconnaissance au Maroc", and few, if any, have been translated into English.

M. Louis Chatelain has dealt with the Roman ruins of Volubilis and M. Tranchant de Lunel, M. Raymond Koechlin, M. Gaillard, M. Ricard, and many other French scholars, have written of Moslem architecture and art in articles published either in "France-Maroc," as introductions to catalogues of exhibitions, or in the reviews and daily papers. Pierre Loti and M. Andre Chevrillon have reflected, with the intensest visual sensibility, the romantic and ruinous Morocco of yesterday, and in the volumes of the "Conferences Marocaines," published by the French government, the experts gathered about the Resident-General have examined the industrial and agricultural Morocco of tomorrow. Lastly, one striking book sums up, with the clearness and consecutiveness of which French scholarship alone possesses the art, the chief things to be said on all these subjects, save that of art and archaeology. This is M. Augustin Bernard's volume, "Le Maroc," the one portable and compact yet full and informing book since Leo Africanus described the bazaars of Fez. But M. Augustin Bernard deals only with the ethnology, the social, religious and political history, and the physical properties, of the country; and this, though "a large order," leaves out the visual and picturesque side, except in so far as the book touches on the always picturesque life of the people.

For the use, therefore, of the happy wanderers who may be planning a Moroccan journey, I have added to the record of my personal impressions a slight sketch of the history and art of the country. In extenuation of the attempt I must add that the chief merit of this sketch will be its absence of originality. Its facts will be chiefly drawn from the pages of M. Augustin Bernard, M. H. Saladin, and M. Gaston Migeon, and the rich sources of the "Conferences Marocaines" and the articles of "France-Maroc." It will also be deeply indebted to information given on the spot by the brilliant specialists of the French administration, to the Marquis de Segonzac, with whom I had the good luck to travel from Rabat to Marrakech and back; to M. Alfred de Tarde, editor of "France-Maroc"; to M. Tranchant de Lunel, director of the French School of Fine Arts in Morocco; to M. Goulven, the historian of Portuguese Mazagan, to M. Louis Chatelain, and to the many other cultivated and cordial French officials, military and civilian, who, at each stage of my journey, did their amiable best to answer my questions and open my eyes.

NOTE

In the writing of proper names and of other Arab words the French spelling has been followed.

In the case of proper names, and names of cities and districts, this seems justified by the fact that they occur in a French colony, where French usage naturally prevails, and to spell Oudjda in the French way, and koubba, for instance, in the English form of kubba, would cause needless confusion as to their respective pronunciation. It seems therefore simpler, in a book written for the ordinary traveller, to conform altogether to French usage.

I - RABAT AND SALE

I

LEAVING TANGIER

To step on board a steamer in a Spanish port, and three hours later to land in a country without a guide-book, is a sensation to rouse the hunger of the repletest sight-seer.

The sensation is attainable by anyone who will take the trouble to row out into the harbour of Algeciras and scramble onto a little black boat headed across the straits. Hardly has the rock of Gibraltar turned to cloud when one's foot is on the soil of an almost unknown Africa. Tangier, indeed, is in the guide-books; but, cuckoo-like, it has had to lays its eggs in strange nests, and the traveller who wants to find out about it must acquire a work dealing with some other country— Spain or Portugal or Algeria. There is no guide-book to Morocco, and no way of knowing, once one has left Tangier behind, where the long trail over the Rif is going to land one, in the sense understood by any one accustomed to European certainties. The air of the unforeseen blows on one from the roadless passes of the Atlas.

This feeling of adventure is heightened by the contrast between Tangier—cosmopolitan, frowsy, familiar Tangier, that every tourist has visited for the last forty years—and the vast unknown just beyond. One has met, of course, travellers who have been to Fez; but they have gone there on special missions, under escort, mysteriously, perhaps perilously; the expedition has seemed, till lately, a considerable affair. And when one opens the records of Moroccan travellers written within the last twenty years, how many, even of the most adventurous, are found to have gone beyond Fez? And what, to this day, do the names of Meknez and Marrakech, of Mogador, Saffi or Rabat, signify to any but a few students of political history, a few explorers and naturalists? Not till within the last year has Morocco been open to travel from Tangier to the Great Atlas, and from Moulay Idriss to the Atlantic. Three years ago Christians were being massacred in the streets of Sale, the pirate town across the river from Rabat, and two years ago no European had been allowed to enter the Sacred City of Moulay Idriss, the burial-place of the lawful descendant of Ali, founder of the Idrissite dynasty. Now, thanks to the energy and the imagination of one of the greatest of colonial administrators, the country, at least in the French zone, is as safe and open as the opposite shore of Spain. All that remains is to tell the traveller how to find his way about it.

Ten years ago there was not a wheeled vehicle in Morocco, now its thousands of miles of trail, and its hundreds of miles of firm French roads, are travelled by countless carts, omnibuses and motor-vehicles. There are light railways from Rabat to Fez in the west, and to a point about eighty-five kilometres from Marrakech in the south, and it is possible to say that within a year a regular railway system will connect eastern Morocco with western Algeria, and the ports of Tangier and Casablanca with the principal points of the interior.

What, then, prevents the tourist from instantly taking ship at Bordeaux or Algeciras and letting loose his motor on this new world? Only the temporary obstacles which the war has everywhere put in the way of travel. Till these are lifted it will hardly be possible to travel in Morocco except by favour of the Resident-General; but, normal conditions once restored, the country will be as accessible, from the straits of Gibraltar to the Great Atlas, as Algeria or Tunisia.

To see Morocco during the war was therefore to see it in the last phase of its curiously abrupt transition from remoteness and danger to security and accessibility; at a moment when its aspect and its customs were still almost unaffected by European influences, and when the "Christian" might taste the transient joy of wandering unmolested in cities of ancient mystery and hostility, whose inhabitants seemed hardly aware of his intrusion.

II

THE TRAIL TO EL-KSAR

With such opportunities ahead it was impossible, that brilliant morning of September, 1917, not to be off quickly from Tangier, impossible to do justice to the pale-blue town piled up within brown walls against the thickly-foliaged gardens of "the Mountain," to the animation of its market-place and the secret beauties of its steep Arab streets. For Tangier swarms with people in European clothes, there are English, French and Spanish signs above its shops, and cab-stands in its squares; it belongs, as much as Algiers, to the familiar dog-eared world of travel—and there, beyond the last dip of "the Mountain," lies the world of mystery, with the rosy dawn just breaking over it. The motor is at the door and we are off.

The so-called Spanish zone, which encloses internationalized Tangier in a wide circuit of territory, extends southward for a distance of about a hundred and fifteen kilometres. Consequently, when good roads traverse it, French Morocco will be reached in less than two hours by motor-travellers bound for the south. But for the present Spanish enterprise dies out after a few miles of macadam (as it does even between Madrid and Toledo), and the tourist is committed to the piste. These pistes—the old caravan-trails from the south—are more available to motors in Morocco than in southern Algeria and Tunisia, since they run mostly over soil which, though sandy in part, is bound together by a tough dwarf vegetation, and not over pure desert sand. This, however, is the utmost that can be said of the Spanish pistes. In the French protectorate constant efforts are made to keep the trails fit for wheeled traffic, but Spain shows no sense of a corresponding obligation.

After leaving the macadamized road which runs south from Tangier one seems to have embarked on a petrified ocean in a boat hardly equal to the adventure. Then, as one leaps and plunges over humps and ruts, down sheer banks into rivers, and up precipices into sand-pits, one gradually gains faith in one's conveyance and in one's spinal column; but both must be sound in every joint to resist the strain of the long miles to Arbaoua, the frontier post of the French protectorate.

Luckily there are other things to think about. At the first turn out of Tangier, Europe and the European disappear, and as soon as the motor begins to dip and rise over the arid little hills beyond the last gardens one is sure that every figure on the road will be picturesque instead of prosaic, every garment graceful instead of grotesque. One knows, too, that there will be no more omnibuses or trams or motorcyclists, but only long lines of camels rising up in brown friezes against the sky, little black donkeys trotting across the scrub under bulging pack-saddles, and noble draped figures walking beside them or majestically perching on their rumps. And for miles and miles there will be no more towns—only, at intervals on the naked slopes, circles of rush-roofed huts in a blue stockade of cactus, or a hundred or two nomad tents of black camel's hair resting on walls of wattled thorn and grouped about a terebinth-tree and a well.

Between these nomad colonies lies the bled, the immense waste of fallow land and palmetto desert: an earth as void of life as the sky above it of clouds. The scenery is always the same; but if one has the love of great emptinesses, and of the play of light on long stretches of parched earth and rock, the sameness is part of the enchantment. In such a scene every landmark takes on an extreme value. For miles one watches the little white dome of a saint's grave rising and disappearing with the undulations of the trail; at last one is abreast of it, and the solitary tomb, alone with its fig-tree and its broken well-curb, puts a meaning into the waste. The same importance, but intensified, marks the appearance of every human figure. The two white-draped riders passing single file up the red slope to that ring of tents on the ridge have a mysterious and inexplicable importance: one follows their progress with eyes that ache with conjecture. More exciting still is the encounter of the first veiled woman heading a little cavalcade from the south. All the mystery that awaits us looks out through the eye-slits in the grave-clothes muffling her. Where have they come from, where are they going, all these slow wayfarers out of the unknown? Probably only from one thatched douar[A] to another; but interminable distances unroll behind them, they breathe of Timbuctoo and the farthest desert. Just such figures must swarm in the Saharan cities, in the Soudan and Senegal. There is no break in the links: these wanderers have looked on at the building of cities that were dust when the Romans pushed their outposts across the Atlas.

[Footnote A: Village of tents. The village of mud-huts is called a nourwal.]

III

EL-KSAR TO RABAT

A town at last—its nearness announced by the multiplied ruts of the trail, the cactus hedges, the fig-trees weighed down by dust leaning over ruinous earthen walls. And here are the first houses of the European El-Ksar—neat white Spanish houses on the slope outside the old Arab settlement. Of the Arab town itself, above reed stockades and brown walls, only a minaret and a few flat roofs are visible. Under the walls drowse the usual gregarious Lazaruses; others, temporarily resuscitated, trail their grave-clothes after a line of camels and donkeys toward the olive-gardens outside the town.

The way to Rabat is long and difficult, and there is no time to visit El-Ksar, though its minaret beckons so alluringly above the fruit-orchards; so we stop for luncheon outside the walls, at a canteen with a corrugated iron roof where skinny Spaniards are serving thick purple wine and eggs fried in oil to a party of French soldiers. The heat has suddenly become intolerable, and a flaming wind straight from the south brings in at the door, with a cloud of blue flies, the smell of camels and trampled herbs and the strong spices of the bazaars.

Luncheon over, we hurry on between the cactus hedges, and then plunge back into the waste. Beyond El-Ksar the last hills of the Rif die away, and there is a stretch of wilderness without an outline till the Lesser Atlas begins to rise in the east. Once in the French protectorate the trail improves, but there are still difficult bits; and finally, on a high plateau, the chauffeur stops in a web of criss-cross trails, throws up his hands, and confesses that he has lost his way. The heat is mortal at the moment. For the last hour the red breath of the sirocco has risen from every hollow into which we dipped, now it hangs about us in the open, as if we had caught it in our wheels and it had to pause above us when we paused.

All around is the featureless wild land, palmetto scrub stretching away into eternity. A few yards off rises the inevitable ruined koubba[A] with its fig-tree: in the shade under its crumbling wall the buzz of the flies is like the sound of frying. Farther off, we discern a cluster of huts, and presently some Arab boys and a tall pensive shepherd come hurrying across the scrub. They are full of good-will, and no doubt of information; but our chauffeur speaks no Arabic and the talk dies down into shrugs and head-shakings. The Arabs retire to the shade of the wall, and we decide to start—for anywhere....

[Footnote A: Saint's tomb. The saint himself is called a marabout.]

The chauffeur turns the crank, but there is no responding quiver. Something has gone wrong; we can't move, and it is not much comfort to remember that, if we could, we should not know where to go. At least we should be cooler in motion than sitting still under the blinding sky.

Such an adventure initiates one at the outset into the stern facts of desert motoring. Every detail of our trip from Tangier to Rabat had been carefully planned to keep us in unbroken contact with civilization. We were to "tub" in one European hotel, and to dine in another, with just enough picnicking between to give a touch of local colour. But let one little cog slip and the whole plan falls to bits, and we are alone in the old untamed Moghreb, as remote from Europe as any mediaeval adventurer. If one lose one's way in Morocco, civilization vanishes as though it were a magic carpet rolled up by a Djinn.

It is a good thing to begin with such a mishap, not only because it develops the fatalism necessary to the enjoyment of Africa, but because it lets one at once into the mysterious heart of the country, a country so deeply conditioned by its miles and miles of uncitied wilderness that until one has known the wilderness one cannot begin to understand the cities.

We came to one at length, after sunset on that first endless day. The motor, cleverly patched up, had found its way to a real road, and speeding along between the stunted cork-trees of the forest of

Mamora brought us to a last rise from which we beheld in the dusk a line of yellow walls backed by the misty blue of the Atlantic. Sale, the fierce old pirate town, where Robinson Crusoe was so long a slave, lay before us, snow-white in its cheese-coloured ramparts skirted by fig and olive gardens. Below its gates a stretch of waste land, endlessly trailed over by mules and camels, sloped down to the mouth of the Bou-Regreg, the blue-brown river dividing it from Rabat. The motor stopped at the landing-stage of the steam-ferry; crowding about it were droves of donkeys, knots of camels, plump-faced merchants on crimson-saddled mules, with negro servants at their bridles, bare-legged water-carriers with hairy goat-skins slung over their shoulders, and Arab women in a heap of veils, cloaks, mufflings, all of the same ashy white, the caftans of clutched children peeping through in patches of old rose and lilac and pale green.

Across the river the native town of Rabat lay piled up on an orange-red cliff beaten by the Atlantic. Its walls, red too, plunged into the darkening breakers at the mouth of the river, and behind it, stretching up to the mighty tower of Hassan, and the ruins of the Great Mosque, the scattered houses of the European city showed their many lights across the plain.

IV

THE KASBAH OF THE OUDAYAS

Sale the white and Rabat the red frown at each other over the foaming bar of the Bou-Regreg, each walled, terraced, minareted, and presenting a singularly complete picture of the two types of Moroccan town, the snowy and the tawny. To the gates of both the Atlantic breakers roll in with the boom of northern seas, and under a misty northern sky. It is one of the surprises of Morocco to find the familiar African pictures bathed in this unfamiliar haze. Even the fierce midday sun does not wholly dispel it—the air remains thick, opalescent, like water slightly clouded by milk. One is tempted to say that Morocco is Tunisia seen by moonlight.

The European town of Rabat, a rapidly developing community, lies almost wholly outside the walls of the old Arab city. The latter, founded in the twelfth century by the great Almohad conqueror of Spain, Yacoub-el-Mansour, stretches its mighty walls to the river's mouth. Thence they climb the cliff to enclose the Kasbah[A] of the Oudayas, a troublesome tribe whom one of the Almohad Sultans, mistrusting their good faith, packed up one day, flocks, tents and camels, and carried across the bled to stow them into these stout walls under his imperial eye. Great crenellated ramparts, cyclopean, superb, follow the curve of the cliff. On the landward side they are interrupted by a gate-tower resting on one of the most nobly decorated of the horseshoe arches that break the mighty walls of Moroccan cities. Underneath the tower the vaulted entrance turns, Arab fashion, at right angles, profiling its red arch against darkness and mystery. This bending of passages, so characteristic a device of the Moroccan builder, is like an architectural expression of the tortuous secret soul of the land.

[Footnote A: Citadel.]

Outside the Kasbah a narrow foot-path is squeezed between the walls and the edge of the cliff. Toward sunset it looks down on a strange scene. To the south of the citadel the cliff descends to a long dune sloping to a sand-beach; and dune and beach are covered with the slanting headstones of the immense Arab cemetery of El Alou. Acres and acres of graves fall away from the red ramparts to the grey sea; and breakers rolling straight from America send their spray across the lowest stones.

There are always things going on toward evening in an Arab cemetery. In this one, travellers from the bled are camping in one corner, donkeys grazing (on heaven knows what), a camel dozing under its pack; in another, about a new-made grave, there are ritual movements of muffled figures and wailings of a funeral hymn half drowned by the waves. Near us, on a fallen headstone, a man with a thoughtful face sits chatting with two friends and hugging to his breast a tiny boy who looks like a grasshopper in his green caftan; a little way off, a solitary philosopher, his eye fixed on the sunset, lies on another grave, smoking his long pipe of kif.

There is infinite sadness in this scene under the fading sky, beside the cold welter of the Atlantic. One seems to be not in Africa itself, but in the Africa that northern crusaders may have dreamed of in snow-bound castles by colder shores of the same ocean. This is what Moghreb must have looked like to the confused imagination of the Middle Ages, to Norman knights burning to ransom the Holy Places, or Hansa merchants devising, in steep-roofed towns, of Barbary and the long caravans bringing apes and gold-powder from the south.

Inside the gate of the Kasbah one comes on more waste land and on other walls—for all Moroccan towns are enclosed in circuit within circuit of battlemented masonry. Then, unexpectedly, a gate in one of the inner walls lets one into a tiled court enclosed in a traceried cloister and overlooking an orange-grove that rises out of a carpet of roses. This peaceful and well-ordered place is the interior of the Medersa (the college) of the Oudayas. Morocco is full of these colleges, or rather lodging-houses of the students frequenting the mosques, for all Mahometan education is given in the mosque itself, only the preparatory work being done in the colleges. The most beautiful of the Medersas date from the earlier years of the long Merinid dynasty (1248-1548), the period at which Moroccan art, freed from too distinctively Spanish and Arab influences, began to develop a delicate grace of its own as far removed from the extravagance of Spanish ornament as from the inheritance of Roman-Byzantine motives that the first Moslem invasion had brought with it from Syria and Mesopotamia.

These exquisite collegiate buildings, though still in use whenever they are near a well-known mosque, have all fallen into a state of sordid disrepair. The Moroccan Arab, though he continues to build—and fortunately to build in the old tradition, which has never been lost—has, like all Orientals, an invincible repugnance to repairing and restoring, and one after another the frail exposed Arab structures, with their open courts and badly constructed terrace-roofs, are crumbling into ruin. Happily the French Government has at last been asked to intervene, and all over Morocco the Medersas are being repaired with skill and discretion. That of the Oudayas is already completely restored, and as it had long fallen into disuse it has been transformed by the Ministry of Fine Arts into a museum of Moroccan art.

The plan of the Medersas is always much the same: the eternal plan of the Arab house, built about one or more arcaded courts, with long narrow rooms enclosing them on the ground floor, and several stories above, reached by narrow stairs, and often opening on finely carved cedar galleries. The chief difference between the Medersa and the private house, or even the fondak,[A] lies in the use to which the rooms are put. In the Medersas, one of the ground-floor apartments is always fitted up as a chapel, and shut off from the court by carved cedar doors still often touched with old gilding and vermilion. There are always a few students praying in the chapel, while others sit in the doors of the upper rooms, their books on their knees, or lean over the carved galleries chatting with their companions who are washing their feet at the marble fountain in the court, preparatory to entering the chapel.

[Footnote A: The Moroccan inn or caravanserai.]

In the Medersa of the Oudayas, these native activities have been replaced by the lifeless hush of a museum. The rooms are furnished with old rugs, pottery, brasses, the curious embroidered hangings which line the tents of the chiefs, and other specimens of Arab art. One room reproduces a barber's shop in the bazaar, its benches covered with fine matting, the hanging mirror inlaid with mother-of-pearl, the razor-handles of silver niello. The horseshoe arches of the outer gallery look out on orange-blossoms, roses and the sea. It is all beautiful, calm and harmonious; and if one is tempted to mourn the absence of life and local colour, one has only to visit an abandoned Medersa to see that, but for French intervention, the charming colonnades and cedar chambers of the college of the Oudayas would by this time be a heap of undistinguished rubbish—for plaster and rubble do not "die in beauty" like the firm stones of Rome.

V

ROBINSON CRUSOE'S "SALLEE"

Before Morocco passed under the rule of the great governor who now administers it, the European colonists made short work of the beauty and privacy of the old Arab towns in which they established themselves.

On the west coast, especially, where the Mediterranean peoples, from the Phenicians to the Portuguese, have had trading-posts for over two thousand years, the harm done to such seaboard towns as Tangier, Rabat and Casablanca is hard to estimate. The modern European colonist apparently imagined that to plant his warehouses, cafes and cinema-palaces within the walls which for so long had fiercely excluded him was the most impressive way of proclaiming his domination.

Under General Lyautey such views are no longer tolerated. Respect for native habits, native beliefs and native architecture is the first principle inculcated in the civil servants attached to his administration. Not only does he require that the native towns shall be kept intact, and no European building erected within them; a sense of beauty not often vouchsafed to Colonial governors causes him to place the administration buildings so far beyond the walls that the modern colony grouped around them remains entirely distinct from the old town, instead of growing out of it like an ugly excrescence.

The Arab quarter of Rabat was already irreparably disfigured when General Lyautey came to Morocco; but ferocious old Sale, Phenician counting-house and breeder of Barbary pirates, had been saved from profanation by its Moslem fanaticism. Few Christian feet had entered its walls except those of the prisoners who, like Robinson Crusoe, slaved for the wealthy merchants in its mysterious terraced houses. Not till two or three years ago was it completely pacified; and when it opened its gates to the infidel it was still, as it is to-day, the type of the untouched Moroccan city—so untouched that, with the sunlight irradiating its cream-coloured walls and the blue-white domes above them, it rests on its carpet of rich fruit-gardens like some rare specimen of Arab art on a strip of old Oriental velvet.

Within the walls, the magic persists: which does not always happen when one penetrates into the mirage-like cities of Arabian Africa. Sale has the charm of extreme compactness. Crowded between the river-mouth and the sea, its white and pale-blue houses almost touch across the narrow streets, and the reed-thatched bazaars seem like miniature reductions of the great trading labyrinths of Tunis or Fez.

Everything that the reader of the Arabian Nights expects to find is here: the whitewashed niches wherein pale youths sit weaving the fine mattings for which the town is still famous; the tunnelled passages where indolent merchants with bare feet crouch in their little kennels hung with richly ornamented saddlery and arms, or with slippers of pale citron leather and bright embroidered babouches, the stalls with fruit, olives, tunny-fish, vague syrupy sweets, candles for saints' tombs, Mantegnesque garlands of red and green peppers, griddle-cakes sizzling on red-hot pans, and all the varied wares and cakes and condiments that the lady in the tale of the Three Calanders went out to buy, that memorable morning in the market of Bagdad.

Only at Sale all is on a small scale: there is not much of any one thing, except of the exquisite matting. The tide of commerce has ebbed from the intractable old city, and one feels, as one watches the listless purchasers in her little languishing bazaars, that her long animosity against the intruder has ended by destroying her own life.

The feeling increases when one leaves the bazaar for the streets adjoining it. An even deeper hush than that which hangs over the well-to-do quarters of all Arab towns broods over these silent thoroughfares, with heavy-nailed doors barring half-ruined houses. In a steep deserted square one of these doors opens its panels of weather-silvered cedar on the court of the frailest, ghostliest of Medersas—mere carved and painted shell of a dead house of learning. Mystic interweavings of endless lines, patient patterns interminably repeated in wood and stone and clay, all are here, from the tessellated paving of the court to the honeycombing of the cedar roof through which a patch of sky shows here and there like an inset of turquoise tiling.

This lovely ruin is in the safe hands of the French Fine Arts administration, and soon the wood-carvers and stucco-workers of Fez will have revived its old perfection; but it will never again be more than a show-Medersa, standing empty and unused beside the mosque behind whose guarded doors and high walls one guesses that the old religious fanaticism of Sale is dying also, as her learning and her commerce have died.

In truth the only life in her is centred in the market-place outside the walls, where big expanding Rabat goes on certain days to provision herself. The market of Sale, though typical of all Moroccan markets, has an animation and picturesqueness of its own. Its rows of white tents pitched on a dusty square between the outer walls and the fruit-gardens make it look as though a hostile tribe had sat down to lay siege to the town, but the army is an army of hucksters, of farmers from the rich black lands along the river, of swarthy nomads and leather-gaitered peasant women from the hills, of slaves and servants and tradesmen from Rabat and Sale; a draped, veiled, turbaned mob shrieking, bargaining, fist-shaking, call on Allah to witness the monstrous villanies of the misbegotten miscreants they are trading with, and then, struck with the mysterious Eastern apathy, sinking down in languid heaps of muslin among the black figs, purple onions and rosy melons, the fluttering hens, the tethered goats, the whinnying foals, that are all enclosed in an outer circle of folded-up camels and of mules dozing under faded crimson saddles.

VI

CHELLA AND THE GREAT MOSQUE

The Merinid Sultans of Rabat had a terribly troublesome neighbour across the Bou-Regreg, and they built Chella to keep an eye on the pirates of Sale. But Chella has fallen like a Babylonian city triumphed over by the prophets; while Sale, sly, fierce and irrepressible, continued till well on in the nineteenth century to breed pirates and fanatics.

The ruins of Chella lie on the farther side of the plateau above the native town of Rabat. The mighty wall enclosing them faces the city wall of Rabat, looking at it across one of those great red powdery wastes which seem, in this strange land, like death and the desert forever creeping up to overwhelm the puny works of man.

The red waste is scored by countless trains of donkeys carrying water from the springs of Chella, by long caravans of mules and camels, and by the busy motors of the French administration; yet there emanates from it an impression of solitude and decay which even the prosaic tinkle of the trams jogging out from the European town to the Exhibition grounds above the sea cannot long dispel.

Perpetually, even in the new thriving French Morocco, the outline of a ruin or the look in a pair of eyes shifts the scene, rends the thin veil of the European Illusion, and confronts one with the old grey Moslem reality. Passing under the gate of Chella, with its richly carved corbels and lofty crenellated towers, one feels one's self thus completely reabsorbed into the past.

Below the gate the ground slopes away, bare and blazing, to a hollow where a little blue-green minaret gleams through fig-trees, and fragments of arch and vaulting reveal the outline of a ruined mosque.

Was ever shade so blue-black and delicious as that of the cork-tree near the spring where the donkey's water-cans are being filled? Under its branches a black man in a blue shirt lies immovably sleeping in the dust. Close by women and children splash and chatter about the spring, and the dome of a saint's tomb shines through lustreless leaves. The black man, the donkeys, the women and children, the saint's dome, are all part of the inimitable Eastern scene in which inertia and agitation are so curiously combined, and a surface of shrill noise flickers over depths of such unfathomable silence.

The ruins of Chella belong to the purest period of Moroccan art. The tracery of the broken arches is all carved in stone or in glazed turquoise tiling, and the fragments of wall and vaulting have the firm elegance of a classic ruin. But what would even their beauty be without the leafy setting of the place? The "unimaginable touch of Time" gives Chella its peculiar charm: the aged fig-tree clamped in uptorn tiles and thrusting gouty arms between the arches; the garlanding of vines flung from column to column; the secret pool to which childless women are brought to bathe, and where the tree springing from a cleft of the steps is always hung with the bright bits of stuff which are the votive offerings of Africa.

The shade, the sound of springs, the terraced orange-garden with irises blooming along channels of running water, all this greenery and coolness in the hollow of a fierce red hill make Chella seem, to the traveller new to Africa, the very type and embodiment of its old contrasts of heat and freshness, of fire and languor. It is like a desert traveller's dream in his last fever.

Yacoub-el-Mansour was the fourth of the great Almohad Sultans who, in the twelfth century, drove out the effete Almoravids, and swept their victorious armies from Marrakech to Tunis and from Tangier to Madrid. His grandfather, Abd-el-Moumen, had been occupied with conquest and civic administration. It was said of his rule that "he seized northern Africa to make order prevail there"; and in fact, out of a welter of wild tribes confusedly fighting and robbing he drew an empire firmly seated and securely governed, wherein caravans travelled from the Atlas to the Straits without fear of attack, and "a soldier wandering through the fields would not have dared to pluck an ear of wheat."

His grandson, the great El-Mansour, was a conqueror too; but where he conquered he planted the undying seed of beauty. The victor of Alarcos, the soldier who subdued the north of Spain, dreamed a great dream of art. His ambition was to bestow on his three capitals, Seville, Rabat and Marrakech, the three most beautiful towers the world had ever seen; and if the tower of Rabat had been completed, and that of Seville had not been injured by Spanish embellishments, his dream would have been realized.

The "Tower of Hassan," as the Sultan's tower is called, rises from the plateau above old Rabat, overlooking the steep cliff that drops down to the last winding of the Bou-Regreg. Truncated at half its height, it stands on the edge of the cliff, a far-off beacon to travellers by land and sea. It is one of the world's great monuments, so sufficient in strength and majesty that until one has seen its fellow, the Koutoubya of Marrakech, one wonders if the genius of the builder could have carried such perfect balance of massive wall-spaces and traceried openings to a triumphant completion.

Near the tower, the red-brown walls and huge piers of the mosque built at the same time stretch their roofless alignment beneath the sky. This mosque, before it was destroyed, must have been one of the finest monuments of Almohad architecture in Morocco: now, with its tumbled red masses of masonry and vast cisterns overhung by clumps of blue aloes, it still forms a ruin of Roman grandeur. The Mosque, the Tower, the citadel of the Oudayas, and the mighty walls and towers of Chella, compose an architectural group as noble and complete as that of some mediaeval Tuscan city. All they need to make the comparison exact is that they should have been compactly massed on a steep hill, instead of lying scattered over the wide spaces between the promontory of the Oudayas and the hill-side of Chella.

The founder of Rabat, the great Yacoub-el-Mansour, called it, in memory of the battle of Alarcos, "The Camp of Victory" (Ribat-el-Path), and the monuments he bestowed on it justified the name in another sense, by giving it the beauty that lives when battles are forgotten.

II - VOLUBILIS, MOULAY IDRISS AND MEKNEZ

I

VOLUBILIS

One day before sunrise we set out from Rabat for the ruins of Roman Volubilis.

From the ferry of the Bou-Regreg we looked backward on a last vision of orange ramparts under a night-blue sky sprinkled with stars; ahead, over gardens still deep in shadow, the walls of Sale were passing from drab to peach-colour in the eastern glow. Dawn is the romantic hour in Africa. Dirt and dilapidation disappear under a pearly haze, and a breeze from the sea blows away the memory of fetid markets and sordid heaps of humanity. At that hour the old Moroccan cities look like the ivory citadels in a Persian miniature, and the fat shopkeepers riding out to their vegetable-gardens like Princes sallying forth to rescue captive maidens.

Our way led along the highroad from Rabat to the modern port of Kenitra, near the ruins of the Phenician colony of Mehedyia. Just north of Kenitra we struck the trail, branching off eastward to a

European village on the light railway between Rabat and Fez, and beyond the railway-sheds and flat-roofed stores the wilderness began, stretching away into clear distances bounded by the hills of the Rarb,[A] above which the sun was rising.

[Footnote A: The high plateau-and-hill formation between Tangier and Fez.]

Range after range these translucent hills rose before us, all around the solitude was complete. Village life, and even tent life, naturally gathers about a river-bank or a spring; and the waste we were crossing was of waterless sand bound together by a loose desert growth. Only an abandoned well-curb here and there cast its blue shadow on the yellow bled, or a saint's tomb hung like a bubble between sky and sand. The light had the preternatural purity which gives a foretaste of mirage: it was the light in which magic becomes real, and which helps to understand how, to people living in such an atmosphere, the boundary between fact and dream perpetually fluctuates.

The sand was scored with tracks and ruts innumerable, for the road between Rabat and Fez is travelled not only by French government motors but by native caravans and trains of pilgrims to and from the sacred city of Moulay Idriss, the founder of the Idrissite dynasty, whose tomb is in the Zerhoun, the mountain ridge above Volubilis. To untrained eyes it was impossible to guess which of the trails one ought to follow; and without much surprise we suddenly found the motor stopping, while its wheels spun round vainly in the loose sand.

The military chauffeur was not surprised either; nor was Captain de M., the French staff-officer who accompanied us.

"It often happens just here," they admitted philosophically. "When the General goes to Meknez he is always followed by a number of motors, so that if his own is stuck he may go on in another."

This was interesting to know, but not particularly helpful, as the General and his motors were not travelling our way that morning. Nor was any one else, apparently. It is curious how quickly the bled empties itself to the horizon if one happens to have an accident in it! But we had learned our lesson between Tangier and Rabat, and were able to produce a fair imitation of the fatalistic smile of the country.

The officer remarked cheerfully that somebody might turn up, and we all sat down in the bled.

A Berber woman, cropping up from nowhere, came and sat beside us. She had the thin suntanned face of her kind, brilliant eyes touched with khol, high cheek-bones, and the exceedingly short upper lip which gives such charm to the smile of the young nomad women. Her dress was the usual faded cotton shift, hooked on the shoulders with brass or silver clasps (still the antique fibulae), and wound about with a vague drapery in whose folds a brown baby wriggled.

The coolness of dawn had vanished and the sun beat down from a fierce sky. The village on the railway was too far off to be reached on foot, and there were probably no mules there to spare. Nearer at hand there was no sign of help, not a fortified farm, or even a circle of nomad tents. It was the unadulterated desert—and we waited.

Not in vain; for after an hour or two, from far off in the direction of the hills, there appeared an army with banners. We stared at it unbelievingly. The mirage, of course! We were too sophisticated to doubt it, and tales of sun-dazed travellers mocked by such visions rose in our well-stocked memories.

The chauffeur thought otherwise. "Good! That's a pilgrimage from the mountains. They're going to Sale to pray at the tomb of the marabout; to-day is his feast-day."

And so they were! And as we hung on their approach, and speculated as to the chances of their stopping to help, I had time to note the beauty of this long train winding toward us under parti-colored banners. There was something celestial, almost diaphanous, in the hundreds of figures turbaned and draped in white, marching slowly through the hot colorless radiance over the hot colorless sand.

The most part were on foot, or bestriding tiny donkeys, but a stately Caid rode alone at the end of the line on a horse saddled with crimson velvet, and to him our officer appealed.

The Caid courteously responded, and twenty or thirty pilgrims were ordered to harness themselves to the motor and haul it back to the trail, while the rest of the procession moved hieratically onward.

I felt scruples at turning from their path even a fraction of this pious company; but they fell to with a saintly readiness, and before long the motor was on the trail. Then rewards were dispensed; and instantly those holy men became a prey to the darkest passions. Even in this land of contrasts the transition from pious serenity to rapacious rage can seldom have been more rapid. The devotees of the marabout fought, screamed, tore their garments and rolled over each other with sanguinary gestures in the struggle for our pesetas; then, perceiving our indifference, they suddenly remembered their religious duties, scrambled to their feet, tucked up their flying draperies, and raced after the tail-end of the procession.

Through a golden heat-haze we struggled on to the hills. The country was fallow, and in great part too sandy for agriculture, but here and there we came on one of the deep-set Moroccan rivers, with a reddish-yellow course channelled between perpendicular banks of red earth, and marked by a thin line of verdure that widened to fruit-gardens wherever a village had sprung up. We traversed several of these "sedentary"[A] villages, nourwals of clay houses with thatched conical roofs, in gardens of fig, apricot and pomegranate that must be so many pink and white paradises after the winter rains.

[Footnote A: So called to distinguish them from the tent villages of the less settled groups.]

One of these villages seemed to be inhabited entirely by blacks, big friendly creatures who came out to tell us by which trail to reach the bridge over the yellow oued. In the oued their womenkind were washing the variegated family rags. They were handsome blue-bronze creatures, bare to the waist, with tight black astrakhan curls and firmly sculptured legs and ankles; and all around them, like a swarm of gnats, danced countless jolly pickaninnies, naked as lizards, with the spindle legs and globular stomachs of children fed only on cereals.

Half terrified but wholly interested, these infants buzzed about the motor while we stopped to photograph them; and as we watched their antics we wondered whether they were the descendants of the little Soudanese boys whom the founder of Meknez, the terrible Sultan Moulay-Ismael, used to carry off from beyond the Atlas and bring up in his military camps to form the nucleus of the Black Guard which defended his frontiers. We were on the line of travel between Meknez and the sea, and it seemed not unlikely that these nourwals were all that remained of scattered outposts of Moulay-Ismael's legionaries.

After a time we left oueds and villages behind us and were in the mountains of the Rarb, toiling across a high sandy plateau. Far off a fringe of vegetation showed promise of shade and water, and at last, against a pale mass of olive-trees, we saw the sight which, at whatever end of the world one comes upon it, wakes the same sense of awe: the ruin of a Roman city.

Volubilis (called by the Arabs the Castle of the Pharaohs) is the only considerable Roman colony so far discovered in Morocco. It stands on the extreme ledge of a high plateau backed by the mountains of the Zerhoun. Below the plateau, the land drops down precipitately to a narrow river-valley green with orchards and gardens, and in the neck of the valley, where the hills meet again, the conical white town of Moulay Idriss, the Sacred City of Morocco, rises sharply against a wooded background.

So the two dominations look at each other across the valley: one, the lifeless Roman ruin, representing a system, an order, a social conception that still run through all our modern ways, the other, the untouched Moslem city, more dead and sucked back into an unintelligible past than any broken architrave of Greece or Rome.

Volubilis seems to have had the extent and wealth of a great military outpost, such as Timgad in Algeria; but in the seventeenth century it was very nearly destroyed by Moulay-Ismael, the Sultan of the Black Guard, who carried off its monuments piece-meal to build his new capital of Meknez, that Mequinez of contemporary travellers which was held to be one of the wonders of the age.

Little remains to Volubilis in the way of important monuments: only the fragments of a basilica, part of an arch of triumph erected in honour of Caracalla, and the fallen columns and architraves which strew the path of Rome across the world. But its site is magnificent; and as the excavation of the ruins was interrupted by the war it is possible that subsequent search may bring forth other treasures comparable to the beautiful bronze sloughi (the African hound) which is now its principal possession.

It was delicious, after seven hours of travel under the African sun, to sit on the shady terrace where the Curator of Volubilis, M. Louis Chatelain, welcomes his visitors. The French Fine Arts have built a charming house with gardens and pergolas for the custodian of the ruins, and have found in M. Chatelain an archaeologist so absorbed in his task that, as soon as conditions permit, every inch of soil in the circumference of the city will be made to yield up whatever secrets it hides.

II

MOULAY IDRISS

We lingered under the pergolas of Volubilis till the heat grew less intolerable, and then our companions suggested a visit to Moulay Idriss.

[Illustration: From a photograph from the Service des Beaux-Arts au Maroc

Volubilis—the western portico of the basilica of Antonius Pius]

Such a possibility had not occurred to us, and even Captain de M. seemed to doubt whether the expedition were advisable. Moulay Idriss was still said to be resentful of Christian intrusion: it was only a year before that the first French officers had entered it.

But M. Chatelain was confident that there would be no opposition to our visit, and with the piled-up terraces and towers of the Sacred City growing golden in the afternoon light across the valley it was impossible to hesitate.

We drove down through an olive-wood as ancient as those of Mitylene and Corfu, and then along the narrowing valley, between gardens luxuriant even in the parched Moroccan autumn. Presently the motor began to climb the steep road to the town, and at a gateway we got out and were met by the native chief of police. Instantly at the high windows of mysterious houses veiled heads appeared and sidelong eyes cautiously inspected us. But the quarter was deserted, and we walked on without meeting any one to the Street of the Weavers, a silent narrow way between low whitewashed niches like the cubicles in a convent. In each niche sat a grave white-robed youth, forming a great amphora-shaped grain-basket out of closely plaited straw. Vine-leaves and tendrils hung through the reed roofing overhead, and grape-clusters cast their classic shadow at our feet. It was like walking on the unrolled frieze of a white Etruscan vase patterned with black vine garlands.

The silence and emptiness of the place began to strike us: there was no sign of the Oriental crowd that usually springs out of the dust at the approach of strangers. But suddenly we heard close by the lament of the rekka (a kind of long fife), accompanied by a wild thrum-thrum of earthenware drums and a curious excited chanting of men's voices. I had heard such a chant before, at the other end of North Africa, in Kairouan, one of the other great Sanctuaries of Islam, where the sect of the Aissaouas celebrate their sanguinary rites in the Zaouia[A] of their confraternity. Yet it seemed incredible that if the Aissaouas of Moulay Idriss were performing their ceremonies that day the chief of police should be placidly leading us through the streets in the very direction from which the chant was coming. The Moroccan, though he has no desire to get into trouble with the Christian, prefers to be left alone on feast-days, especially in such a stronghold of the faith as Moulay Idriss.

[Footnote A: Sacred college.]

But "Geschehen ist geschehen" is the sum of Oriental philosophy. For centuries Moulay Idriss had held out fanatically on its holy steep; then, suddenly, in 1916, its chiefs saw that the game was up, and surrendered without a pretense of resistance. Now the whole thing was over, the new conditions were accepted, and the chief of police assured us that with the French uniform at our side we should be safe anywhere.

"The Aissaouas?" he explained. "No, this is another sect, the Hamadchas, who are performing their ritual dance on the feast-day of their patron, the marabout Hamadch, whose tomb is in the Zerhoun. The feast is celebrated publicly in the market-place of Moulay Idriss."

As he spoke we came out into the market-place, and understood why there had been no crowd at the gate. All the population was in the square and on the roofs that mount above it, tier by tier, against the wooded hillside: Moulay Idriss had better to do that day than to gape at a few tourists in dust-coats.

Short of Sfax, and the other coast cities of eastern Tunisia, there is surely not another town in North Africa as white as Moulay Idriss. Some are pale blue and pinky yellow, like the Kasbah of Tangier, or cream and blue like Sale, but Tangier and Sale, for centuries continuously subject to European influences, have probably borrowed their colors from Genoa and the Italian Riviera. In the interior of the country, and especially in Morocco, where the whole color-scheme is much soberer than in Algeria and Tunisia, the color of the native houses is always a penitential shade of mud and ashes.

But Moulay Idriss, that afternoon, was as white as if its arcaded square had been scooped out of a big cream cheese. The late sunlight lay like gold-leaf on one side of the square, the other was in pure blue shade, and above it, the crowded roofs, terraces and balconies packed with women in bright dresses looked like a flower-field on the edge of a marble quarry.

The bright dresses were as unusual a sight as the white walls, for the average Moroccan crowd is the color of its houses. But the occasion was a special one, for these feasts of the Hamadchas occur only twice a year, in spring and autumn, and as the ritual dances take place out of doors, instead of being performed inside the building of the confraternity, the feminine population seizes the opportunity to burst into flower on the housetops.

It is rare, in Morocco, to see in the streets or the bazaars any women except of the humblest classes, household slaves, servants, peasants from the country or small tradesmen's wives; and even they (with the exception of the unveiled Berber women) are wrapped in the prevailing grave-clothes. The filles de joie and dancing-girls whose brilliant dresses enliven certain streets of the Algerian and Tunisian towns are invisible, or at least unnoticeable, in Morocco, where life, on the whole, seems so much less gay and brightly-tinted; and the women of the richer classes, mercantile or aristocratic, never leave their harems except to be married or buried. A throng of women dressed in light colors is therefore to be seen in public only when some street festival draws them to the roofs. Even then it is probable that the throng is mostly composed of slaves, household servants, and women of the lower bourgeoisie; but as they are all dressed in mauve and rose and pale green, with long earrings and jewelled head-bands flashing through their parted veils, the illusion, from a little distance, is as complete as though they were the ladies in waiting of the Queen of Sheba; and that radiant afternoon at Moulay Idriss, above the vine-garlanded square, and against the background of piled-up terraces, their vivid groups were in such contrast to the usual gray assemblages of the East that the scene seemed like a setting for some extravagantly staged ballet.

For the same reason the spectacle unrolling itself below us took on a blessed air of unreality. Any normal person who has seen a dance of the Aissaouas and watched them swallow thorns and hot coals, slash themselves with knives, and roll on the floor in epilepsy must have privately longed, after the first excitement was over, to fly from the repulsive scene. The Hamadchas are much more savage than Aissaouas, and carry much farther their display of cataleptic anaesthesia, and, knowing this, I had wondered how long I should be able to stand the sight of what was going on below our terrace. But the beauty of the setting redeemed the bestial horror. In that unreal golden light the scene became merely symbolical: it was like one of those strange animal masks which the Middle Ages brought down from antiquity by way of the satyr-plays of Greece, and of which the half-human protagonists still grin and contort themselves among the Christian symbols of Gothic cathedrals.

At one end of the square the musicians stood on a stone platform above the dancers. Like the musicians in a bas-relief they were flattened side by side against a wall, the fife-players with lifted arms and inflated cheeks, the drummers pounding frantically on long earthenware drums shaped like enormous hour-glasses and painted in barbaric patterns; and below, down the length of the market-place, the dance unrolled itself in a frenzied order that would have filled with envy a Paris or London impresario.

In its centre an inspired-looking creature whirled about on his axis, the black ringlets standing out in snaky spirals from his haggard head, his cheek-muscles convulsively twitching. Around him, but a long way off, the dancers rocked and circled with long raucous cries dominated by the sobbing booming music, and in the sunlit space between dancers and holy man, two or three impish children bobbed about with fixed eyes and a grimace of comic frenzy, solemnly parodying his contortions.

Meanwhile a tall grave personage in a doge-like cap, the only calm figure in the tumult, moved gravely here and there, regulating the dance, stimulating the frenzy, or calming some devotee who had broken the ranks and lay tossing and foaming on the stones. There was something far more sinister in this passionless figure, holding his hand on the key that let loose such crazy forces, than in the poor central whirligig who merely set the rhythm of the convulsions.

The dancers were all dressed in white caftans or in the blue shirts of the lowest classes. In the sunlight something that looked like fresh red paint glistened on their shaved black or yellow skulls and made dark blotches on their garments. At first these stripes and stains suggested only a gaudy ritual ornament like the pattern on the drums; then one saw that the paint, or whatever it was, kept dripping down from the whirling caftans and forming fresh pools among the stones, that as one of the pools dried up another formed, redder and more glistening, and that these pools were fed from great gashes which the dancers hacked in their own skulls and breasts with hatchets and sharpened stones. The dance was a blood-rite, a great sacrificial symbol, in which blood flowed so freely that all the rocking feet were splashed with it.

Gradually, however, it became evident that many of the dancers simply rocked and howled, without hacking themselves, and that most of the bleeding skulls and breasts belonged to negroes. Every now and then the circle widened to let in another figure, black or dark yellow, the figure of some humble blue-shirted spectator suddenly "getting religion" and rushing forward to snatch a weapon and baptize himself with his own blood; and as each new recruit joined the dancers the music shrieked louder and the devotees howled more wolfishly. And still, in the centre, the mad marabout spun, and the children bobbed and mimicked him and rolled their diamond eyes.

Such is the dance of the Hamadchas, of the confraternity of the marabout Hamadch, a powerful saint of the seventeenth century, whose tomb is in the Zerhoun above Moulay Idriss. Hamadch, it appears, had a faithful slave, who, when his master died, killed himself in despair, and the self-inflicted wounds of the brotherhood are supposed to symbolize the slave's suicide; though no doubt the origin of the ceremony might be traced back to the depths of that ensanguined grove where Mr. Fraser plucked the Golden Bough.

The more naive interpretation, however, has its advantages, since it enables the devotees to divide their ritual duties into two classes, the devotions of the free men being addressed to the saint who died in his bed, while the slaves belong to the slave, and must therefore simulate his horrid end. And this is the reason why most of the white caftans simply rock and writhe, while the humble blue shirts drip with blood.

The sun was setting when we came down from our terrace above the market-place. To find a lodging for the night we had to press on to Meknez, where we were awaited at the French military post; therefore we were reluctantly obliged to refuse an invitation to take tea with the Caid, whose high-perched house commands the whole white amphitheatre of the town. It was disappointing to leave Moulay Idriss with the Hamadchas howling their maddest, and so much besides to see; but as we drove away under the long shadows of the olives we counted ourselves lucky to have entered the sacred town, and luckier still to have been there on the day of the dance which, till a year ago, no foreigner had been allowed to see.

A fine French road runs from Moulay Idriss to Meknez, and we flew on through the dusk between wooded hills and open stretches on which the fires of nomad camps put orange splashes in the darkness. Then the moon rose, and by its light we saw a widening valley, and gardens and orchards that stretched up to a great walled city outlined against the stars.

MEKNEZ

All that evening, from the garden of the Military Subdivision on the opposite height, we sat and looked across at the dark tree-clumps and moonlit walls of Meknez, and listened to its fantastic history.

Meknez was built by the Sultan Moulay-Ismael, around the nucleus of a small town of which the site happened to please him, at the very moment when Louis XIV was creating Versailles. The coincidence of two contemporary autocrats calling cities out of the wilderness has caused persons with a taste for analogy to describe Meknez as the Versailles of Morocco: an epithet which is about as instructive as it would be to call Phidias the Benvenuto Cellini of Greece.

There is, however, a pretext for the comparison in the fact that the two sovereigns took a lively interest in each other's affairs. Moulay-Ismael sent several embassies to treat with Louis XIV on the eternal question of piracy and the ransom of Christian captives, and the two rulers were continually exchanging gifts and compliments.

The governor of Tetouan, who was sent to Paris in 1680, having brought as presents to the French King a lion, a lioness, a tigress, and four ostriches, Louis XIV shortly afterward despatched M. de Saint-Amand to Morocco with two dozen watches, twelve pieces of gold brocade, a cannon six feet long and other firearms. After this the relations between the two courts remained friendly till 1693, at which time they were strained by the refusal of France to return the Moorish captives who were employed on the king's galleys, and who were probably as much needed there as the Sultan's Christian slaves for the building of Moorish palaces.

Six years later the Sultan despatched Abdallah-ben-Aissa to France to reopen negotiations. The ambassador was as brilliantly received and as eagerly run after as a modern statesman on an official mission, and his candidly expressed admiration for the personal charms of the Princesse de Conti, one of the French monarch's legitimatized children, is supposed to have been mistaken by the court for an offer of marriage from the Emperor of Barbary. But he came back without a treaty.

Moulay-Ismael, whose long reign (1673 to 1727) and extraordinary exploits make him already a legendary figure, conceived, early in his career, a passion for Meknez; and through all his troubled rule, with its alternations of barbaric warfare and far-reaching negotiations, palace intrigue, crazy bloodshed and great administrative reforms, his heart perpetually reverted to the wooded slopes on which he dreamed of building a city more splendid than Fez or Marrakech.

"The Sultan" (writes his chronicler Aboul Kasim-ibn-Ahmad, called "Ezziani") "loved Meknez, the climate of which had enchanted him, and he would have liked never to leave it." He left it, indeed, often, left it perpetually, to fight with revolted tribes in the Atlas, to defeat one Berber army after another, to carry his arms across the High Atlas into the Souss, to adorn Fez with the heads of seven hundred vanquished chiefs, to put down his three rebellious brothers, to strip all the cities of his empire of their negroes and transport them to Meknez ("so that not a negro, man, woman or child, slave or free, was left in any part of the country"); to fight and defeat the Christians (1683), to take Tangier, to conduct a campaign on the Moulouya, to lead the holy war against the Spanish (1689), to take Larache, the Spanish commercial post on the west coast (which furnished eighteen hundred captives for Meknez); to lay siege to Ceuta, conduct a campaign against the Turks of Algiers, repress the pillage in his army, subdue more tribes, and build forts for his Black Legionaries from Oudjda to the Oued Noun. But almost each year's bloody record ends with the placid phrase: "Then the Sultan returned to Meknez."

In the year 1701, Ezziani writes, the indomitable old man "deprived his rebellious sons of their principalities; after which date he consecrated himself exclusively to the building of his palaces and the planting of his gardens. And in 1720 (nineteen years later in this long reign!) he ordered the destruction of the mausoleum of Moulay Idriss for the purpose of enlarging it. And to gain the necessary space he bought all the adjacent land, and the workmen did not leave these new labors till they were entirely completed."

In this same year there was levied on Fez a new tax which was so heavy that the inhabitants were obliged to abandon the city.

Yet it is written of this terrible old monarch, who devastated whole districts, and sacrificed uncounted thousands of lives for his ruthless pleasure, that under his administration of his chaotic and turbulent empire "the country rejoiced in the most complete security. A Jew or a woman might travel alone from Oudjda to the Oued Noun without any one's asking their business. Abundance reigned throughout the land: grain, food, cattle were to be bought for the lowest prices. Nowhere in the whole of Morocco was a highwayman or a robber to be found."

And probably both sides of the picture are true.

What, then, was the marvel across the valley, what were the "lordly pleasure-houses" to whose creation and enlargement Moulay-Ismael returned again and again amid the throes and violences of a nearly centenarian life?

The chronicler continues: "The Sultan caused all the houses near the Kasbah[A] to be demolished, and compelled the inhabitants to carry away the ruins of their dwellings. All the eastern end of the town was also torn down, and the ramparts were rebuilt. He also built the Great Mosque next to the palace of Nasr.... He occupied himself personally with the construction of his palaces, and before one was finished he caused another to be begun. He built the mosque of Elakhdar; the walls of the new town were pierced with twenty fortified gates and surmounted with platforms for cannon. Within the walls he made a great artificial lake where one might row in boats. There was also a granary with immense subterranean reservoirs of water, and a stable three miles long for the Sultan's horses and mules; twelve thousand horses could be stabled in it. The flooring rested on vaults in which the grain for the horses was stored.... He also built the palace of Elmansour, which had twenty cupolas; from the top of each cupola one could look forth on the plain and the mountains around Meknez. All about the stables the rarest trees were planted. Within the walls were fifty palaces, each with its own mosque and its baths. Never was such a thing known in any country, Arab or foreign, pagan or Moslem. The guarding of the doors of these palaces was intrusted to twelve hundred black eunuchs."

[Footnote A: The citadel of old Meknez.]

Such were the wonders that seventeenth century travellers toiled across the desert to see, and from which they came back dazzled and almost incredulous, as if half-suspecting that some djinn had deluded them with the vision of a phantom city. But for the soberer European records, and the evidence of the ruins themselves (for the whole of the new Meknez is a ruin), one might indeed be inclined to regard Ezziani's statements as an Oriental fable; but the briefest glimpse of Moulay-

Ismael's Meknez makes it easy to believe all his chronicler tells of it, even to the three miles of stables.

Next morning we drove across the valley and, skirting the old town on the hill, entered, by one of the twenty gates of Moulay-Ismael, a long empty street lined with half-ruined arcades. Beyond was another street of beaten red earth bordered by high red walls blotched with gray and mauve. Ahead of us this road stretched out interminably (Meknez, before Washington, was the "city of magnificent distances"), and down its empty length only one or two draped figures passed, like shadows on the way to Shadowland. It was clear that the living held no further traffic with the Meknez of Moulay-Ismael.

Here it was at last. Another great gateway let us, under a resplendently bejewelled arch of turquoise-blue and green, into another walled emptiness of red clay, a third gate opened into still vaster vacancies, and at their farther end rose a colossal red ruin, something like the lower stories of a Roman amphitheatre that should stretch out indefinitely instead of forming a circle, or like a series of Roman aqueducts built side by side and joined into one structure. Below this indescribable ruin the arid ground sloped down to an artificial water which was surely the lake that the Sultan had made for his boating-parties; and beyond it more red earth stretched away to more walls and gates, with glimpses of abandoned palaces and huge crumbling angle-towers.

The vastness, the silence, the catastrophic desolation of the place, were all the more impressive because of the relatively recent date of the buildings. As Moulay-Ismael had dealt with Volubilis, so time had dealt with his own Meknez; and the destruction which it had taken thousands of lash-driven slaves to inflict on the stout walls of the Roman city, neglect and abandonment had here rapidly accomplished. But though the sun-baked clay of which the impatient Sultan built his pleasure-houses will not suffer comparison with the firm stones of Rome, "the high Roman fashion" is visible in the shape and outline of these ruins. What they are no one knows. In spite of Ezziani's text (written when the place was already partly destroyed) archaeologists disagree as to the uses of the crypt of rose-flushed clay whose twenty rows of gigantic arches are so like an alignment of Roman aqueducts. Were these the vaulted granaries, or the subterranean reservoirs under the three miles of stabling which housed the twelve thousand horses? The stables, at any rate, were certainly near this spot, for the lake adjoins the ruins as in the chronicler's description; and between it and old Meknez, behind walls within walls, lie all that remains of the fifty palaces with their cupolas, gardens, mosques and baths.

This inner region is less ruined than the mysterious vaulted structure, and one of the palaces, being still reserved for the present Sultan's use, cannot be visited; but we wandered unchallenged through desert courts, gardens of cypress and olive where dried fountains and painted summer-houses are falling into dust, and barren spaces enclosed in long empty facades. It was all the work of an eager and imperious old man, who, to realize his dream quickly, built in perishable materials, but the design, the dimensions, the whole conception, show that he had not only heard of Versailles but had looked with his own eyes on Volubilis.

To build on such a scale, and finish the work in a single lifetime, even if the materials be malleable and the life a long one, implies a command of human labor that the other Sultan at Versailles must have envied. The imposition of the corvee was of course even simpler in Morocco than in France, since the material to draw on was unlimited, provided one could assert one's power over it; and for that purpose Ismael had his Black Army, the hundred and fifty thousand disciplined legionaries who enabled him to enforce his rule over all the wild country from Algiers to Agadir.

The methods by which this army were raised and increased are worth recounting in Ezziani's words:

"A taleb[A] of Marrakech having shown the Sultan a register containing the names of the negroes who had formed part of the army of El-Mansour, Moulay-Ismael ordered his agents to collect all that remained of these negroes and their children.... He also sent to the tribes of the Beni-Hasen, and into the mountains, to purchase all the negroes to be found there. Thus all that were in the whole of Moghreb were assembled, from the cities and the countryside, till not one was left, slave or free.

[Footnote A: Learned man.]

"These negroes were armed and clothed, and sent to Mechra Erremel (north of Meknez) where they were ordered to build themselves houses, plant gardens and remain till their children were ten years old. Then the Sultan caused all the children to be brought to him, both boys and girls. The boys were apprenticed to masons, carpenters, and other tradesmen; others were employed to make mortar. The next year they were taught to drive the mules, the third to make adobe for building; the fourth year they learned to ride horses bareback, the fifth they were taught to ride in the saddle while using firearms. At the age of sixteen these boys became soldiers. They were then married to the young negresses who had meanwhile been taught cooking and washing in the Sultan's palaces— except those who were pretty, and these were given a musical education, after which each one received a wedding-dress and a marriage settlement, and was handed over to her husband.

"All the children of these couples were in due time destined for the Black Army, or for domestic service in the palaces. Every year the Sultan went to the camp at Mechra Erremel and brought back the children. The Black Army numbered one hundred and fifty thousand men, of whom part were at Erremel, part at Meknez, and the rest in the seventy-six forts which the Sultan built for them throughout his domain. May the Lord be merciful to his memory!"

Such was the army by means of which Ismael enforced the corvee on his undisciplined tribes. Many thousands of lives went to the building of imperial Meknez; but his subjects would scarcely have sufficed if he had not been able to add to them twenty-five thousand Christian captives.

M. Augustin Bernard, in his admirable book on Morocco, says that the seventeenth century was "the golden age of piracy" in Morocco; and the great Ismael was no doubt one of its chief promoters. One understands his unwillingness to come to an agreement with his great friend and competitor, Louis XIV, on the difficult subject of the ransom of Christian captives when one reads in the admiring Ezziani that it took fifty-five thousand prisoners and captives to execute his architectural conceptions. "These prisoners, by day, were occupied on various tasks; at night they were locked into subterranean dungeons. Any prisoner who died at his task was built into the wall he was building." (This statement is confirmed by John Windus, the English traveller who visited the court of Moulay-Ismael in the Sultan's old age.) Many Europeans must have succumbed quickly to the heat and the lash, for the wall-builders were obliged to make each stroke in time with their neighbors, and were bastinadoed mercilessly if they broke the rhythm; and there is little doubt that the expert artisans of France, Italy and Spain were even dearer to the old architectural madman than the friendship of the palace-building despot across the sea.

Ezziani's chronicle dates from the first part of the nineteenth century, and is an Arab's colorless panegyric of a great Arab ruler; but John Windus, the Englishman who accompanied Commodore Stewart's embassy to Meknez in 1721, saw the imperial palaces and their builder with his own eyes, and described them with the vivacity of a foreigner struck by every contrast.

Moulay-Ismael was then about eighty-seven years old, "a middle-sized man, who has the remains of a good face, with nothing of a negro's features, though his mother was a black. He has a high nose, which is pretty long from the eyebrows downward, and thin. He has lost all his teeth, and breathes short, as if his lungs were bad, coughs and spits pretty often, which never falls to the ground, men being always ready with handkerchiefs to receive it. His beard is thin and very white, his eyes seem to have been sparkling, but their vigor decayed through age, and his cheeks very much sunk in."

Such was the appearance of this extraordinary man, who deceived, tortured, betrayed, assassinated, terrorized and mocked his slaves, his subjects, his women and children and his ministers like any other half-savage Arab despot, but who yet managed through his long reign to maintain a barbarous empire, to police the wilderness, and give at least an appearance of prosperity and security where all had before been chaos.

The English emissaries appear to have been much struck by the magnificence of his palaces, then in all the splendor of novelty, and gleaming with marbles brought from Volubilis and Sale. Windus extols in particular the sunken gardens of cypress, pomegranate and orange trees, some of them laid out seventy feet below the level of the palace-courts; the exquisite plaster fretwork; the miles of tessellated walls and pavement made in the finely patterned mosaic work of Fez; and the long terrace walk trellised with "vines and other greens" leading from the palace to the famous stables, and over which it was the Sultan's custom to drive in a chariot drawn by women and eunuchs.

Moulay-Ismael received the English ambassador with every show of pomp and friendship, and immediately "made him a present" of a handful of young English captives; but just as the negotiations were about to be concluded Commodore Stewart was privately advised that the Sultan had no intention of allowing the rest of the English to be ransomed. Luckily a diplomatically composed letter, addressed by the English envoy to one of the favorite wives, resulted in Ismael's changing his mind, and the captives were finally given up, and departed with their rescuers. As one stands in the fiery sun, among the monstrous ruins of those tragic walls, one pictures the other Christian captives pausing for a second, at the risk of death, in the rhythmic beat of their labor, to watch the little train of their companions winding away across the desert to freedom.

On the way back through the long streets that lead to the ruins we noticed, lying by the roadside, the shafts of fluted columns, blocks of marble, Roman capitals: fragments of the long loot of Sale and Volubilis. We asked how they came there, and were told that, according to a tradition still believed in the country, when the prisoners and captives who were dragging the building materials toward the palace under the blistering sun heard of the old Sultan's death, they dropped their loads with one accord and fled. At the same moment every worker on the walls flung down his trowel or hod, every slave of the palaces stopped grinding or scouring or drawing water or carrying faggots or polishing the miles of tessellated floors, so that, when the tyrant's heart stopped beating, at that very instant life ceased to circulate in the huge house he had built, and in all its members it became a carcass for his carcass.

III - FEZ

I

THE FIRST VISION

Many-walled Fez rose up before us out of the plain toward the end of the day.

The walls and towers we saw were those of the upper town, Fez Eldjid (the New), which lies on the edge of the plateau and hides from view Old Fez tumbling down below it into the ravine of the Oued Fez. Thus approached, the city presents to view only a long line of ramparts and fortresses, merging into the wide, tawny plain and framed in barren mountains. Not a house is visible outside the walls, except, at a respectful distance, the few unobtrusive buildings of the European colony, and not a village breaks the desolation of the landscape.

As we drew nearer, the walls towered close over us, and skirting them we came to a bare space outside a great horseshoe gate, and found ourselves suddenly in the foreground of a picture by Carpaccio or Bellini. Where else had one seen just those rows of white-turbaned majestic figures, squatting in the dust under lofty walls, all the pale faces ringed in curling beards turned to the story-teller in the centre of the group? Transform the story-teller into a rapt young Venetian, and you have the audience and the foreground of Carpaccio's "Preaching of St. Stephen," even to the camels craning inquisitive necks above the turbans. Every step of the way in North Africa corroborates the close observation of the early travellers, whether painters or narrators, and shows the unchanged character of the Oriental life that the Venetians pictured, and Leo Africanus and Windus and Charles Cochelet described.

There was time, before sunset, to go up to the hill from which the ruined tombs of the Merinid Sultans look down over the city they made glorious. After the savage massacre of foreign residents in 1912 the French encircled the heights commanding Fez with one of their admirably engineered military roads, and in a few minutes our motor had climbed to the point from which the great dynasty of artist-Sultans dreamed of looking down forever on their capital.

Nothing endures in Islam, except what human inertia has left standing and its own solidity has preserved from the elements. Or rather, nothing remains intact, and nothing wholly perishes, but the architecture, like all else, lingers on half-ruined and half-unchanged. The Merinid tombs, however, are only hollow shells and broken walls, grown part of the brown cliff they cling to. No one thinks of them save as an added touch of picturesqueness where all is picturesque: they survive as the best point from which to look down at Fez.

There it lies, outspread in golden light, roofs, terraces, and towers sliding over the plain's edge in a rush dammed here and there by barriers of cypress and ilex, but growing more precipitous as the ravine of the Fez narrows downward with the fall of the river. It is as though some powerful enchanter, after decreeing that the city should be hurled into the depths, had been moved by its beauty, and with a wave of his wand held it suspended above destruction.

At first the eye takes in only this impression of a great city over a green abyss, then the complex scene begins to define itself. All around are the outer lines of ramparts, walls beyond walls, their crenellations climbing the heights, their angle fortresses dominating the precipices. Almost on a level with us lies the upper city, the aristocratic Fez Eldjid of painted palaces and gardens, then, as the houses close in and descend more abruptly, terraces, minarets, domes, and long reed-thatched roofs of the bazaars, all gather around the green-tiled tomb of Moulay Idriss and the tower of the Almohad mosque of El Kairouiyin, which adjoin each other in the depths of Fez, and form its central sanctuary.

From the Merinid hill we had noticed a long facade among the cypresses and fruit-trees of Eldjid. This was Bou-Jeloud, the old summer-palace of the Sultan's harem, now the house of the Resident-General, where lodgings had been prepared for us.

The road descended again, crossing the Oued Fez by one of the fine old single-arch bridges that mark the architectural link between Morocco and Spain. We skirted high walls, wayside pools, and dripping mill-wheels; then one of the city gates engulfed us, and we were in the waste spaces of intramural Fez, formerly the lines of defense of a rich and perpetually menaced city, now chiefly used for refuse-heaps, open-air fondaks, and dreaming-places for rows of Lazaruses rolled in their cerements in the dust.

Through another gate and more walls we came to an arch in the inner line of defense. Beyond that, the motor paused before a green door, where a Cadi in a silken caftan received us. Across squares of orange-trees divided by running water we were led to an arcaded apartment hung with Moroccan embroideries and lined with wide divans; the hall of reception of the Resident-General. Through its arches were other tiled distances, fountains, arcades, beyond, in greener depths, the bright blossoms of a flower-garden. Such was our first sight of Bou-Jeloud, once the summer-palace of the wives of Moulay Hafid.

Upstairs, from a room walled and ceiled with cedar, and decorated with the bold rose-pink embroideries of Sale and the intricate old needlework of Fez, I looked out over the upper city toward the mauve and tawny mountains.

Just below the window the flat roofs of a group of little houses descended like the steps of an irregular staircase. Between them rose a few cypresses and a green minaret, out of the court of one house an ancient fig-tree thrust its twisted arms. The sun had set, and one after another bright figures appeared on the roofs. The children came first, hung with silver amulets and amber beads, and pursued by negresses in striped turbans, who bustled up with rugs and matting, then the mothers followed more indolently, released from their ashy mufflings and showing, under their light veils, long earrings from the Mellah[A] and caftans of pale green or peach color.

[Footnote A: The Ghetto in African towns. All the jewellers in Morocco are Jews.]

The houses were humble ones, such as grow up in the cracks of a wealthy quarter, and their inhabitants doubtless small folk, but in the enchanted African twilight the terraces blossomed like gardens, and when the moon rose and the muezzin called from the minaret, the domestic squabbles and the shrill cries from roof to roof became part of a story in Bagdad, overheard a thousand years ago by that arch-detective Haroun-al-Raschid.

II

FEZ ELDJID

It is usual to speak of Fez as very old, and the term seems justified when one remembers that the palace of Bou-Jeloud stands on the site of an Almoravid Kasbah of the eleventh century, that when that Kasbah was erected Fez Elbali had already existed for three hundred years, that El Kairouiyin is the contemporary of Sant' Ambrogio of Milan, and that the original mosque of Moulay Idriss II was built over his grave in the eighth century.

Fez is, in fact, the oldest city in Morocco without a Phenician or a Roman past, and has preserved more traces than any other of its architectural flowering-time, yet it would be truer to say of it, as of all Moroccan cities, that it has no age, since its seemingly immutable shape is forever crumbling and being renewed on the old lines.

When we rode forth the next day to visit some of the palaces of Eldjid our pink-saddled mules carried us at once out of the bounds of time. How associate anything so precise and Occidental as years or centuries with these visions of frail splendor seen through cypresses and roses? The Cadis in their multiple muslins, who received us in secret doorways and led us by many passages into the sudden wonder of gardens and fountains; the bright-earringed negresses peering down from painted balconies, the pilgrims and clients dozing in the sun against hot walls, the deserted halls with plaster lace-work and gold pendentives in tiled niches; the Venetian chandeliers and tawdry rococo beds, the terraces from which pigeons whirled up in a white cloud while we walked on a carpet of their feathers—were all these the ghosts of vanished state, or the actual setting of the life of some rich merchant with "business connections" in Liverpool and Lyons, or some government official at that very moment speeding to Meknez or Casablanca in his sixty h.p. motor?

We visited old palaces and new, inhabited and abandoned, and over all lay the same fine dust of oblivion, like the silvery mould on an overripe fruit. Overripeness is indeed the characteristic of this rich and stagnant civilization. Buildings, people, customs, seem all about to crumble and fall of their own weight: the present is a perpetually prolonged past. To touch the past with one's hands is realized only in dreams, and in Morocco the dream-feeling envelopes one at every step. One trembles continually lest the "Person from Porlock" should step in.

He is undoubtedly on the way, but Fez had not heard of him when we rode out that morning. Fez Eldjid, the "New Fez" of palaces and government buildings, was founded in the fourteenth century by the Merinid princes, and probably looks much as it did then. The palaces in their overgrown gardens, with pale-green trellises dividing the rose-beds from the blue-and-white tiled paths, and fountains in fluted basins of Italian marble, all had the same drowsy charm, yet the oldest were built not more than a century or two ago, others within the last fifty years; and at Marrakech, later in our journey, we were to visit a sumptuous dwelling where plaster-cutters and ceramists from Fez were actually repeating with wonderful skill and spontaneity, the old ornamentation of which the threads run back to Rome and Damascus.

Of really old private dwellings, palaces or rich men's houses, there are surprisingly few in Morocco. It is hard to guess the age of some of the featureless houses propping each other's flanks in old Fez or old Sale, but people rich enough to rebuild have always done so, and the passion for building seems allied, in this country of inconsequences, to the supine indifference that lets existing constructions crumble back to clay. "Dust to dust" should have been the motto of the Moroccan palace-builders.

Fez possesses one old secular building, a fine fondak of the fifteenth century, but in Morocco, as a rule, only mosques and the tombs of saints are preserved—none too carefully—and even the strong stone buildings of the Almohads have been allowed to fall to ruin, as at Chella and Rabat. This indifference to the completed object—which is like a kind of collective exaggeration of the artist's indifference to his completed work—has resulted in the total disappearance of the furniture and works of art which must have filled the beautiful buildings of the Merinid period. Neither pottery nor brasswork nor enamels nor fine hangings survive; there is no parallel in Morocco to the textiles of Syria, the potteries of Persia, the Byzantine ivories or enamels. It has been said that the Moroccan is always a nomad, who lives in his house as if it were a tent; but this is not a conclusive answer to any one who knows the passion of the modern Moroccan for European furniture. When one reads the list of the treasures contained in the palaces of the mediaeval Sultans of Egypt one feels sure that, if artists were lacking in Morocco, the princes and merchants who brought skilled craftsmen across the desert to build their cities must also have imported treasures to adorn them. Yet, as far as is known, the famous fourteenth-century bronze chandelier of Tetuan, and the fine old ritual furniture reported to be contained in certain mosques, are the only important works of art in Morocco later in date than the Roman sloughi of Volubilis.

FEZ ELBALI

The distances in Fez are so great and the streets so narrow, and in some quarters so crowded, that all but saints or humble folk go about on mule-back.

In the afternoon, accordingly, the pink mules came again, and we set out for the long tunnel-like street that leads down the hill to the Fez Elbali.

"Look out—'ware heads!" our leader would call back at every turn, as our way shrank to a black passage under a house bestriding the street, or a caravan of donkeys laden with obstructive reeds or branches of dates made the passers-by flatten themselves against the walls.

On each side of the street the houses hung over us like fortresses, leaning across the narrow strip of blue and throwing out great beams and buttresses to prop each other's bulging sides. Windows there were none on the lower floors; only here and there an iron-barred slit stuffed with rags and immemorial filth, from which a lean cat would suddenly spring out, and scuttle off under an archway like a witch's familiar.

Some of these descending lanes were packed with people, others as deserted as a cemetery; and it was strange to pass from the thronged streets leading to the bazaars to the profound and secretive silence of a quarter of well-to-do dwelling-houses, where only a few veiled women attended by negro slaves moved noiselessly over the clean cobblestones, and the sound of fountains and runnels came from hidden courtyards and over garden-walls.

This noise of water is as characteristic of Fez as of Damascus. The Oued Fez rushes through the heart of the town, bridged, canalized, built over, and ever and again bursting out into tumultuous falls and pools shadowed with foliage. The central artery of the city is not a street but a waterfall, and tales are told of the dark uses to which, even now, the underground currents are put by some of the dwellers behind the blank walls and scented gardens of those highly respectable streets.

The crowd in Oriental cities is made up of many elements, and in Morocco Turks, Jews and infidels, Berbers of the mountains, fanatics of the confraternities, Soudanese blacks and haggard Blue Men of the Souss, jostle the merchants and government officials with that democratic familiarity which goes side by side with abject servility in this land of perpetual contradictions. But Fez is above all the city of wealth and learning, of universities and counting-houses, and the merchant and the oulama[A]— the sedentary and luxurious types—prevail.

[Footnote A: Learned man, doctor of the university.]

The slippered Fazi merchant, wrapped in white muslins and securely mounted on a broad velvet saddle-cloth anchored to the back of a broad mule, is as unlike the Arab horseman of the desert as Mr. Tracy Tupman was unlike the Musketeers of Dumas. Ease, music, money-making, the affairs of his harem and the bringing-up of his children, are his chief interests, and his plump pale face with long-lashed hazel eyes, his curling beard and fat womanish hands, recall the portly potentates of Hindu miniatures, dreaming among houris beside lotus-tanks.

These personages, when they ride abroad, are preceded by a swarthy footman, who keeps his hand on the embroidered bridle; and the government officers and dignitaries of the Makhzen[A] are usually escorted by several mounted officers of their household, with a servant to each mule. The cry of the runners scatters the crowd, and even the panniered donkeys and perpetually astonished camels somehow contrive to become two-dimensional while the white procession goes by.

[Footnote A: The Sultan's government.]

Then the populace closes in again, so quickly and densely that it seems impossible it could ever have been parted, and negro water-carriers, muffled women, beggars streaming with sores, sinewy and greasy "saints," Soudanese sorcerers hung with amulets made of sardine-boxes and hares'-feet, long-lashed boys of the Chleuh in clean embroidered caftans, Jews in black robes and skull-caps, university students carrying their prayer-carpets, bangled and spangled black women, scrofulous children with gazelle eyes and mangy skulls, and blind men tapping along with linked arms and howling out verses of the Koran, surge together in a mass drawn by irresistible suction to the point where the bazaars converge about the mosques of Moulay Idriss and El Kairouiyin.

Seen from a terrace of the upper town, the long thatched roofing of El Attarine, the central bazaar of Fez, promises fantastic revelations of native life; but the dun-colored crowds moving through its checkered twilight, the lack of carved shop-fronts and gaily adorned coffee-houses, and the absence of the painted coffers and vivid embroideries of Tunis, remind one that Morocco is a melancholy country, and Fez a profoundly melancholy city.

Dust and ashes, dust and ashes, echoes from the gray walls, the mouldering thatch of the souks, the long lamentable song of the blind beggars sitting in rows under the feet of the camels and asses. No young men stroll through the bazaar in bright caftans, with roses and jasmine behind their ears, no pedlars offer lemonade and sweetmeats and golden-fritters, no flower-sellers pursue one with tight bunches of orange-blossom and little pink roses. The well-to-do ride by in white, and the rest of the population goes mournfully in earth-color.

But gradually one falls under the spell of another influence—the influence of the Atlas and the desert. Unknown Africa seems much nearer to Morocco than to the white towns of Tunis and the smiling oases of South Algeria. One feels the nearness of Marrakech at Fez, and at Marrakech that of Timbuctoo.

Fez is sombre, and the bazaars clustered about its holiest sanctuaries form its most sombre quarter. Dusk falls there early, and oil-lanterns twinkle in the merchants' niches while the clear African daylight still lies on the gardens of upper Fez. This twilight adds to the mystery of the souks, making them, in spite of profane noise and crowding and filth, an impressive approach to the sacred places.

Until a year or two ago, the precincts around Moulay Idriss and El Kairouiyin were horm, that is, cut off from the unbeliever. Heavy beams of wood barred the end of each souk, shutting off the sanctuaries, and the Christian could only conjecture what lay beyond. Now he knows in part; for, though the beams have not been lowered, all comers may pass under them to the lanes about the mosques, and even pause a moment in their open doorways. Farther one may not go, for the shrines of Morocco are still closed to unbelievers; but whoever knows Cordova, or has stood under the arches of the Great Mosque of Kairouan, can reconstruct something of the hidden beauties of its namesake, the "Mosque Kairouan" of western Africa.

Once under the bars, the richness of the old Moorish Fez presses upon one with unexpected beauty. Here is the graceful tiled fountain of Nedjarine, glittering with the unapproachable blues and greens of ceramic mosaics, near it, the courtyard of the Fondak Nedjarine, oldest and stateliest of Moroccan inns, with triple galleries of sculptured cedar rising above arcades of stone. A little farther on lights and incense draw one to a threshold where it is well not to linger unduly. Under a deep archway, between booths where gay votive candles are sold, the glimmer of hanging lamps falls on patches of gilding and mosaic, and on veiled women prostrating themselves before an invisible shrine—for this is the vestibule of the mosque of Moulay Idriss, where, on certain days of the week, women are admitted to pray.

Moulay Idriss was not built over the grave of the Fatimite prophet, first of the name, whose bones lie in the Zerhoun above his sacred town. The mosque of Fez grew up around the tomb of his posthumous son, Moulay Idriss II, who, descending from the hills, fell upon a camp of Berbers on an affluent of the Sebou, and there laid the foundations of Fez, and of the Moroccan Empire.

Of the original monument it is said that little remains. The zaouia[A] which encloses it dates from the reign of Moulay-Ismael, the seventeenth-century Sultan of Meknez, and the mosque itself, and the green minaret shooting up from the very centre of old Fez, were not built until 1820. But a rich surface of age has already formed on all these disparate buildings, and the over-gorgeous details of the shrines and fountains set in their outer walls are blended into harmony by a film of incense-smoke, and the grease of countless venerating lips and hands.

[Footnote A: Moslem monastery.]

Featureless walls of mean houses close in again at the next turn; but a few steps farther another archway reveals another secret scene. This time it is a corner of the jealously guarded court of ablutions in the great mosque El Kairouiyin, with the twin green-roofed pavilions that are so like those of the Alhambra.

Those who have walked around the outer walls of the mosque of the other Kairouan, and recall the successive doors opening into the forecourt and into the mosque itself, will be able to guess at the plan of the church of Fez. The great Almohad sanctuary of Tunisia is singularly free from parasitic buildings, and may be approached as easily as that of Cordova, but the approaches of El Kairouiyin are so built up that one never knows at which turn of the labyrinth one may catch sight of its court of fountains, or peep down the endless colonnades of which the Arabs say: "The man who should try to count the columns of Kairouiyin would go mad."

Marble floors, heavy whitewashed piers, prostrate figures in the penumbra, rows of yellow slippers outside in the sunlight—out of such glimpses one must reconstruct a vision of the long vistas of arches, the blues and golds of the mirhab,[A] the lustre of bronze chandeliers, and the ivory inlaying of the twelfth-century minbar[B] of ebony and sandalwood.

[Footnote A: Niche in the sanctuary of mosques.]

[Footnote B: Movable pulpit.]

No Christian footstep has yet profaned Kairouiyin, but fairly definite information as to its plan has been gleaned by students of Moroccan art. The number of its "countless" columns has been counted, and it is known that, to the right of the mirhab, carved cedar doors open into a mortuary chapel called "the mosque of the dead"—and also that in this chapel, on Fridays, old books and precious manuscripts are sold by auction.

This odd association of uses recalls the fact that Kairouiyin is not only a church but a library, the University of Fez as well as its cathedral. The beautiful Medersas with which the Merinids adorned the city are simply the lodging-houses of the students, the classes are all held in the courts and galleries adjoining the mosque.

El Kairouiyin was originally an oratory built in the ninth century by Fatmah, whose father had migrated from Kairouan to Fez. Later it was enlarged, and its cupola was surmounted by the talismans which protect sacred edifices against rats, scorpions and serpents, but in spite of these precautions all animal life was not successfully exorcised from it. In the twelfth century, when the great gate Ech Chemmain was building, a well was discovered under its foundations. The mouth of the well was obstructed by an immense tortoise, but when the workmen attempted to take the tortoise out she said: "Burn me rather than take me away from here." They respected her wishes and built her into the foundations; and since then women who suffer from the back-ache have only to come and sit on the bench above the well to be cured.

The actual mosque, or "praying-hall," is said to be formed of a rectangle or double cube of 90 metres by 45, and this vast space is equally divided by rows of horseshoe arches resting on whitewashed piers on which the lower part is swathed in finely patterned matting from Sale. Fifteen monumental doorways lead into the mosque. Their doors are of cedar, heavily barred and ornamented with wrought iron, and one of them bears the name of the artisan, and the date 531 of the Hegira (the first half of the twelfth century). The mosque also contains the two halls of audience of the Cadi, of which one has a graceful exterior facade with coupled lights under horseshoe arches; the library, whose 20,000 volumes are reported to have dwindled to about a thousand, the chapel where the Masters of the Koran recite the sacred text in fulfilment of pious bequests; the "museum" in the upper part of the minaret, wherein a remarkable collection of ancient astronomical instruments is said to be preserved; and the mestonda, or raised hall above the court, where women come to pray.

But the crown of El Kairouiyin is the Merinid court of ablutions. This inaccessible wonder lies close under the Medersa Attarine, one of the oldest and most beautiful collegiate buildings of Fez, and through the kindness of the Director of Fine Arts, who was with us, we were taken up to the roof of the Medersa and allowed to look down into the enclosure.

It is so closely guarded from below that from our secret coign of vantage we seemed to be looking down into the heart of forbidden things. Spacious and serene the great tiled cloister lay beneath us, water spilling over from a central basin of marble with a cool sound to which lesser fountains made answer from under the pyramidal green roofs of the twin pavilions. It was near the prayer-hour, and worshippers were flocking in, laying off their shoes and burnouses, washing their faces at the fountains and their feet in the central tank, or stretching themselves out in the shadow of the enclosing arcade.

This, then, was the famous court "so cool in the great heats that seated by thy beautiful jet of water I feel the perfection of bliss"—as the learned doctor Abou Abd Allah el Maghili sang of it, the court in which the students gather from the adjoining halls after having committed to memory the principles of grammar in prose and verse, the "science of the reading of the Koran," the invention, exposition and ornaments of style, law, medicine, theology, metaphysics and astronomy, as well as the talismanic numbers, and the art of ascertaining by calculation the influences of the angels, the spirits and the heavenly bodies, "the names of the victor and the vanquished, and of the desired object and the person who desires it."

Such is the twentieth-century curriculum of the University of Fez. Repetition is the rule of Arab education as it is of Arab ornament. The teaching of the University is based entirely on the mediaeval principle of mnemonics, and as there are no examinations, no degrees, no limits to the duration of any given course, nor is any disgrace attached to slowness in learning, it is not surprising that many students, coming as youths, linger by the fountain of Kairouiyin till their hair is gray. One well-known oulama has lately finished his studies after twenty-seven years at the University, and is justly proud of the length of his stay. The life of the scholar is easy, the way of knowledge is long, the contrast exquisite between the foul lanes and noisy bazaars outside and this cool heaven of learning. No wonder the students of Kairouiyin say with the tortoise, "Burn me rather than take me away."

IV

EL ANDALOUS AND THE POTTERS' FIELD

Outside the sacred precincts of Moulay Idriss and Kairouiyin, on the other side of the Oued Fez, lies El Andalous, the mosque which the Andalusian Moors built when they settled in Fez in the ninth century.

It stands apart from the bazaars, on higher ground, and though it is not horm we found it less easy to see than the more famous mosques, since the Christian loiterer in its doorways is more quickly noticed. The Fazi are not yet used to seeing unbelievers near their sacred places. It is only in the tumult and confusion of the souks that one can linger on the edge of the inner mysteries without becoming aware of attracting sullen looks, and my only impression of El Andalous is of a magnificent Almohad door and the rich blur of an interior in which there was no time to single out the details.

Turning from its forbidden and forbidding threshold we rode on through a poor quarter which leads to the great gate of Bab F'touh. Beyond the gate rises a dusty rocky slope extending to the outer walls—one of those grim intramural deserts that girdle Fez with desolation. This one is strewn with gravestones, not enclosed, but, as in most Moroccan cemeteries, simply cropping up like nettles between the rocks and out of the flaming dust. Here and there among the slabs rises a well-curb or a crumbling koubba. A solitary palm shoots up beside one of the shrines. And between the crowded graves the caravan trail crosses from the outer to the inner gate, and perpetual lines of camels and donkeys trample the dead a little deeper into the dusty earth.

This Bab F'touh cemetery is also a kind of fondak. Poor caravans camp there under the walls in a mire of offal and chicken-feathers and stripped date-branches prowled through by wolfish dogs and buzzed over by fat blue flies. Camel-drivers squat beside iron kettles over heaps of embers, sorcerers from the Sahara offer their amulets to negro women, peddlers with portable wooden booths sell greasy cakes that look as if they had been made out of the garbage of the caravans, and in and out among the unknown dead and sleeping saints circulates the squalid indifferent life of the living poor.

A walled lane leads down from Bab F'touh to a lower slope, where the Fazi potters have their baking-kilns. Under a series of grassy terraces overgrown with olives we saw the archaic ovens and dripping wheels which produce the earthenware sold in the souks. It is a primitive and homely ware, still fine in shape, though dull in color and monotonous in pattern; and stacked on the red earth under the olives, the rows of jars and cups, in their unglazed and unpainted state, showed their classical descent more plainly than after they have been decorated.

This green quiet hollow, where turbaned figures were moving attentively among the primitive ovens, so near to the region of flies and offal we had just left, woke an old phrase in our memories, and as our mules stumbled back over the graves of Bab F'touh we understood the grim meaning of the words: "They carried him out and buried him in the Potters' Field."

V

MEDERSAS, BAZAARS AND AN OASIS

Fez, for two centuries and more, was in a double sense the capital of Morocco: the centre of its trade as well as of its culture.

Culture, in fact, came to northwest Africa chiefly through the Merinid princes. The Almohads had erected great monuments from Rabat to Marrakech, and had fortified Fez, but their "mighty wasteful empire" fell apart like those that had preceded it. Stability had to come from the west; it was not till the Arabs had learned it through the Moors that Morocco produced a dynasty strong and enlightened enough to carry out the dream of its founders.

Whichever way the discussion sways as to the priority of eastern or western influences on Moroccan art—whether it came to her from Syria, and was thence passed on to Spain, or was first formed in Spain, and afterward modified by the Moroccan imagination—there can at least be no doubt that Fazi art and culture, in their prime, are partly the reflection of European civilization.

Fugitives from Spain came to the new city when Moulay Idriss founded it. One part of the town was given to them, and the river divided the Elbali of the Almohads into the two quarters of Kairouiyin and Andalous, which still retain their old names. But the full intellectual and artistic flowering of Fez was delayed till the thirteenth and fourteenth centuries. It seems as though the seeds of the new springtime of art, blown across the sea from reawakening Europe, had at last given the weltering tribes of the desert the force to create their own type of beauty.

Nine Medersas sprang up in Fez, six of them built by the princes who were also creating the exquisite collegiate buildings of Sale, Rabat and old Meknez, and the enchanting mosque and minaret of Chella. The power of these rulers also was in perpetual flux, they were always at war with the Sultans of Tlemcen, the Christians of Spain, the princes of northern Algeria and Tunis. But during the fourteenth century they established a rule wide and firm enough to permit of the great outburst of art and learning which produced the Medersas of Fez.

Until a year or two ago these collegiate buildings were as inaccessible as the mosques, but now that the French government has undertaken their restoration strangers may visit them under the guidance of the Fine Arts Department.

All are built on the same plan, the plan of Sale and Rabat, which (as M. Tranchant de Lunel[A] has pointed out) became, with slight modifications, that of the rich private houses of Morocco. But interesting as they are in plan and the application of ornament, their main beauty lies in their details, in the union of chiselled plaster with the delicate mosaic work of niches and revetements, the web-like arabesques of the upper walls and the bold, almost Gothic sculpture of the cedar architraves and corbels supporting them. And when all these details are enumerated, and also the fretted panels of cedar, the bronze doors with their great shield-like bosses, and the honeycombings and rufflings of the gilded ceilings, there still remains the general tinge of dry disintegration, as though all were perishing of a desert fever—that, and the final wonder of seeing before one, in such a setting, the continuance of the very life that went on there when the tiles were set and the gold was new on the ceilings.

[Footnote A: In France-Maroc, No. 1.]

For these tottering Medersas, already in the hands of the restorers, are still inhabited. As long as the stairway holds and the balcony has not rotted from its corbels, the students of the University see no reason for abandoning their lodgings above the cool fountain and the house of prayer. The strange men giving incomprehensible orders for unnecessary repairs need not disturb their meditations, and when the hammering grows too loud the oulamas have only to pass through the silk market or the souk of the embroiderers to the mosque of Kairouiyin, and go on weaving the pattern of their dreams by the fountain of perfect bliss.

One reads of the bazaars of Fez that they have been for centuries the central market of the country. Here are to be found not only the silks and pottery, the Jewish goldsmiths' work, the arms and embroidered saddlery which the city itself produces, but "morocco" from Marrakech, rugs, tent-hangings and matting from Rabat and Sale, grain baskets from Moulay Idriss, daggers from the Souss, and whatever European wares the native markets consume. One looks, on the plan of Fez, at the space covered by the bazaars, one breasts the swarms that pour through them from dawn to dusk—and one remains perplexed, disappointed. They are less "Oriental" than one had expected, if "Oriental" means color and gaiety.

Sometimes, on occasion, it does mean that: as, for instance, when a procession passes bearing the gifts for a Jewish wedding. The gray crowd makes way for a group of musicians in brilliant caftans, and following them comes a long file of women with uncovered faces and bejewelled necks, balancing on their heads the dishes the guests have sent to the feast—kouskous, sweet creams and syrups, "gazelles' horns" of sugar and almonds—in delicately woven baskets, each covered with several squares of bright gauze edged with gold. Then one remembers the marketing of the Lady of "The Three Calendars," and Fez again becomes the Bagdad of Al Raschid.

But when no exceptional events, processions, ceremonies and the like brighten the underworld of the souks, their look is uniformly melancholy. The gay bazaars, the gaily-painted houses, the flowers and flute-playing of North Africa, are found in her Mediterranean ports, in contact with European influences. The farther west she extends, the more she becomes self-contained, sombre, uninfluenced, a gloomy fanatic with her back to the walls of the Atlantic and the Atlas. Color and laughter lie mostly along the trade-routes, where the peoples of the world come and go in curiosity and rivalry. This ashen crowd swarming gloomily through the dark tunnels represents the real Moghreb that is close to the wild tribes of the "hinterland" and the grim feudal fortresses of the Atlas. How close, one has only to go out to Sefrou on a market-day to see.

Sefrou is a military outpost in an oasis under the Atlas, about forty miles south of Fez. To most people the word "oasis" evokes palms and sand; but though Morocco possesses many oases it has no pure sand and few palms. I remember it as a considerable event when I discovered one from my lofty window at Bou-Jeloud.

The bled is made of very different stuff from the sand-ocean of the Sahara. The light plays few tricks with it. Its monotony is wearisome rather than impressive, and the fact that it is seldom without some form of dwarfish vegetation makes the transition less startling when the alluvial green is finally reached. One had always half expected it, and it does not spring at a djinn's wave out of sterile gold.

But the fact brings its own compensations. Moroccan oases differ one from another far more than those of South Algeria and Tunisia. Some have no palms, others but a few, others are real palm-oases, though even in the south (at least on the hither side of the great Atlas) none spreads out a dense uniform roofing of metal-blue fronds like the date-oases of Biskra or Tozeur. As for Sefrou, which Foucauld called the most beautiful oasis of Morocco, it is simply an extremely fertile valley with vineyards and orchards stretching up to a fine background of mountains. But the fact that it lies just below the Atlas makes it an important market-place and centre of caravans.

Though so near Fez it is still almost on the disputed border between the loyal and the "unsubmissive" tribes, those that are Blad-Makhzen (of the Sultan's government) and those that are against it. Until recently, therefore, it has been inaccessible to visitors, and even now a strongly fortified French post dominates the height above the town. Looking down from the fort, one distinguishes, through masses of many-tinted green, a suburb of Arab houses in gardens, and below, on the river, Sefrou itself, a stout little walled town with angle-towers defiantly thrust forth toward the Atlas. It is just outside these walls that the market is held.

It was swarming with hill-people the day we were there, and strange was the contrast between the crowd inside the circle of picketed horses and the white-robed cockneys from Rabat who fill the market-place of Sale. Here at last we were in touch with un-Arab Morocco, with Berbers of the bled and the hills, whose women know no veils and no seclusion, and who, under a thin surface of Mahometanism, preserve their old stone and animal worship, and all the gross fetichistic beliefs from which Mahomet dreamed of freeing Africa.

The men were lean and weather-bitten, some with negroid lips, others with beaked noses and gaunt cheek-bones, all muscular and fierce-looking. Some were wrapped in the black cloaks worn by the Blue Men of the Sahara,[A] with a great orange sun embroidered on the back, some tunicked like the Egyptian fellah, under a rough striped outer garment trimmed with bright tufts and tassels of wool. The men of the Rif had a braided lock on the shoulder, those of the Atlas a ringlet over each ear, and brown woollen scarfs wound round their temples, leaving the shaven crown bare.

[Footnote A: So called because of the indigo dye of their tunics, which leaves a permanent stain on their bodies.]

The women, squatting among their kids and poultry and cheeses, glanced at us with brilliant hennaed eyes and smiles that lifted their short upper lips maliciously. Their thin faces were painted in stripes and patterns of indigo. Silver necklets covered their throats, long earrings dangled under the wool-embroidered kerchiefs bound about their temples with a twist of camel's hair, and below the cotton shifts fastened on their shoulders with silver clasps their legs were bare to the knee, or covered with leather leggings to protect them from the thorny bled.

They seemed abler bargainers than the men, and the play of expression on their dramatic and intensely feminine faces as they wheedled the price of a calf out of a fierce hillsman, or haggled over a heap of dates that a Jew with greasy ringlets was trying to secure for his secret distillery, showed that they knew their superiority and enjoyed it.

Jews abounded in the market-place and also in the town. Sefrou contains a large Israelite colony, and after we had wandered through the steep streets, over gushing waterfalls spanned by "ass-backed" Spanish bridges, and through a thatched souk smelling strong of camels and the desert, the French commissioner (the only European in Sefrou) suggested that it might interest us to visit the Mellah.

It was our first sight of a typical Jewish quarter in Africa. The Mellah of Fez was almost entirely destroyed during the massacres of 1912 (which incidentally included a pogrom), and its distinctive character, happily for the inhabitants, has disappeared in the rebuilding. North African Jews are still compelled to live in ghettos, into which they are locked at night, as in France and Germany in the Middle Ages, and until lately the men have been compelled to go unarmed, to wear black gabardines and black slippers, to take off their shoes when they passed near a mosque or a saint's tomb, and in various other ways to manifest their subjection to the ruling race. Nowhere else do they live in conditions of such demoralizing promiscuity as in some of the cities of Morocco. They have so long been subject to unrestricted extortion on the part of the Moslems that even the wealthy Jews (who are numerous) have sunk to the habits and appearance of the poorest; and Sefrou, which has come so recently under French control, offers a good specimen of a Mellah before foreign sanitation has lighted up its dark places.

Dark indeed they were. After wandering through narrow and malodorous lanes, and slipping about in the offal of the souks, we were suddenly led under an arch over which should have been written "All light abandon—" and which made all we had seen before seem clean and bright and airy.

The beneficent African sun dries up and purifies the immemorial filth of Africa, where that sun enters there is none of the foulness of damp. But into the Mellah of Sefrou it never comes, for the streets form a sort of subterranean rabbit-warren under the upper stories of a solid agglomeration of tall houses—a buried city lit even at midday by oil-lamps hanging in the goldsmiths' shops and under the archways of the black and reeking staircases.

It was a Jewish feast-day. The Hebrew stalls in the souks were closed, and the whole population of the Mellah thronged its tunnels in holiday dress. Hurrying past us were young women with plump white faces and lovely eyes, turbaned in brilliant gauzes, with draperies of dirty curtain muslin over tawdry brocaded caftans. Their paler children swarmed about them, little long-earringed girls like wax dolls dressed in scraps of old finery, little boys in tattered caftans with long-lashed eyes and wily smiles, and, waddling in the rear, their unwieldy grandmothers, huge lumps of tallowy flesh who were probably still in the thirties.

With them were the men of the family, in black gabardines and skull-caps, sallow striplings, incalculably aged ancestors, round-bellied husbands and fathers bumping along like black balloons, all hastening to the low doorways dressed with lamps and paper garlands behind which the feast was spread.

One is told that in cities like Fez and Marrakech the Hebrew quarter conceals flowery patios and gilded rooms with the heavy European furniture that rich Jews delight in. Perhaps even in the Mellah of Sefrou, among the ragged figures shuffling past us, there were some few with bags of gold in their walls and rich stuffs hid away in painted coffers, but for patios and flowers and daylight there seemed no room in the dark bolgia they inhabit. No wonder the babies of the Moroccan ghettos are nursed on date-brandy, and their elders doze away to death under its consoling spell.

VI

THE LAST GLIMPSE

It is well to bid good-by to Fez at night—a moonlight night for choice.

Then, after dining at the Arab inn of Fez Eldjid—where it might be inconvenient to lodge, but where it is extremely pleasant to eat kouskous under a grape-trellis in a tiled and fountained patio—this pleasure over, one may set out on foot and stray down the lanes toward Fez Elbali.

Not long ago the gates between the different quarters of the city used to be locked every night at nine o'clock, and the merchant who went out to dine in another part of the town had to lodge with his host. Now this custom has been given up, and one may roam about untroubled through the old quarters, grown as silent as the grave after the intense life of the bazaars has ceased at nightfall.

Nobody is in the streets wandering from ghostly passage to passage, one hears no step but that of the watchman with staff and lantern. Presently there appears, far off, a light like a low-flying firefly, as it comes nearer, it is seen to proceed from the Mellah lamp of open-work brass that a servant carries ahead of two merchants on their way home from Elbali. The merchants are grave men, they move softly and slowly on their fat slippered feet, pausing from time to time in confidential talk. At last they stop before a house wall with a low blue door barred by heavy hasps of iron. The servant lifts the lamp and knocks. There is a long delay, then, with infinite caution, the door is opened a few inches, and another lifted light shines faintly on lustrous tiled walls, and on the face of a woman slave who quickly veils herself. Evidently the master is a man of standing, and the house well guarded. The two merchants touch each other on the right shoulder, one of them passes in, and his friend goes on through the moonlight, his servant's lantern dancing ahead.

But here we are in an open space looking down one of the descents to El Attarine. A misty radiance washes the tall houses, the garden-walls, the archways, even the moonlight does not whiten Fez, but only turns its gray to tarnished silver. Overhead in a tower window a single light twinkles: women's voices rise and fall on the roofs. In a rich man's doorway slaves are sleeping, huddled on the tiles. A cock crows from somebody's dunghill, a skeleton dog prowls by for garbage.

Everywhere is the loud rush or the low crooning of water, and over every wall comes the scent of jasmine and rose. Far off, from the red purgatory between the walls, sounds the savage thrum-thrum of a negro orgy, here all is peace and perfume. A minaret springs up between the roofs like a palm, and from its balcony the little white figure bends over and drops a blessing on all the loveliness and all the squalor.

IV - MARRAKECH

I

THE WAY THERE

There are countless Arab tales of evil Djinns who take the form of sandstorms and hot winds to overwhelm exhausted travellers.

In spite of the new French road between Rabat and Marrakech the memory of such tales rises up insistently from every mile of the level red earth and the desolate stony stretches of the bled. As long as the road runs in sight of the Atlantic breakers they give the scene freshness and life, but when it bends inland and stretches away across the wilderness the sense of the immensity and immobility of Africa descends on one with an intolerable oppression.

The road traverses no villages, and not even a ring of nomad tents is visible in the distance on the wide stretches of arable land. At infrequent intervals our motor passed a train of laden mules, or a group of peasants about a well, and sometimes, far off, a fortified farm profiled its thick-set angle-towers against the sky, or a white koubba floated like a mirage above the brush, but these rare signs of life intensified the solitude of the long miles between.

At midday we were refreshed by the sight of the little oasis around the military-post of Settat. We lunched there with the commanding officer, in a cool Arab house about a flowery patio, but that brief interval over, the fiery plain began again. After Settat the road runs on for miles across the waste to the gorge of the Oued Ouem, and beyond the river it climbs to another plain so desperate in its calcined aridity that the prickly scrub of the wilderness we had left seemed like the vegetation of an oasis. For fifty kilometres the earth under our wheels was made up of a kind of glistening red slag covered with pebbles and stones. Not the scantest and toughest of rock-growths thrust a leaf through its brassy surface, not a well-head or a darker depression of the rock gave sign of a trickle of water. Everything around us glittered with the same unmerciful dryness.

A long way ahead loomed the line of the Djebilets, the Djinn-haunted mountains guarding Marrakech on the north. When at last we reached them the wicked glister of their purple flanks seemed like a volcanic upheaval of the plain. For some time we had watched the clouds gathering over them, and as we got to the top of the defile rain was falling from a fringe of thunder to the south. Then the vapours lifted, and we saw below us another red plain with an island of palms in its centre. Mysteriously, from the heart of the palms, a tower shot up, as if alone in the wilderness, behind it stood the sun-streaked cliffs of the Atlas, with snow summits appearing and vanishing through the storm.

As we drove downward the rock gradually began to turn to red earth fissured by yellow streams, and stray knots of palms sprang up, lean and dishevelled, about well-heads where people were watering camels and donkeys. To the east, dominating the oasis, the twin peaked hills of the Ghilis, fortified to the crest, mounted guard over invisible Marrakech; but still, above the palms, we saw only that lonely and triumphant tower.

Presently we crossed the Oued Tensif on an old bridge built by Moroccan engineers. Beyond the river were more palms, then olive-orchards, then the vague sketch of the new European settlement, with a few shops and cafes on avenues ending suddenly in clay pits, and at last Marrakech itself appeared to us, in the form of a red wall across a red wilderness.

We passed through a gate and were confronted by other ramparts. Then we entered an outskirt of dusty red lanes bordered by clay hovels with draped figures slinking by like ghosts. After that more walls, more gates, more endlessly winding lanes, more gates again, more turns, a dusty open space with donkeys and camels and negroes; a final wall with a great door under a lofty arch—and suddenly we were in the palace of the Bahia, among flowers and shadows and falling water.

II

THE BAHIA

Whoever would understand Marrakech must begin by mounting at sunset to the roof of the Bahia.

Outspread below lies the oasis-city of the south, flat and vast as the great nomad camp it really is, its low roofs extending on all sides to a belt of blue palms ringed with desert. Only two or three minarets and a few noblemen's houses among gardens break the general flatness; but they are hardly noticeable, so irresistibly is the eye drawn toward two dominant objects—the white wall of the Atlas and the red tower of the Koutoubya.

Foursquare, untapering, the great tower lifts its flanks of ruddy stone. Its large spaces of unornamented wall, its triple tier of clustered openings, lightening as they rise from the severe rectangular lights of the first stage to the graceful arcade below the parapet, have the stern harmony of the noblest architecture. The Koutoubya would be magnificent anywhere; in this flat desert it is grand enough to face the Atlas.

The Almohad conquerors who built the Koutoubya and embellished Marrakech dreamed a dream of beauty that extended from the Guadalquivir to the Sahara; and at its two extremes they placed their watch-towers. The Giralda watched over civilized enemies in a land of ancient Roman culture, the Koutoubya stood at the edge of the world, facing the hordes of the desert.

The Almoravid princes who founded Marrakech came from the black desert of Senegal, themselves were leaders of wild hordes. In the history of North Africa the same cycle has perpetually repeated itself. Generation after generation of chiefs have flowed in from the desert or the mountains, overthrown their predecessors, massacred, plundered, grown rich, built sudden palaces, encouraged their great servants to do the same, then fallen on them, and taken their wealth and their palaces. Usually some religious fury, some ascetic wrath against the self-indulgence of the cities, has been the motive of these attacks, but invariably the same results followed, as they followed when the Germanic barbarians descended on Italy. The conquerors, infected with luxury and mad with power, built vaster palaces, planned grander cities, but Sultans and Viziers camped in their golden houses as if on the march, and the mud huts of the tribesmen within their walls were but one degree removed from the mud-walled tents of the bled.

This was more especially the case with Marrakech, a city of Berbers and blacks, and the last outpost against the fierce black world beyond the Atlas from which its founders came. When one looks at its site, and considers its history, one can only marvel at the height of civilization it attained.

The Bahia itself, now the palace of the Resident General, though built less than a hundred years ago, is typical of the architectural megalomania of the great southern chiefs. It was built by Ba-Ahmed, the all-powerful black Vizier of the Sultan Moulay-el-Hassan.[A] Ba-Ahmed was evidently an artist and an archaeologist. His ambition was to re-create a Palace of Beauty such as the Moors had built in the prime of Arab art, and he brought to Marrakech skilled artificers of Fez, the last surviving masters of the mystery of chiselled plaster and ceramic mosaics and honeycombing of gilded cedar. They came, they built the Bahia, and it remains the loveliest and most fantastic of Moroccan palaces.

[Footnote A: Moulay-el-Hassan reigned from 1873 to 1894.]

Court within court, garden beyond garden, reception halls, private apartments, slaves' quarters, sunny prophets' chambers on the roofs and baths in vaulted crypts, the labyrinth of passages and rooms stretches away over several acres of ground. A long court enclosed in pale-green trellis-work, where pigeons plume themselves about a great tank and the dripping tiles glitter with refracted sunlight, leads to the fresh gloom of a cypress garden, or under jasmine tunnels bordered with running water; and these again open on arcaded apartments faced with tiles and stucco-work, where, in a languid twilight, the hours drift by to the ceaseless music of the fountains.

The beauty of Moroccan palaces is made up of details of ornament and refinements of sensuous delight too numerous to record, but to get an idea of their general character it is worth while to cross the Court of Cypresses at the Bahia and follow a series of low-studded passages that turn on themselves till they reach the centre of the labyrinth. Here, passing by a low padlocked door leading to a crypt, and known as the "Door of the Vizier's Treasure-House," one comes on a painted portal that opens into a still more secret sanctuary: The apartment of the Grand Vizier's Favourite.

This lovely prison, from which all sight and sound of the outer world are excluded, is built about an atrium paved with disks of turquoise and black and white. Water trickles from a central vasca of alabaster into an hexagonal mosaic channel in the pavement. The walls, which are at least twenty-five feet high, are roofed with painted beams resting on panels of traceried stucco in which is set a clerestory of jewelled glass. On each side of the atrium are long recessed rooms closed by vermilion doors painted with gold arabesques and vases of spring flowers, and into these shadowy inner rooms, spread with rugs and divans and soft pillows, no light comes except when their doors are opened into the atrium. In this fabulous place it was my good luck to be lodged while I was at Marrakech.

In a climate where, after the winter snow has melted from the Atlas, every breath of air for long months is a flame of fire, these enclosed rooms in the middle of the palaces are the only places of refuge from the heat. Even in October the temperature of the favourite's apartment was deliciously reviving after a morning in the bazaars or the dusty streets, and I never came back to its wet tiles and perpetual twilight without the sense of plunging into a deep sea-pool.

From far off, through circuitous corridors, came the scent of citron-blossom and jasmine, with sometimes a bird's song before dawn, sometimes a flute's wail at sunset, and always the call of the muezzin in the night, but no sunlight reached the apartment except in remote rays through the clerestory, and no air except through one or two broken panes.

Sometimes, lying on my divan, and looking out through the vermilion doors, I used to surprise a pair of swallows dropping down from their nest in the cedar-beams to preen themselves on the fountain's edge or in the channels of the pavement, for the roof was full of birds who came and went through the broken panes of the clerestory. Usually they were my only visitors, but one morning just at daylight I was waked by a soft tramp of bare feet, and saw, silhouetted against the cream-coloured walls, a procession of eight tall negroes in linen tunics, who filed noiselessly across the atrium like a moving frieze of bronze. In that fantastic setting, and the hush of that twilight hour, the vision was so like the picture of a "Seraglio Tragedy," some fragment of a Delacroix or Decamps floating up into the drowsy brain, that I almost fancied I had seen the ghosts of Ba-Ahmed's executioners revisiting with dagger and bowstring the scene of an unavenged crime.

A cock crew, and they vanished ... and when I made the mistake of asking what they had been doing in my room at that hour I was told (as though it were the most natural thing in the world) that they were the municipal lamp-lighters of Marrakech, whose duty it is to refill every morning the two hundred acetylene lamps lighting the palace of the Resident General. Such unforeseen aspects, in this mysterious city, do the most ordinary domestic functions wear.

III

THE BAZAARS

Passing out of the enchanted circle of the Bahia it is startling to plunge into the native life about its gates.

Marrakech is the great market of the south, and the south means not only the Atlas with its feudal chiefs and their wild clansmen, but all that lies beyond of heat and savagery, the Sahara of the veiled Touaregs, Dakka, Timbuctoo, Senegal and the Soudan. Here come the camel caravans from Demnat and Tameslout, from the Moulouya and the Souss, and those from the Atlantic ports and the confines of Algeria. The population of this old city of the southern march has always been even more mixed than that of the northerly Moroccan towns. It is made up of the descendants of all the peoples conquered by a long line of Sultans who brought their trains of captives across the sea from Moorish Spain and across the Sahara from Timbuctoo. Even in the highly cultivated region on the lower slopes of the Atlas there are groups of varied ethnic origin, the descendants of tribes transplanted by long-gone rulers and still preserving many of their original characteristics.

In the bazaars all these peoples meet and mingle: cattle-dealers, olive-growers, peasants from the Atlas, the Souss and the Draa, Blue Men of the Sahara, blacks from Senegal and the Soudan, coming in to trade with the wool-merchants, tanners, leather-merchants, silk-weavers, armourers, and makers of agricultural implements.

Dark, fierce and fanatical are these narrow souks of Marrakech. They are mere mud lanes roofed with rushes, as in South Tunisia and Timbuctoo, and the crowds swarming in them are so dense that it is hardly possible, at certain hours, to approach the tiny raised kennels where the merchants sit like idols among their wares. One feels at once that something more than the thought of bargaining—dear as this is to the African heart—animates these incessantly moving throngs. The Souks of Marrakech seem, more than any others, the central organ of a native life that extends far beyond the city walls into secret clefts of the mountains and far-off oases where plots are hatched and holy wars fomented—farther still, to yellow deserts whence negroes are secretly brought across the Atlas to that inmost recess of the bazaar where the ancient traffic in flesh and blood still surreptitiously goes on.

All these many threads of the native life, woven of greed and lust, of fetichism and fear and blind hate of the stranger, form, in the souks, a thick network in which at times one's feet seem literally to stumble. Fanatics in sheepskins glowering from the guarded thresholds of the mosques, fierce tribesmen with inlaid arms in their belts and the fighters' tufts of wiry hair escaping from camel's-hair turbans, mad negroes standing stark naked in niches of the walls and pouring down Soudanese incantations upon the fascinated crowd, consumptive Jews with pathos and cunning in their large eyes and smiling lips, lusty slave-girls with earthen oil-jars resting against swaying hips, almond-eyed boys leading fat merchants by the hand, and bare-legged Berber women, tattooed and insolently gay, trading their striped blankets, or bags of dried roses and irises, for sugar, tea or Manchester cottons—from all these hundreds of unknown and unknowable people, bound together by secret affinities, or intriguing against each other with secret hate, there emanates an atmosphere of mystery and menace more stifling than the smell of camels and spices and black bodies and smoking fry which hangs like a fog under the close roofing of the souks.

And suddenly one leaves the crowd and the turbid air for one of those quiet corners that are like the back-waters of the bazaars, a small square where a vine stretches across a shop-front and hangs ripe clusters of grapes through the reeds. In the patterning of grape-shadows a very old donkey, tethered to a stone-post, dozes under a pack-saddle that is never taken off; and near by, in a matted niche, sits a very old man in white. This is the chief of the Guild of "morocco" workers of Marrakech, the most accomplished craftsman in Morocco in the preparing and using of the skins to which the city gives its name. Of these sleek moroccos, cream-white or dyed with cochineal or pomegranate skins, are made the rich bags of the Chleuh dancing-boys, the embroidered slippers for the harem, the belts and harnesses that figure so largely in Moroccan trade—and of the finest, in old days, were made the pomegranate-red morocco bindings of European bibliophiles.

From this peaceful corner one passes into the barbaric splendor of a souk hung with innumerable plumy bunches of floss silk—skeins of citron yellow, crimson, grasshopper green and pure purple. This is the silk-spinners' quarter, and next to it comes that of the dyers, with great seething vats into which the raw silk is plunged, and ropes overhead where the rainbow masses are hung out to dry.

Another turn leads into the street of the metal-workers and armourers, where the sunlight through the thatch flames on round flanks of beaten copper or picks out the silver bosses of ornate powder-flasks and pistols, and near by is the souk of the plough-shares, crowded with peasants in rough Chleuh cloaks who are waiting to have their archaic ploughs repaired, and that of the smiths, in an outer lane of mud huts where negroes squat in the dust and sinewy naked figures in tattered loincloths bend over blazing coals. And here ends the maze of the bazaars.

IV

THE AGDAL

One of the Almohad Sultans who, during their hundred years of empire, scattered such great monuments from Seville to the Atlas, felt the need of coolness about his southern capital, and laid out the olive-yards of the Agdal.

To the south of Marrakech the Agdal extends for many acres between the outer walls of the city and the edge of the palm-oasis—a continuous belt of silver foliage traversed by deep red lanes, and enclosing a wide-spreading summer palace and two immense reservoirs walled with masonry, and the vision of these serene sheets of water, in which the olives and palms are motionlessly reflected, is one of the most poetic impressions in that city of inveterate poetry.

On the edge of one of the reservoirs a sentimental Sultan built in the last century a little pleasure-house called the Menara. It is composed of a few rooms with a two-storied loggia looking across the water to the palm-groves, and surrounded by a garden of cypresses and orange-trees. The Menara, long since abandoned, is usually uninhabited, but on the day when we drove through the Agdal we noticed, at the gate, a group of well-dressed servants holding mules with embroidered saddle-clothes.

The French officer who was with us asked the porter what was going on, and he replied that the Chief of the Guild of Wool-Merchants had hired the pavilion for a week and invited a few friends to visit him. They were now, the porter added, taking tea in the loggia above the lake, and the host, being informed of our presence, begged that we should do him and his friends the honour of visiting the pavilion.

In reply to this amiable invitation we crossed an empty saloon surrounded with divans and passed out onto the loggia where the wool-merchant and his guests were seated. They were evidently persons of consequence: large bulky men wrapped in fresh muslins and reclining side by side on muslin-covered divans and cushions. Black slaves had placed before them brass trays with pots of mint-tea, glasses in filigree stands, and dishes of gazelles' horns and sugar-plums, and they sat serenely absorbing these refreshments and gazing with large calm eyes upon the motionless water and the reflected trees.

So, we were told, they would probably spend the greater part of their holiday. The merchant's cooks had taken possession of the kitchens, and toward sunset a sumptuous repast of many courses would be carried into the saloon on covered trays, and the guests would squat about it on rugs of Rabat, tearing with their fingers the tender chicken wings and small artichokes cooked in oil, plunging their fat white hands to the wrist into huge mounds of saffron and rice, and washing off the traces of each course in the brass basin of perfumed water carried about by a young black slave-girl with hoop-earrings and a green-and-gold scarf about her hips.

Then the singing-girls would come out from Marrakech, squat round-faced young women heavily hennaed and bejewelled, accompanied by gaunt musicians in bright caftans; and for hours they would sing sentimental or obscene ballads to the persistent maddening twang of violin and flute and drum. Meanwhile fiery brandy or sweet champagne would probably be passed around between the steaming glasses of mint-tea which the slaves perpetually refilled; or perhaps the sultry air, the heavy meal, the scent of the garden and the vertiginous repetition of the music would suffice to plunge these sedentary worthies into the delicious coma in which every festive evening in Morocco ends.

The next day would be spent in the same manner, except that probably the Chleuh boys with sidelong eyes and clean caftans would come instead of the singing-girls, and weave the arabesque of their dance in place of the runic pattern of the singing. But the result would always be the same: a prolonged state of obese ecstasy culminating in the collapse of huge heaps of snoring muslin on the divans against the wall. Finally at the week's end the wool-merchant and his friends would all ride back with dignity to the bazaar.

V

ON THE ROOFS

"Should you like to see the Chleuh boys dance?" someone asked.

"There they are," another of our companions added, pointing to a dense ring of spectators on one side of the immense dusty square at the entrance of the souks—the "Square of the Dead" as it is called, in memory of the executions that used to take place under one of its grim red gates.

It is the square of the living now, the centre of all the life, amusement and gossip of Marrakech, and the spectators are so thickly packed about the story-tellers, snake-charmers and dancers who frequent it that one can guess what is going on within each circle only by the wailing monologue or the persistent drum-beat that proceeds from it.

Ah, yes—we should indeed like to see the Chleuh boys dance, we who, since we had been in Morocco, had seen no dancing, heard no singing, caught no single glimpse of merry-making! But how were we to get within sight of them?

On one side of the "Square of the Dead" stands a large house, of European build, but modelled on Oriental lines: the office of the French municipal administration. The French Government no longer allows its offices to be built within the walls of Moroccan towns, and this house goes back to the epic days of the Caid Sir Harry Maclean, to whom it was presented by the fantastic Abd-el-Aziz when the Caid was his favourite companion as well as his military adviser.

At the suggestion of the municipal officials we mounted the stairs and looked down on the packed square. There can be no more Oriental sight this side of the Atlas and the Sahara. The square is surrounded by low mud-houses, fondaks, cafes, and the like. In one corner, near the archway leading into the souks, is the fruit-market, where the red-gold branches of unripe dates[A] for animal fodder are piled up in great stacks, and dozens of donkeys are coming and going, their panniers laden with fruits and vegetables which are being heaped on the ground in gorgeous pyramids: purple egg-plants, melons, cucumbers, bright orange pumpkins, mauve and pink and violet onions, rusty crimson pomegranates and the gold grapes of Sefrou and Sale, all mingled with fresh green sheaves of mint and wormwood.

[Footnote A: Dates do not ripen in Morocco.]

In the middle of the square sit the story-tellers' turbaned audiences. Beyond these are the humbler crowds about the wild-ringleted snake-charmers with their epileptic gestures and hissing incantations, and farther off, in the densest circle of all, we could just discern the shaved heads and waving surpliced arms of the dancing-boys. Under an archway near by an important personage in white muslin, mounted on a handsome mule and surrounded by his attendants, sat with motionless face and narrowed eyes gravely following the movements of the dancers.

Suddenly, as we stood watching the extraordinary animation of the scene, a reddish light overspread it, and one of our companions exclaimed: "Ah—a dust-storm!"

In that very moment it was upon us: a red cloud rushing across the square out of nowhere, whirling the date-branches over the heads of the squatting throngs, tumbling down the stacks of fruits and vegetables, rooting up the canvas awnings over the lemonade-sellers' stalls and before the cafe doors, huddling the blinded donkeys under the walls of the fondak, and stripping to the hips the black slave-girls scudding home from the souks.

Such a blast would instantly have scattered any western crowd, but "the patient East" remained undisturbed, rounding its shoulders before the storm and continuing to follow attentively the motions of the dancers and the turns of the story-tellers. By and bye, however, the gale grew too furious, and the spectators were so involved in collapsing tents, eddying date-branches and stampeding mules that the square began to clear, save for the listeners about the most popular story-teller, who continued to sit on unmoved. And then, at the height of the storm, they too were abruptly scattered by the rush of a cavalcade across the square. First came a handsomely dressed man, carrying before him on his peaked saddle a tiny boy in a gold-embroidered orange caftan, in front of whom he held an open book, and behind them a train of white-draped men on showily harnessed mules, followed by musicians in bright dresses. It was only a Circumcision procession on its way to the mosque; but the dust-enveloped rider in his rich dress, clutching the bewildered child to his breast, looked like some Oriental prince trying to escape with his son from the fiery embraces of desert Erl-maidens.

As swiftly as it rose the storm subsided, leaving the fruit-market in ruins under a sky as clear and innocent as an infant's eye. The Chleuh boys had vanished with the rest, like marionettes swept into a drawer by an impatient child, but presently, toward sunset, we were told that we were to see them after all, and our hosts led us up to the roof of the Caid's house.

The city lay stretched before us like one immense terrace circumscribed by palms. The sky was pure blue, verging to turquoise green where the Atlas floated above mist; and facing the celestial snows stood the Koutoubya, red in the sunset.

People were beginning to come out on the roofs: it was the hour of peace, of ablutions, of family life on the house-tops. Groups of women in pale tints and floating veils spoke to each other from terrace to terrace, through the chatter of children and the guttural calls of bedizened negresses. And presently, on the roof adjoining ours, appeared the slim dancing-boys with white caftans and hennaed feet.

The three swarthy musicians who accompanied them crossed their lean legs on the tiles and set up their throb-throb and thrum-thrum, and on a narrow strip of terrace the youths began their measured steps.

It was a grave static dance, such as David may have performed before the Ark; untouched by mirth or folly, as beseemed a dance in that sombre land, and borrowing its magic from its gravity. Even when the pace quickened with the stress of the music the gestures still continued to be restrained and hieratic, only when, one by one, the performers detached themselves from the round and knelt before us for the peseta it is customary to press on their foreheads, did one see, by the moisture which made the coin adhere, how quick and violent their movements had been.

The performance, like all things Oriental, like the life, the patterns, the stories, seemed to have no beginning and no end: it just went monotonously and indefatigably on till fate snipped its thread by calling us away to dinner. And so at last we went down into the dust of the streets refreshed by that vision of white youths dancing on the house-tops against the gold of a sunset that made them look— in spite of ankle-bracelets and painted eyes—almost as guileless and happy as the round of angels on the roof of Fra Angelico's Nativity.

VI

THE SAADIAN TOMBS

On one of the last days of our stay in Marrakech we were told, almost mysteriously, that permission was to be given us to visit the tombs of the Saadian Sultans.

Though Marrakech has been in the hands of the French since 1912, the very existence of these tombs was unknown to the authorities till 1917. Then the Sultan's government privately informed the Resident General that an unsuspected treasure of Moroccan art was falling into ruin, and after some hesitation it was agreed that General Lyautey and the Director of Fine Arts should be admitted to the mosque containing the tombs, on the express condition that the French Government undertook to repair them. While we were at Rabat General Lyautey had described his visit to us, and it was at his request that the Sultan authorized us to see the mosque, to which no travellers had as yet been admitted.

With a good deal of ceremony, and after the customary pourparlers with the great Pasha who controls native affairs at Marrakech, an hour was fixed for our visit, and we drove through long lanes of mud-huts to a lost quarter near the walls. At last we came to a deserted square on one side of which stands the long low mosque of Mansourah with a turquoise-green minaret embroidered with traceries of sculptured terra cotta. Opposite the mosque is a gate in a crumbling wall; and at this gate the Pasha's Cadi was to meet us with the keys of the mausoleum. But we waited in vain. Oriental dilatoriness, or a last secret reluctance to admit unbelievers to a holy place, had caused the Cadi to forget his appointment, and we drove away disappointed.

The delay drove us to wondering about these mysterious Saadian Sultans, who, though coming so late in the annals of Morocco, had left at least one monument said to be worthy of the Merinid tradition. And the tale of the Saadians is worth telling.

They came from Arabia to the Draa (the fruitful country south of the Great Atlas) early in the fifteenth century, when the Merinid empire was already near disintegration. Like all previous invaders they preached the doctrine of a pure Islamism to the polytheistic and indifferent Berbers, and found a ready hearing because they denounced the evils of a divided empire, and also because the whole of Morocco was in revolt against the Christian colonies of Spain and Portugal, which had encircled the coast from Ceuta to Agadir with a chain of fortified counting-houses. To bouter dehors the money-making unbeliever was an object that found adherents from the Rif to the Sahara, and the Saadian cherifs soon rallied a mighty following to their standard. Islam, though it never really gave a creed to the Berbers, supplied them with a war-cry as potent to-day as when it first rang across Barbary.

The history of the Saadians is a foreshortened record of that of all their predecessors. They overthrew the artistic and luxurious Merinids, and in their turn became artistic and luxurious. Their greatest Sultan, Abou-el-Abbas, surnamed "The Golden," after defeating the Merinids and putting an end to Christian rule in Morocco by the crushing victory of El-Ksar (1578), bethought him in his turn of enriching himself and beautifying his capital, and with this object in view turned his attention to the black kingdoms of the south.

Senegal and the Soudan, which had been Mohammedan since the eleventh century, had attained in the sixteenth century a high degree of commercial wealth and artistic civilization. The Sultanate of Timbuctoo seems in reality to have been a thriving empire, and if Timbuctoo was not the Claude-like vision of Carthaginian palaces which it became in the tales of imaginative travellers, it apparently had something of the magnificence of Fez and Marrakech.

The Saadian army, after a march of four and a half months across the Sahara, conquered the whole black south. Senegal, the Soudan and Bornou submitted to Abou-el-Abbas, the Sultan of Timbuctoo was dethroned, and the celebrated negro jurist Ahmed-Baba was brought a prisoner to Marrakech, where his chief sorrow appears to have been for the loss of his library of 1,600 volumes—though he declared that, of all the numerous members of his family, it was he who possessed the smallest number of books.

Besides this learned bibliophile, the Sultan Abou-el-Abbas brought back with him an immense booty, principally of ingots of gold, from which he took his surname of "The Golden"; and as the result of the expedition Marrakech was embellished with mosques and palaces for which the Sultan brought marble from Carrara, paying for it with loaves of sugar from the sugar-cane that the Saadians grew in the Souss.

In spite of these brilliant beginnings the rule of the dynasty was short and without subsequent interest. Based on a fanatical antagonism against the foreigner, and fed by the ever-wakeful hatred of the Moors for their Spanish conquerors, it raised ever higher the Chinese walls of exclusiveness which the more enlightened Almohads and Merinids had sought to overthrow. Henceforward less and less daylight and fresh air were to penetrate into the souks of Morocco.

The day after our unsuccessful attempt to see the tombs of these ephemeral rulers we received another message, naming an hour for our visit; and this time the Pasha's representative was waiting in the archway. We followed his lead, under the openly mistrustful glances of the Arabs who hung about the square, and after picking our way through a twisting land between walls, we came out into a filthy nettle-grown space against the ramparts. At intervals of about thirty feet splendid square towers rose from the walls, and facing one of them lay a group of crumbling buildings masked behind other ruins.

We were led first into a narrow mosque or praying-chapel, like those of the Medersas, with a coffered cedar ceiling resting on four marble columns, and traceried walls of unusually beautiful design. From this chapel we passed into the hall of the tombs, a cube about forty feet square. Fourteen columns of colored marble sustain a domed ceiling of gilded cedar, with an exterior deambulatory under a tunnel-vaulting also roofed with cedar. The walls are, as usual, of chiselled stucco, above revetements of ceramic mosaic, and between the columns lie the white marble cenotaphs of the Saadian Sultans, covered with Arabic inscriptions in the most delicate low-relief. Beyond this central mausoleum, and balancing the praying-chapel, lies another long narrow chamber, gold-ceilinged also, and containing a few tombs.

It is difficult, in describing the architecture of Morocco, to avoid producing an impression of monotony. The ground-plan of mosques and Medersas is always practically the same, and the same elements, few in number and endlessly repeated, make up the materials and the form of the ornament. The effect upon the eye is not monotonous, for a patient art has infinitely varied the combinations of pattern and the juxtapositions of color; while the depth of undercutting of the stucco, and the treatment of the bronze doors and of the carved cedar corbels, necessarily varies with the periods which produced them.

But in the Saadian mausoleum a new element has been introduced which makes this little monument a thing apart. The marble columns supporting the roof appear to be unique in Moroccan architecture, and they lend themselves to a new roof-plan which relates the building rather to the tradition of Venice or Byzantine by way of Kairouan and Cordova.

The late date of the monument precludes any idea of a direct artistic tradition. The most probable explanation seems to be that the architect of the mausoleum was familiar with European Renaissance architecture, and saw the beauty to be derived from using precious marbles not merely as ornament, but in the Roman and Italian way, as a structural element. Panels and fountain-basins are ornament, and ornament changes nothing essential in architecture; but when, for instance, heavy square piers are replaced by detached columns, a new style results.

It is not only the novelty of its plan that makes the Saadian mausoleum singular among Moroccan monuments. The details of its ornament are of the most intricate refinement: it seems as though the last graces of the expiring Merinid art had been gathered up into this rare blossom. And the slant of sunlight on lustrous columns, the depths of fretted gold, the dusky ivory of the walls and the pure white of the cenotaphs, so classic in spareness of ornament and simplicity of design—this subtle harmony of form and color gives to the dim rich chapel an air of dream-like unreality.

And how can it seem other than a dream? Who can have conceived, in the heart of a savage Saharan camp, the serenity and balance of this hidden place? And how came such fragile loveliness to survive, preserving, behind a screen of tumbling walls, of nettles and offal and dead beasts, every curve of its traceries and every cell of its honeycombing?

Such questions inevitably bring one back to the central riddle of the mysterious North African civilization: the perpetual flux and the immovable stability, the barbarous customs and sensuous refinements, the absence of artistic originality and the gift for regrouping borrowed motives, the patient and exquisite workmanship and the immediate neglect and degradation of the thing once made.

Revering the dead and camping on their graves, elaborating exquisite monuments only to abandon and defile them, venerating scholarship and wisdom and living in ignorance and grossness, these gifted races, perpetually struggling to reach some higher level of culture from which they have always been swept down by a fresh wave of barbarism, are still only a people in the making.

It may be that the political stability which France is helping them to acquire will at last give their higher qualities time for fruition; and when one looks at the mausoleum of Marrakech and the Medersas of Fez one feels that, were the experiment made on artistic grounds alone, it would yet be well worth making.

V - HAREMS AND CEREMONIES

I

THE CROWD IN THE STREET

To occidental travellers the most vivid impression produced by a first contact with the Near East is the surprise of being in a country where the human element increases instead of diminishing the delight of the eye.

After all, then, the intimate harmony between nature and architecture and the human body that is revealed in Greek art was not an artist's counsel of perfection but an honest rendering of reality: there were, there still are, privileged scenes where the fall of a green-grocer's draperies or a milkman's cloak or a beggar's rags are part of the composition, distinctly related to it in line and colour, and where the natural unstudied attitudes of the human body are correspondingly harmonious, however humdrum the acts it is engaged in. The discovery, to the traveller returning from the East, robs the most romantic scenes of western Europe of half their charm: in the Piazza of San Marco, in the market-place of Siena, where at least the robes of the Procurators or the gay tights of Pinturicchio's striplings once justified man's presence among his works, one can see, at first, only the outrage inflicted on beauty by the "plentiful strutting manikins" of the modern world.

Moroccan crowds are always a feast to the eye. The instinct of skilful drapery, the sense of colour (subdued by custom, but breaking out in subtle glimpses under the universal ashy tints) make the humblest assemblage of donkey-men and water-carriers an ever-renewed delight. But it is only on rare occasions, and in the court ceremonies to which so few foreigners have had access, that the hidden sumptuousness of the native life is revealed. Even then, the term sumptuousness may seem ill-chosen, since the nomadic nature of African life persists in spite of palaces and chamberlains and all the elaborate ritual of the Makhzen, and the most pompous rites are likely to end in a dusty gallop of wild tribesmen, and the most princely processions to tail off in a string of half-naked urchins riding bareback on donkeys.

As in all Oriental countries, the contact between prince and beggar, vizier and serf is disconcertingly free and familiar, and one must see the highest court officials kissing the hem of the Sultan's robe, and hear authentic tales of slaves given by one merchant to another at the end of a convivial evening, to be reminded that nothing is as democratic in appearance as a society of which the whole structure hangs on the whim of one man.

AID-EL-KEBIR

In the verandah of the Residence of Rabat I stood looking out between posts festooned with gentian-blue ipomeas at the first shimmer of light on black cypresses and white tobacco-flowers, on the scattered roofs of the new town, and the plain stretching away to the Sultan's palace above the sea.

We had been told, late the night before, that the Sultan would allow Madame Lyautey, with the three ladies of her party, to be present at the great religious rite of the Aid-el-Kebir (the Sacrifice of the Sheep). The honour was an unprecedented one, a favour probably conceded only at the last moment: for as a rule no women are admitted to these ceremonies. It was an opportunity not to be missed, and all through the short stifling night I had lain awake wondering if I should be ready early enough. Presently the motors assembled, and we set out with the French officers in attendance on the Governor's wife.

The Sultan's palace, a large modern building on the familiar Arab lines, lies in a treeless and gardenless waste enclosed by high walls and close above the blue Atlantic. We motored past the gates, where the Sultan's Black Guard was drawn up, and out to the msalla,[A] a sort of common adjacent to all the Sultan's residences where public ceremonies are usually performed. The sun was already beating down on the great plain thronged with horsemen and with the native population of Rabat on mule-back and foot. Within an open space in the centre of the crowd a canvas palissade dyed with a bold black pattern surrounded the Sultan's tents. The Black Guard, in scarlet tunics and white and green turbans, were drawn up on the edge of the open space, keeping the spectators at a distance; but under the guidance of our companions we penetrated to the edge of the crowd.

[Footnote A: The msalla is used for the performance of religious ceremonies when the crowd is too great to be contained in the court of the mosque.]

The palissade was open on one side, and within it we could see moving about among the snowy-robed officials a group of men in straight narrow gowns of almond-green, peach-blossom, lilac and pink; they were the Sultan's musicians, whose coloured dresses always flower out conspicuously among the white draperies of all the other court attendants.

In the tent nearest the opening, against a background of embroidered hangings, a circle of majestic turbaned old men squatted placidly on Rabat rugs. Presently the circle broke up, there was an agitated coming and going, and someone said: "The Sultan has gone to the tent at the back of the enclosure to kill the sheep."

A sense of the impending solemnity ran through the crowd. The mysterious rumour which is the Voice of the Bazaar rose about us like the wind in a palm-oasis; the Black Guard fired a salute from an adjoining hillock; the clouds of red dust flung up by wheeling horsemen thickened and then parted, and a white-robed rider sprang out from the tent of the Sacrifice with something red and dripping across his saddle-bow, and galloped away toward Rabat through the shouting. A little shiver ran over the group of occidental spectators, who knew that the dripping red thing was a sheep with its throat so skilfully slit that, if the omen were favourable, it would live on through the long race to Rabat and gasp out its agonized life on the tiles of the Mosque.

The Sacrifice of the Sheep, one of the four great Moslem rites, is simply the annual propitiatory offering made by every Mahometan head of a family, and by the Sultan as such. It is based not on a Koranic injunction, but on the "Souna" or record of the Prophet's "custom" or usages, which forms an authoritative precedent in Moslem ritual. So far goes the Moslem exegesis. In reality, of course, the Moslem blood-sacrifice comes, by way of the Semitic ritual, from far beyond and behind it, and the belief that the Sultan's prosperity for the coming year depends on the animal's protracted agony seems to relate the ceremony to the dark magic so deeply rooted in the mysterious tribes peopling North Africa long ages before the first Phoenician prows had rounded its coast.

Between the Black Guard and the tents, five or six horses were being led up and down by muscular grooms in snowy tunics. They were handsome animals, as Moroccan horses go, and each of a different colour, and on the bay horse was a red saddle embroidered in gold, on the piebald a saddle of peach-colour and silver, on the chestnut, grass-green encrusted with seed-pearls, on the white mare purple housings, and orange velvet on the grey. The Sultan's band had struck up a shrill hammering and twanging, the salute of the Black Guard continued at intervals, and the caparisoned steeds began to rear and snort and drag back from the cruel Arab bits with their exquisite niello incrustations. Someone whispered that these were His Majesty's horses—and that it was never known till he appeared which one he would mount.

Presently the crowd about the tents thickened, and when it divided again there emerged from it a grey horse bearing a motionless figure swathed in blinding white. Marching at the horse's bridle, lean brown grooms in white tunics rhythmically waved long strips of white linen to keep off the flies from the Imperial Presence, and beside the motionless rider, in a line with his horse's flank, rode the Imperial Parasol-bearer, who held above the sovereign's head a great sunshade of bright green velvet. Slowly the grey horse advanced a few yards before the tent; behind rode the court dignitaries, followed by the musicians, who looked, in their bright scant caftans, like the slender music-making angels of a Florentine fresco.

The Sultan, pausing beneath his velvet dome, waited to receive the homage of the assembled tribes. An official, riding forward, drew bridle and called out a name. Instantly there came storming across the plain a wild cavalcade of tribesmen, with rifles slung across their shoulders, pistols and cutlasses in their belts, and twists of camel's-hair bound about their turbans. Within a few feet of the Sultan they drew in, their leader uttered a cry and sprang forward, bending to the saddle-bow, and with a great shout the tribe galloped by, each man bowed over his horse's neck as he flew past the hieratic figure on the grey horse.

Again and again this ceremony was repeated, the Sultan advancing a few feet as each new group thundered toward him. There were more than ten thousand horsemen and chieftains from the Atlas and the wilderness, and as the ceremony continued the dust-clouds grew denser and more fiery-golden, till at last the forward-surging lines showed through them like blurred images in a tarnished mirror.

As the Sultan advanced we followed, abreast of him and facing the oncoming squadrons. The contrast between his motionless figure and the wild waves of cavalry beating against it typified the strange soul of Islam, with its impetuosity forever culminating in impassiveness. The sun hung high, a brazen ball in a white sky, darting down metallic shafts on the dust-enveloped plain and the serene white figure under its umbrella. The fat man with a soft round beard-fringed face, wrapped in spirals of pure white, one plump hand on his embroidered bridle, his yellow-slippered feet thrust heel-down in big velvet-lined stirrups, became, through sheer immobility, a symbol, a mystery, a God. The human flux beat against him, dissolved, ebbed away, another spear-crested wave swept up behind it and dissolved in turn; and he sat on, hour after hour, under the white-hot sky, unconscious of the heat, the dust, the tumult, embodying to the wild factious precipitate hordes a long tradition of serene aloofness.

III

THE IMPERIAL MIRADOR

As the last riders galloped up to do homage we were summoned to our motors and driven rapidly to the palace. The Sultan had sent word to Mme. Lyautey that the ladies of the Imperial harem would entertain her and her guests while his Majesty received the Resident General, and we had to hasten back in order not to miss the next act of the spectacle.

We walked across a long court lined with the Black Guard, passed under a gateway, and were met by a shabbily dressed negress. Traversing a hot dazzle of polychrome tiles we reached another archway guarded by the chief eunuch, a towering black with the enamelled eyes of a basalt bust. The eunuch delivered us to other negresses, and we entered a labyrinth of inner passages and patios, all murmuring and dripping with water. Passing down long corridors where slaves in dim greyish garments flattened themselves against the walls, we caught glimpses of great dark rooms, laundries, pantries, bakeries, kitchens, where savoury things were brewing and stewing, and where more negresses, abandoning their pots and pans, came to peep at us from the threshold. In one corner, on a bench against a wall hung with matting, grey parrots in tall cages were being fed by a slave.

A narrow staircase mounted to a landing where a princess out of an Arab fairy-tale awaited us. Stepping softly on her embroidered slippers she led us to the next landing, where another golden-slippered being smiled out on us, a little girl this one, blushing and dimpling under a jewelled diadem and pearl-woven braids. On a third landing a third damsel appeared, and encircled by the three graces we mounted to the tall mirador in the central tower from which we were to look down at the coming ceremony. One by one, our little guides, kicking off their golden shoes, which a slave laid neatly outside the door, led us on soft bare feet into the upper chamber of the harem.

It was a large room, enclosed on all sides by a balcony glazed with panes of brightly-coloured glass. On a gaudy modern Rabat carpet stood gilt armchairs of florid design and a table bearing a commercial bronze of the "art goods" variety. Divans with muslin-covered cushions were ranged against the walls and down an adjoining gallery-like apartment which was otherwise furnished only with clocks. The passion for clocks and other mechanical contrivances is common to all unmechanical races, and every chief's palace in North Africa contains a collection of time-pieces which might be called striking if so many had not ceased to go. But those in the Sultan's harem of Rabat are remarkable for the fact that, while designed on current European models, they are proportioned in size to the Imperial dignity, so that a Dutch "grandfather" becomes a wardrobe, and the box-clock of the European mantelpiece a cupboard that has to be set on the floor. At the end of this avenue of time-pieces a European double-bed with a bright silk quilt covered with Nottingham lace stood majestically on a carpeted platform.

But for the enchanting glimpses of sea and plain through the lattices of the gallery, the apartment of the Sultan's ladies falls far short of occidental ideas of elegance. But there was hardly time to think of this, for the door of the mirador was always opening to let in another fairy-tale figure, till at last we were surrounded by a dozen houris, laughing, babbling, taking us by the hand, and putting shy questions while they looked at us with caressing eyes. They were all (our interpretess whispered) the Sultan's "favourites," round-faced apricot-tinted girls in their teens, with high cheek-bones, full red lips, surprised brown eyes between curved-up Asiatic lids, and little brown hands fluttering out like birds from their brocaded sleeves.

In honour of the ceremony, and of Mme. Lyautey's visit, they had put on their finest clothes, and their freedom of movement was somewhat hampered by their narrow sumptuous gowns, with over-draperies of gold and silver brocade and pale rosy gauze held in by corset-like sashes of gold tissue of Fez, and the heavy silken cords that looped their voluminous sleeves. Above their foreheads the hair was shaven like that of an Italian fourteenth-century beauty, and only a black line as narrow as a pencilled eyebrow showed through the twist of gauze fastened by a jewelled clasp above the real eye-brows. Over the forehead-jewel rose the complicated structure of the headdress. Ropes of black wool were plaited through the hair, forming, at the back, a double loop that stood out above the nape like the twin handles of a vase, the upper veiled in airy shot gauzes and fastened with jewelled bands and ornaments. On each side of the red cheeks other braids were looped over the ears hung with broad earrings of filigree set with rough pearls and emeralds, or gold loops and pendants of coral, and an unexpected tulle ruff, like that of a Watteau shepherdess, framed the round chin above a torrent of necklaces, necklaces of amber, coral, baroque pearls, hung with mysterious barbaric amulets and fetiches. As the young things moved about us on soft hennaed feet the light played on shifting gleams of gold and silver, blue and violet and apple-green, all harmonized and bemisted by clouds of pink and sky-blue, and through the changing group capered a little black picaninny in a caftan of silver-shot purple with a sash of raspberry red.

But presently there was a flutter in the aviary. A fresh pair of babouches clicked on the landing, and a young girl, less brilliantly dressed and less brilliant of face than the others, came in on bare painted feet. Her movements were shy and hesitating, her large lips pale, her eye-brows less vividly dark, her head less jewelled. But all the little humming-birds gathered about her with respectful rustlings as she advanced toward us leaning on one of the young girls, and holding out her ringed hand to Mme. Lyautey's curtsey. It was the young Princess, the Sultan's legitimate daughter. She examined us with sad eyes, spoke a few compliments through the interpretess, and seated herself in silence, letting the others sparkle and chatter.

Conversation with the shy Princess was flagging when one of the favourites beckoned us to the balcony. We were told we might push open the painted panes a few inches, but as we did so the butterfly group drew back lest they should be seen looking out on the forbidden world.

Salutes were crashing out again from the direction of the msalla: puffs of smoke floated over the slopes like thistle-down. Farther off, a pall of red vapour veiled the gallop of the last horsemen wheeling away toward Rabat. The vapour subsided, and moving out of it we discerned a slow procession. First rode a detachment of the Black Guard, mounted on black horses, and, comically fierce in their British scarlet and Meccan green, a uniform invented at the beginning of the nineteenth century by a retired English army officer. After the Guard came the standard-bearers and the great dignitaries, then the Sultan, still aloof, immovable, as if rapt in the contemplation of his mystic office. More court officials followed, then the bright-gowned musicians on foot, then a confused irrepressible crowd of pilgrims, beggars, saints, mountebanks, and the other small folk of the Bazaar, ending in a line of boys jamming their naked heels into the ribs of world-weary donkeys.

The Sultan rode into the court below us, and Vizier and chamberlains, snowy-white against the scarlet line of the Guards, hurried forward to kiss his draperies, his shoes, his stirrup. Descending from his velvet saddle, still entranced, he paced across the tiles between a double line of white servitors bowing to the ground. White pigeons circled over him like petals loosed from a great orchard, and he disappeared with his retinue under the shadowy arcade of the audience chamber at the back of the court.

At this point one of the favourites called us in from the mirador. The door had just opened to admit an elderly woman preceded by a respectful group of girls. From the newcomer's round ruddy face, her short round body, the round hands emerging from her round wrists, an inexplicable majesty emanated; and though she too was less richly arrayed than the favourites she carried her headdress of striped gauze like a crown.

This impressive old lady was the Sultan's mother. As she held out her plump wrinkled hand to Mme. Lyautey and spoke a few words through the interpretess one felt that at last a painted window of the mirador had been broken, and a thought let into the vacuum of the harem. What thought, it would have taken deep insight into the processes of the Arab mind to discover; but its honesty was manifest in the old Empress's voice and smile. Here at last was a woman beyond the trivial dissimulations, the childish cunning, the idle cruelties of the harem. It was not a surprise to be told that she was her son's most trusted adviser, and the chief authority in the palace. If such a woman deceived and intrigued it would be for great purposes and for ends she believed in; the depth of her soul had air and daylight in it, and she would never willingly shut them out.

The Empress Mother chatted for a while with Mme. Lyautey, asking about the Resident General's health, enquiring for news of the war, and saying, with an emotion perceptible even through the unintelligible words: "All is well with Morocco as long as all is well with France." Then she withdrew, and we were summoned again to the mirador.

This time it was to see a company of officers in brilliant uniforms advancing at a trot across the plain from Rabat. At sight of the figure that headed them, so slim, erect and young on his splendid chestnut, with a pale blue tunic barred by the wide orange ribbon of the Cherifian Order, salutes pealed forth again from the slope above the palace and the Black Guard presented arms. A moment later General Lyautey and his staff were riding in at the gates below us. On the threshold of the inner court they dismounted, and moving to the other side of our balcony we followed the next stage of the ceremony. The Sultan was still seated in the audience chamber. The court officials still stood drawn up in a snow-white line against the snow-white walls. The great dignitaries advanced across the tiles to greet the General, then they fell aside, and he went forward alone, followed at a little distance by his staff. A third of the way across the court he paused, in accordance with the Moroccan court ceremonial, and bowed in the direction of the arcaded room; a few steps farther he bowed again, and a third time on the threshold of the room. Then French uniforms and Moroccan draperies closed in about him, and all vanished into the shadows of the audience hall.

Our audience too seemed to be over. We had exhausted the limited small talk of the harem, had learned from the young beauties that, though they were forbidden to look on at the ceremony, the dancers and singers would come to entertain them presently, and had begun to take leave when a negress hurried in to say that his Majesty begged Mme. Lyautey and her friends to await his arrival. This was the crowning incident of our visit, and I wondered with what Byzantine ritual the Anointed One fresh from the exercise of his priestly functions would be received among his women.

The door opened, and without any announcement or other preliminary flourish a fat man with a pleasant face, his djellabah stretched over a portly front, walked in holding a little boy by the hand. Such was his Majesty the Sultan Moulay Youssef, despoiled of sacramental burnouses and turban, and shuffling along on bare yellow-slippered feet with the gait of a stout elderly gentleman who has taken off his boots in the passage preparatory to a domestic evening.

The little Prince, one of his two legitimate sons, was dressed with equal simplicity, for silken garments are worn in Morocco only by musicians, boy-dancers and other hermaphrodite fry. With his ceremonial raiment the Sultan had put off his air of superhuman majesty, and the expression of his round pale face corresponded with the plainness of his dress. The favourites fluttered about him, respectful but by no means awestruck, and the youngest began to play with the little Prince. We could well believe the report that his was the happiest harem in Morocco, as well as the only one into which a breath of the outer world ever came.

Moulay Youssef greeted Mme. Lyautey with friendly simplicity, made the proper speeches to her companions, and then, with the air of the business-man who has forgotten to give an order before leaving his office, he walked up to a corner of the room, and while the flower-maidens ruffled about him, and through the windows we saw the last participants in the mystic rites galloping away toward the crenellated walls of Rabat, his Majesty the Priest and Emperor of the Faithful unhooked a small instrument from the wall and applied his sacred lips to the telephone.

IV

IN OLD RABAT

Before General Lyautey came to Morocco Rabat had been subjected to the indignity of European "improvements," and one must traverse boulevards scored with tram-lines, and pass between hotel-terraces and cafes and cinema-palaces, to reach the surviving nucleus of the once beautiful native town. Then, at the turn of a commonplace street, one comes upon it suddenly. The shops and cafes cease, the jingle of trams and the trumpeting of motor-horns die out, and here, all at once, are silence and solitude, and the dignified reticence of the windowless Arab house-fronts.

We were bound for the house of a high government official, a Moroccan dignitary of the old school, who had invited us to tea, and added a message to the effect that the ladies of his household would be happy to receive me.

The house we sought was some distance down the quietest of white-walled streets. Our companion knocked at a low green door, and we were admitted to a passage into which a wooden stairway descended. A brother-in-law of our host was waiting for us; in his wake we mounted the ladder-like stairs and entered a long room with a florid French carpet and a set of gilt furniture to match. There were no fretted walls, no painted cedar doors, no fountains rustling in unseen courts: the house was squeezed in between others, and such traces of old ornament as it may have possessed had vanished.

But presently we saw why its inhabitants were indifferent to such details. Our host, a handsome white-bearded old man, welcomed us in the doorway, then he led us to a raised oriel window at one end of the room, and seated us in the gilt armchairs face to face with one of the most beautiful views in Morocco.

Below us lay the white and blue terrace-roofs of the native town, with palms and minarets shooting up between them, or the shadows of a vine-trellis patterning a quiet lane. Beyond, the Atlantic sparkled, breaking into foam at the mouth of the Bou-Regreg and under the towering ramparts of the Kasbah of the Oudayas. To the right, the ruins of the great Mosque rose from their plateau over the river; and, on the farther side of the troubled flood, old Salé, white and wicked, lay like a jewel in its gardens. With such a scene beneath their eyes, the inhabitants of the house could hardly feel its lack of architectural interest.

After exchanging the usual compliments, and giving us time to enjoy the view, our host withdrew, taking with him the men of our party. A moment later he reappeared with a rosy fair-haired girl, dressed in Arab costume, but evidently of European birth. The brother-in-law explained that this young woman, who had "studied in Algeria," and whose mother was French, was the intimate friend of the ladies of the household, and would act as interpreter. Our host then again left us, joining the men visitors in another room, and the door opened to admit his wife and daughters-in-law.

The mistress of the house was a handsome Algerian with sad expressive eyes, the younger women were pale, fat and amiable. They all wore sober dresses, in keeping with the simplicity of the house, and but for the vacuity of their faces the group might have been that of a Professor's family in an English or American University town, decently costumed for an Arabian Nights' pageant in the college grounds. I was never more vividly reminded of the fact that human nature, from one pole to the other, falls naturally into certain categories, and that Respectability wears the same face in an Oriental harem as in England or America.

My hostesses received me with the utmost amiability, we seated ourselves in the oriel facing the view, and the interchange of questions and compliments began.

Had I any children? (They asked it all at once.)

Alas, no.

"In Islam" (one of the ladies ventured) "a woman without children is considered the most unhappy being in the world."

I replied that in the western world also childless women were pitied. (The brother-in-law smiled incredulously.)

Knowing that European fashions are of absorbing interest to the harem I next enquired: "What do these ladies think of our stiff tailor-dresses? Don't they find them excessively ugly?"

"Yes, they do;" (it was again the brother-in-law who replied.) "But they suppose that in your own homes you dress less badly."

"And have they never any desire to travel, or to visit the Bazaars, as the Turkish ladies do?"

"No, indeed. They are too busy to give such matters a thought. In our country women of the highest class occupy themselves with their household and their children, and the rest of their time is devoted to needlework." (At this statement I gave the brother-in-law a smile as incredulous as his own.)

All this time the fair-haired interpretess had not been allowed by the vigilant guardian of the harem to utter a word.

I turned to her with a question.

"So your mother is French, Mademoiselle?"

"Oui, Madame."

"From what part of France did she come?"

A bewildered pause. Finally, "I don't know . . . from Switzerland, I think," brought out this shining example of the Higher Education. In spite of Algerian "advantages" the poor girl could speak only a few words of her mother's tongue. She had kept the European features and complexion, but her soul was the soul of Islam. The harem had placed its powerful imprint upon her, and she looked at me with the same remote and passive eyes as the daughters of the house.

After struggling for a while longer with a conversation which the watchful brother-in-law continued to direct as he pleased, I felt my own lips stiffening into the resigned smile of the harem, and it was a relief when at last their guardian drove the pale flock away, and the handsome old gentleman who owned them reappeared on the scene, bringing back my friends, and followed by slaves and tea.

V

IN FEZ

What thoughts, what speculations, one wonders, go on under the narrow veiled brows of the little creatures destined to the high honour of marriage or concubinage in Moroccan palaces?

Some are brought down from mountains and cedar forests, from the free life of the tents where the nomad women go unveiled. Others come from harems in the turreted cities beyond the Atlas, where blue palm-groves beat all night against the stars and date-caravans journey across the desert from Timbuctoo. Some, born and bred in an airy palace among pomegranate gardens and white terraces, pass thence to one of the feudal fortresses near the snows, where for half the year the great chiefs of the south live in their clan, among fighting men and falconers and packs of sloughis. And still others grow up in a stifling Mellah, trip unveiled on its blue terraces overlooking the gardens of the great, and, seen one day at sunset by a fat vizier or his pale young master, are acquired for a handsome sum and transferred to the painted sepulchre of the harem.

Worst of all must be the fate of those who go from tents and cedar forests, or from some sea-blown garden above Rabat, into one of the houses of Old Fez. They are well-nigh impenetrable, these palaces of Elbali; the Fazi dignitaries do not welcome the visits of strange women. On the rare occasions when they are received, a member of the family (one of the sons, or a brother-in-law who has "studied in Algeria") usually acts as interpreter; and perhaps it is as well that no one from the outer world should come to remind these listless creatures that somewhere the gulls dance on the Atlantic and the wind murmurs through olive-yards and clatters the metallic fronds of palm-groves.

We had been invited, one day, to visit the harem of one of the chief dignitaries of the Makhzen at Fez, and these thoughts came to me as I sat among the pale women in their mouldering prison. The descent through the steep tunnelled streets gave one the sense of being lowered into the shaft of a mine. At each step the strip of sky grew narrower, and was more often obscured by the low vaulted passages into which we plunged. The noises of the Bazaar had died out, and only the sound of fountains behind garden walls and the clatter of our mules' hoofs on the stones went with us. Then fountains and gardens ceased also, the towering masonry closed in, and we entered an almost subterranean labyrinth which sun and air never reach. At length our mules turned into a cul-de-sac blocked by a high building. On the right was another building, one of those blind mysterious house-fronts of Fez that seem like a fragment of its ancient fortifications. Clients and servants lounged on the stone benches built into the wall; it was evidently the house of an important person. A charming youth with intelligent eyes waited on the threshold to receive us; he was one of the sons of the house, the one who had "studied in Algeria" and knew how to talk to visitors. We followed him into a small arcaded patio hemmed in by the high walls of the house. On the right was the usual long room with archways giving on the court. Our host, a patriarchal personage, draped in fat as in a toga, came toward us, a mountain of majestic muslins, his eyes sparkling in a swarthy silver-bearded face. He seated us on divans and lowered his voluminous person to a heap of cushions on the step leading into the court, and the son who had studied in Algeria instructed a negress to prepare the tea.

Across the patio was another arcade closely hung with unbleached cotton. From behind it came the sound of chatter, and now and then a bare brown child in a scant shirt would escape, and be hurriedly pulled back with soft explosions of laughter, while a black woman came out to readjust the curtains.

There were three of these negresses, splendid bronze creatures, wearing white djellabahs over bright-coloured caftans, striped scarves knotted about their large hips, and gauze turbans on their crinkled hair. Their wrists clinked with heavy silver bracelets, and big circular earrings danced in their purple ear-lobes. A languor lay on all the other inmates of the household, on the servants and hangers-on squatting in the shade under the arcade, on our monumental host and his smiling son; but the three negresses, vibrating with activity, rushed continually from the curtained chamber to the kitchen, and from the kitchen to the master's reception-room, bearing on their pinky-blue palms trays of Britannia metal with tall glasses and fresh bunches of mint, shouting orders to dozing menials, and calling to each other from opposite ends of the court; and finally the stoutest of the three, disappearing from view, reappeared suddenly on a pale green balcony overhead, where, profiled against a square of blue sky, she leaned over in a Veronese attitude and screamed down to the others like an excited parrot.

In spite of their febrile activity and tropical bird-shrieks, we waited in vain for tea; and after a while our host suggested to his son that I might like to visit the ladies of the household. As I had expected, the young man led me across the patio, lifted the cotton hanging and introduced me into an apartment exactly like the one we had just left. Divans covered with striped mattress-ticking stood against the white walls, and on them sat seven or eight passive-looking women over whom a number of pale children scrambled.

The eldest of the group, and evidently the mistress of the house, was an Algerian lady, probably of about fifty, with a sad and delicately-modelled face; the others were daughters, daughters-in-law and concubines. The latter word evokes to occidental ears images of sensual seduction which the Moroccan harem seldom realizes. All the ladies of this dignified official household wore the same look of somewhat melancholy respectability. In their stuffy curtained apartment they were like cellar-grown flowers, pale, heavy, fuller but frailer than the garden sort. Their dresses, rich but sober, the veils and diadems put on in honour of my visit, had a dignified dowdiness in odd contrast to the frivolity of the Imperial harem. But what chiefly struck me was the apathy of the younger women. I asked them if they had a garden, and they shook their heads wistfully, saying that there were no gardens in Old Fez. The roof was therefore their only escape: a roof overlooking acres and acres of other roofs, and closed in by the naked fortified mountains which stand about Fez like prison-walls.

After a brief exchange of compliments silence fell. Conversing through interpreters is a benumbing process, and there are few points of contact between the open-air occidental mind and beings imprisoned in a conception of sexual and domestic life based on slave-service and incessant espionage. These languid women on their muslin cushions toil not, neither do they spin. The Moroccan lady knows little of cooking, needlework or any household arts. When her child is ill she can only hang it with amulets and wail over it, the great lady of the Fazi palace is as ignorant of hygiene as the peasant-woman of the bled. And all these colourless eventless lives depend on the favour of one fat tyrannical man, bloated with good living and authority, himself almost as inert and sedentary as his women, and accustomed to impose his whims on them ever since he ran about the same patio as a little short-smocked boy.

The redeeming point in this stagnant domesticity is the tenderness of the parents for their children, and western writers have laid so much stress on this that one would suppose children could be loved only by inert and ignorant parents. It is in fact charming to see the heavy eyes of the Moroccan father light up when a brown grass-hopper baby jumps on his knee, and the unfeigned tenderness with which the childless women of the harem caress the babies of their happier rivals. But the sentimentalist moved by this display of family feeling would do well to consider the lives of these much-petted children. Ignorance, unhealthiness and a precocious sexual initiation prevail in all classes. Education consists in learning by heart endless passages of the Koran, and amusement in assisting at spectacles that would be unintelligible to western children, but that the pleasantries of the harem make perfectly comprehensible to Moroccan infancy. At eight or nine the little girls are married, at twelve the son of the house is "given his first negress"; and thereafter, in the rich and leisured class, both sexes live till old age in an atmosphere of sensuality without seduction.

The young son of the house led me back across the court, where the negresses were still shrieking and scurrying, and passing to and fro like a stage-procession with the vain paraphernalia of a tea that never came. Our host still smiled from his cushions, resigned to Oriental delays. To distract the impatient westerners, a servant unhooked from the wall the cage of a gently-cooing dove. It was brought to us, still cooing, and looked at me with the same resigned and vacant eyes as the ladies I had just left. As it was being restored to its hook the slaves lolling about the entrance scattered respectfully at the approach of a handsome man of about thirty, with delicate features and a black beard. Crossing the court, he stooped to kiss the shoulder of our host, who introduced him as his eldest son, the husband of one or two of the little pale wives with whom I had been exchanging platitudes.

From the increasing agitation of the negresses it became evident that the ceremony of tea-making had been postponed till his arrival. A metal tray bearing a Britannia samovar and tea-pot was placed on the tiles of the court, and squatting beside it the newcomer gravely proceeded to infuse the mint. Suddenly the cotton hangings fluttered again, and a tiny child in the scantest of smocks rushed out and scampered across the court. Our venerable host, stretching out rapturous arms, caught the fugitive to his bosom, where the little boy lay like a squirrel, watching us with great sidelong eyes. He was the last-born of the patriarch, and the youngest brother of the majestic bearded gentleman engaged in tea-making. While he was still in his father's arms two more sons appeared: charming almond-eyed schoolboys returning from their Koran-class, escorted by their slaves. All the sons greeted each other affectionately, and caressed with almost feminine tenderness the dancing baby so lately added to their ranks; and finally, to crown this scene of domestic intimacy, the three negresses, their gigantic effort at last accomplished, passed about glasses of steaming mint and trays of gazelles' horns and white sugar-cakes.

VI

The farther one travels from the Mediterranean and Europe the closer the curtains of the women's quarters are drawn. The only harem in which we were allowed an interpreter was that of the Sultan himself, in the private harems of Fez and Rabat a French-speaking relative transmitted (or professed to transmit) our remarks; in Marrakech, the great nobleman and dignitary who kindly invited me to visit his household was deaf to our hint that the presence of a lady from one of the French government schools might facilitate our intercourse.

When we drove up to his palace, one of the stateliest in Marrakech, the street was thronged with clansmen and clients. Dignified merchants in white muslin, whose grooms held white mules saddled with rose-coloured velvet, warriors from the Atlas wearing the corkscrew ringlets which are a sign of military prowess, Jewish traders in black gabardines, leather-gaitered peasant-women with chickens and cheese, and beggars rolling their blind eyes or exposing their fly-plastered sores, were gathered in Oriental promiscuity about the great man's door; while under the archway stood a group of youths and warlike-looking older men who were evidently of his own clan.

The Caid's chamberlain, a middle-aged man of dignified appearance, advanced to meet us between bowing clients and tradesmen. He led us through cool passages lined with the intricate mosaic-work of Fez, past beggars who sat on stone benches whining out their blessings, and pale Fazi craftsmen laying a floor of delicate tiles. The Caid is a lover of old Arab architecture. His splendid house, which is not yet finished, has been planned and decorated on the lines of the old Imperial palaces, and when a few years of sun and rain and Oriental neglect have worked their way on its cedar-wood and gilding and ivory stucco it will have the same faded loveliness as the fairy palaces of Fez.

In a garden where fountains splashed and roses climbed among cypresses, the Caid himself awaited us. This great fighter and loyal friend of France is a magnificent eagle-beaked man, brown, lean and sinewy, with vigilant eyes looking out under his carefully draped muslin turban, and negroid lips half-hidden by a close black beard.

Tea was prepared in the familiar setting; a long arcaded room with painted ceiling and richly stuccoed walls. All around were ranged the usual mattresses covered with striped ticking and piled with muslin cushions. A bedstead of brass, imitating a Louis XVI cane bed, and adorned with brass garlands and bows, throned on the usual platform; and the only other ornaments were a few clocks and bunches of wax flowers under glass. Like all Orientals, this hero of the Atlas, who spends half his life with his fighting clansmen in a mediaeval stronghold among the snows, and the other half rolling in a 60 h.p. motor over smooth French roads, seems unaware of any degrees of beauty or appropriateness in objects of European design, and places against the exquisite mosaics and traceries of his Fazi craftsmen the tawdriest bric-a-brac of the cheap department-store.

While tea was being served I noticed a tiny negress, not more than six or seven years old, who stood motionless in the embrasure of an archway. Like most of the Moroccan slaves, even in the greatest households, she was shabbily, almost raggedly, dressed. A dirty gandourah of striped muslin covered her faded caftan, and a cheap kerchief was wound above her grave and precocious little face. With preternatural vigilance she watched each movement of the Caid, who never spoke to her, looked at her, or made her the slightest perceptible sign, but whose least wish she instantly divined, refilling his tea-cup, passing the plates of sweets, or removing our empty glasses, in obedience to some secret telegraphy on which her whole being hung.

The Caid is a great man. He and his famous elder brother, holding the southern marches of Morocco against alien enemies and internal rebellion, played a preponderant part in the defence of the French colonies in North Africa during the long struggle of the war. Enlightened, cultivated, a friend of the arts, a scholar and diplomatist, he seems, unlike many Orientals, to have selected the best in assimilating European influences. Yet when I looked at the tiny creature watching him with those anxious joyless eyes I felt once more the abyss that slavery and the seraglio put between the most Europeanized Mahometan and the western conception of life. The Caid's little black slaves are well-known in Morocco, and behind the sad child leaning in the archway stood all the shadowy evils of the social system that hangs like a millstone about the neck of Islam.

Presently a handsome tattered negress came across the garden to invite me to the harem. Captain de S. and his wife, who had accompanied me, were old friends of the Chief's, and it was owing to this that the jealously-guarded doors of the women's quarters were opened to Mme. de S. and myself. We followed the negress to a marble-paved court where pigeons fluttered and strutted about the central fountain. From under a trellised arcade hung with linen curtains several ladies came forward. They greeted my companion with exclamations of delight; then they led us into the usual commonplace room with divans and whitewashed walls. Even in the most sumptuous Moroccan palaces little care seems to be expended on the fittings of the women's quarters: unless, indeed, the room in which visitors are received corresponds with a boarding-school "parlour," and the personal touch is reserved for the private apartments.

The ladies who greeted us were more richly dressed than any I had seen except the Sultan's favourites, but their faces were more distinguished, more European in outline, than those of the round-cheeked beauties of Rabat. My companions had told me that the Caid's harem was recruited from Georgia, and that the ladies receiving us had been brought up in the relative freedom of life in Constantinople; and it was easy to read in their wistfully smiling eyes memories of a life unknown to the passive daughters of Morocco.

They appeared to make no secret of their regrets, for presently one of them, with a smile, called my attention to some faded photographs hanging over the divan. They represented groups of plump provincial-looking young women in dowdy European ball-dresses; and it required an effort of the imagination to believe that the lovely creatures in velvet caftans, with delicately tattooed temples under complicated head-dresses, and hennaed feet crossed on muslin cushions, were the same as the beaming frumps in the photographs. But to the sumptuously-clad exiles these faded photographs and ugly dresses represented freedom, happiness, and all they had forfeited when fate (probably in the shape of an opulent Hebrew couple "travelling with their daughters") carried them from the Bosphorus to the Atlas.

As in the other harems I had visited, perfect equality seemed to prevail between the ladies, and while they chatted with Mme. de S. whose few words of Arabic had loosed their tongues, I tried to guess which was the favourite, or at least the first in rank. My choice wavered between the pretty pale creature with a ferronniere across her temples and a tea-rose caftan veiled in blue gauze, and the nut-brown beauty in red velvet hung with pearls whose languid attitudes and long-lidded eyes were so like the Keepsake portraits of Byron's Haidee. Or was it perhaps the third, less pretty but more vivid and animated, who sat behind the tea-tray, and mimicked so expressively a soldier shouldering his rifle, and another falling dead, in her effort to ask us "when the dreadful war would be over"? Perhaps ... unless, indeed, it were the handsome octoroon, slightly older than the others, but even more richly dressed, so free and noble in her movements, and treated by the others with such friendly deference.

I was struck by the fact that among them all there was not a child; it was the first harem without babies that I had seen in that prolific land. Presently one of the ladies asked Mme. de S. about her children, in reply, she enquired for the Caid's little boy, the son of his wife who had died. The ladies' faces lit up wistfully, a slave was given an order, and presently a large-eyed ghost of a child was brought into the room.

Instantly all the bracelet-laden arms were held out to the dead woman's son; and as I watched the weak little body hung with amulets and the heavy head covered with thin curls pressed against a brocaded bosom, I was reminded of one of the coral-hung child-Christs of Crivelli, standing livid and waxen on the knee of a splendidly dressed Madonna.

The poor baby on whom such hopes and ambitions hung stared at us with a solemn unamused gaze. Would all his pretty mothers, his eyes seemed to ask, succeed in bringing him to maturity in spite of the parched summers of the south and the stifling existence of the harem? It was evident that no precaution had been neglected to protect him from maleficent influences and the danger that walks by night, for his frail neck and wrists were hung with innumerable charms: Koranic verses, Soudanese incantations, and images of forgotten idols in amber and coral and horn and ambergris. Perhaps they will ward off the powers of evil, and let him grow up to shoulder the burden of the great Caids of the south.

VI - GENERAL LYAUTEY'S WORK IN MOROCCO

I

It is not too much to say that General Lyautey has twice saved Morocco from destruction: once in 1912, when the inertia and double-dealing of Abd-el-Hafid abandoned the country to the rebellious tribes who had attacked him in Fez, and the second time in August, 1914, when Germany declared war on France.

In 1912, in consequence of the threatening attitude of the dissident tribes and the generally disturbed condition of the country, the Sultan Abd-el-Hafid had asked France to establish a protectorate in Morocco. The agreement entered into, called the "Convention of Fez," stipulated that a French Resident-General should be sent to Morocco with authority to act as the Sultan's sole representative in treating with the other powers. The convention was signed in March, 1912, and a few days afterward an uprising more serious than any that had gone before took place in Fez. This sudden outbreak was due in part to purely local and native difficulties, in part to the intrinsic weakness of the French situation. The French government had imagined that a native army commanded by French officers could be counted on to support the Makhzen and maintain order, but Abd-el-Hafid's growing unpopularity had estranged his own people from him, and the army turned on the government and on the French. On the 17th of April, 1912, the Moroccan soldiers massacred their French officers after inflicting horrible tortures on them, the population of Fez rose against the European civilians, and for a fortnight the Oued Fez ran red with the blood of harmless French colonists. It was then that France appointed General Lyautey Resident-General in Morocco.

When he reached Fez it was besieged by twenty thousand Berbers. Rebel tribes were flocking in to their support, to the cry of the Holy War, and the terrified Sultan, who had already announced his intention of resigning, warned the French troops who were trying to protect him that unless they guaranteed to get him safely to Rabat he would turn his influence against them. Two days afterward the Berbers attacked Fez and broke in at two gates. The French drove them out and forced them back twenty miles. The outskirts of the city were rapidly fortified, and a few weeks later General Gouraud, attacking the rebels in the valley of the Sebou, completely disengaged Fez.

The military danger overcome. General Lyautey began his great task of civilian administration. His aim was to support and strengthen the existing government, to reassure and pacify the distrustful and antagonistic elements, and to assert French authority without irritating or discouraging native ambitions.

Meanwhile a new Mahdi (Ahmed-el-Hiba) had risen in the south. Treacherously supported by Abd-el-Hafid, he was proclaimed Sultan at Tiznit, and acknowledged by the whole of the Souss. In Marrakech, native unrest had caused the Europeans to fly to the coast, and in the north a new group of rebellious tribes menaced Fez.

El-Hiba entered Marrakech in August, 1912, and the French consul and several other French residents were taken prisoner. El-Hiba's forces then advanced to a point half way between Marrakech and Mazagan, where General Mangin, at that time a colonial colonel, met and utterly routed them. The disorder in the south, and the appeals of the native population for protection against the savage depredations of the new Mahdist rebels, made it necessary for the French troops to follow up their success, and in September Marrakech was taken.

Such were the swift and brilliant results of General Lyautey's intervention. The first difficulties had been quickly overcome; others, far more complicated, remained. The military occupation of Morocco had to be followed up by its civil reorganization. By the Franco-German treaty of 1911 Germany had finally agreed to recognize the French protectorate in Morocco; but in spite of an apparently explicit acknowledgment of this right, Germany, as usual, managed to slip into the contract certain ambiguities of form that were likely to lead to future trouble.

To obtain even this incomplete treaty France had had to sacrifice part of her colonies in equatorial Africa; and in addition to the uncertain relation with Germany there remained the dead weight of the Spanish zone and the confused international administration of Tangier. The disastrously misgoverned Spanish zone has always been a centre for German intrigue and native conspiracies, as well as a permanent obstacle to the economic development of Morocco.

Such were the problems that General Lyautey found awaiting him. A long colonial experience, and an unusual combination of military and administrative talents, prepared him for the almost impossible task of dealing with them. Swift and decisive when military action is required, he has above all the long views and endless patience necessary to the successful colonial governor. The policy of France in Morocco had been weak and spasmodic; in his hands it became firm and consecutive. A sympathetic understanding of the native prejudices, and a real affection for the native character, made him try to build up an administration which should be, not an application of French ideas to African conditions, but a development of the best native aspirations. The difficulties were immense. The attempt to govern as far as possible through the Great Chiefs was a wise one, but it was hampered by the fact that these powerful leaders, however loyal to the Protectorate, knew no methods of administration but those based on extortion. It was necessary at once to use them and to educate them; and one of General Lyautey's greatest achievements has been the successful employment of native ability in the government of the country.

The first thing to do was to create a strong frontier against the dissident tribes of the Blad-es-Siba. To do this it was necessary that the French should hold the natural defenses of the country, the foothills of the Little and of the Great Atlas, and the valley of the Moulouya, which forms the corridor between western Algeria and Morocco. This was nearly accomplished in 1914 when war broke out.

At that moment the home government cabled the Resident-General to send all his available troops to France, abandoning the whole of conquered territory except the coast towns. To do so would have been to give France's richest colonies[A] outright to Germany at a moment when what they could supply—meat and wheat—was exactly what the enemy most needed.

[Footnote A: The loss of Morocco would inevitably have been followed by that of the whole of French North Africa.]

General Lyautey took forty-eight hours to consider. He then decided to "empty the egg without breaking the shell", and the reply he sent was that of a great patriot and a great general. In effect he said: "I will give you all the troops you ask, but instead of abandoning the interior of the country I will hold what we have already taken, and fortify and enlarge our boundaries." No other military document has so nearly that ring as Marshal Foch's immortal Marne despatch (written only a few weeks later): "My centre is broken, my right wing is wavering, the situation is favorable and I am about to attack."

General Lyautey had framed his answer in a moment of patriotic exaltation, when the soul of every Frenchman was strung up to a superhuman pitch. But the pledge once made, it had to be carried out, and even those who most applauded his decision wondered how he would meet the almost insuperable difficulties it involved. Morocco, when he was called there, was already honeycombed by German trading interests and secret political intrigue, and the fruit seemed ready to fall when the declaration of war shook the bough. The only way to save the colony for France was to keep its industrial and agricultural life going, and give to the famous "business as usual" a really justifiable application.

General Lyautey completely succeeded, and the first impression of all travellers arriving in Morocco two years later was that of suddenly returning to a world in normal conditions. There was even, so complete was the illusion, a first moment of almost painful surprise on entering an active prosperous community, seemingly absorbed in immediate material interests to the exclusion of all thought of the awful drama that was being played out in the mother country, and it was only on reflection that this absorption in the day's task, and this air of smiling faith in the future, were seen to be Morocco's truest way of serving France.

For not only was France to be supplied with provisions, but the confidence in her ultimate triumph was at all costs to be kept up in the native mind. German influence was as deep-seated as a cancer: to cut it out required the most drastic of operations. And that operation consisted precisely in letting it be seen that France was strong and prosperous enough for her colonies to thrive and expand without fear while she held at bay on her own frontier the most formidable foe the world has ever seen. Such was the "policy of the smile," consistently advocated by General Lyautey from the beginning of the war, and of which he and his household were the first to set the example.

The General had said that he would not "break the egg-shell"; but he knew that this was not enough, and that he must make it appear unbreakable if he were to retain the confidence of the natives.

How this was achieved, with the aid of the few covering troops left him, is still almost incomprehensible. To hold the line was virtually impossible: therefore he pushed it forward. An anonymous writer in L'Afrique Francaise (January, 1917) has thus described the manoeuvre: "General Henrys was instructed to watch for storm-signals on the front, to stop up the cracks, to strengthen weak points and to rectify doubtful lines. Thanks to these operations, which kept the rebels perpetually harassed by always forestalling their own plans, the occupied territory was enlarged by a succession of strongly fortified positions." While this was going on in the north, General Lamothe was extending and strengthening, by means of pacific negotiations, the influence of the Great Chiefs in the south, and other agents of the Residency were engaged in watching and thwarting the incessant German intrigues in the Spanish zone.

General Lyautey is quoted as having said that "a work-shop is worth a battalion." This precept he managed to put into action even during the first dark days of 1914, and the interior development of Morocco proceeded side by side with the strengthening of its defenses. Germany had long foreseen what an asset northwest Africa would be during the war; and General Lyautey was determined to prove how right Germany had been. He did so by getting the government, to whom he had given nearly all his troops, to give him in exchange an agricultural and industrial army, or at least enough specialists to form such an army out of the available material in the country. For every battle fought a road was made;[A] for every rebel fortress shelled a factory was built, a harbor developed, or more miles of fallow land ploughed and sown.

[Footnote A: During the first year of the war roads were built in Morocco by German prisoners, and it was because Germany was so thoroughly aware of the economic value of the country, and so anxious not to have her prestige diminished, that she immediately protested, on the absurd plea of the unwholesomeness of the climate, and threatened reprisals unless the prisoners were withdrawn.]

But this economic development did not satisfy the Resident. He wished Morocco to enlarge her commercial relations with France and the other allied countries, and with this object in view he organized and carried out with brilliant success a series of exhibitions at Casablanca, Fez and Rabat. The result of this bold policy surpassed even its creator's hopes. The Moroccans of the plain are an industrious and money-loving people, and the sight of these rapidly improvised exhibitions, where the industrial and artistic products of France and other European countries were shown in picturesque buildings grouped about flower-filled gardens, fascinated their imagination and strengthened their confidence in the country that could find time for such an effort in the midst of a great war. The Voice of the Bazaar carried the report to the farthest confines of Moghreb, and one by one the notabilities of the different tribes arrived, with delegations from Algeria and Tunisia. It was even said that several rebel chiefs had submitted to the Makhzen in order not to miss the Exhibition.

At the same time as the "Miracle of the Marne" another, less famous but almost as vital to France, was being silently performed at the other end of her dominions. It will not seem an exaggeration to speak of General Lyautey's achievement during the first year of the war as the "Miracle of Morocco" if one considers the immense importance of doing what he did at the moment when he did it. And to understand this it is only needful to reckon what Germany could have drawn in supplies and men from a German North Africa, and what would have been the situation of France during the war with a powerful German colony in control of the western Mediterranean.

General Lyautey has always been one of the clear-sighted administrators who understand that the successful government of a foreign country depends on many little things, and not least on the administrator's genuine sympathy with the traditions, habits and tastes of the people. A keen feeling for beauty had prepared him to appreciate all that was most exquisite and venerable in the Arab art of Morocco, and even in the first struggle with political and military problems he found time to gather about him a group of archaeologists and artists who were charged with the inspection and preservation of the national monuments and the revival of the languishing native art-industries. The old pottery, jewelry, metal-work, rugs and embroideries of the different regions were carefully collected and classified, schools of decorative art were founded, skilled artisans sought out, and every effort was made to urge European residents to follow native models and use native artisans in building and furnishing.

At the various Exhibitions much space was allotted to these revived industries, and the matting of Sale, the rugs of Rabat, the embroideries of Fez and Marrakech have already found a ready market in France, besides awakening in the educated class of colonists an appreciation of the old buildings and the old arts of the country that will be its surest safeguard against the destructive effects of colonial expansion. It is only necessary to see the havoc wrought in Tunisia and Algeria by the heavy hand of the colonial government to know what General Lyautey has achieved in saving Morocco from this form of destruction also.

All this has been accomplished by the Resident-General during five years of unexampled and incessant difficulty; and probably the true explanation of the miracle is that which he himself gives when he says, with the quiet smile that typifies his Moroccan war-policy: "It was easy to do because I loved the people."

THE WORK OF THE FRENCH PROTECTORATE, 1912-1918

PORTS

Owing to the fact that the neglected and roadless Spanish zone intervened between the French possessions and Tangier, which is the natural port of Morocco, one of the first preoccupations of General Lyautey was to make ports along the inhospitable Atlantic coast, where there are no natural harbours.

Since 1912, in spite of the immense cost and the difficulty of obtaining labour, the following has been done:

Casablanca. A jetty 1900 metres long has been planned: 824 metres finished December, 1917.

Small jetty begun 1916, finished 1917—length 330 metres. Small harbour thus created shelters small boats (150 tons) in all weathers.

Quays 747 metres long already finished.

16 steam-cranes working.

Warehouses and depots covering 41,985 square metres completed.

Rabat. Work completed December, 1917.

A quay 200 metres long, to which boats with a draught of three metres can tie up.

Two groups of warehouses, steam-cranes, etc., covering 22,600 square metres.

A quay 100 metres long on the Sale side of the river.

Kenitra. The port of Kenitra is at the mouth of the Sebou River, and is capable of becoming a good river port.

The work up to December, 1917, comprises:

A channel 100 metres long and three metres deep, cut through the bar of the Sebou.

Jetties built on each side of the channel.

Quay 100 metres long.

Building of sheds, depots, warehouses, steam-cranes, etc.

At the ports of Fedalah, Mazagan, Safi, Mogador and Agadir similar plans are in course of execution.

COMMERCE

COMPARATIVE TABLES

	1912	1918
Total Commerce		
Total Commerce	Fcs 177,737,723	Fcs 386,238,618
Exports		
Exports	Fcs 67,080,383	Fcs 116,148,081

ROADS BUILT

National roads	2,074 kilometres
Secondary roads	569 kilometers

RAILWAYS BUILT
622 kilometres

LAND CULTIVATED
Approximate area

1915	1918
21,165 17 hectares	1,681,308 03 hectares

JUSTICE

1. Creation of French courts for French nationals and those under French protection. These take cognizance of civil cases where both parties, or even one, are amenable to French jurisdiction.

2. Moroccan law is Moslem, and administered by Moslem magistrates. Private law, including that of inheritance, is based on the Koran. The Sultan has maintained the principle whereby real property and administrative cases fall under native law. These courts are as far as possible supervised and controlled by the establishment of a Cherifian Ministry of Justice to which the native Judges are responsible. Special care is taken to prevent the alienation of property held collectively, or any similar transactions likely to produce political and economic disturbances.

3. Criminal jurisdiction is delegated to Pashas and Cadis by the Sultan, except of offenses committed against, or in conjunction with, French nationals and those under French protection. Such cases come before the tribunals of the French Protectorate.

EDUCATION

The object of the Protectorate has been, on the one hand, to give to the children of French colonists in Morocco the same education as they would have received at elementary and secondary schools in France; on the other, to provide the indigenous population with a system of education that shall give to the young Moroccans an adequate commercial or manual training, or prepare them for administrative posts, but without interfering with their native customs or beliefs.

Before 1912 there existed in Morocco only a few small schools supported by the French Legation at Tangier and by the Alliance Francaise, and a group of Hebrew schools in the Mellahs, maintained by the Universal Israelite Alliance.

1912. Total number of schools 37	1918. Total number of schools 191
1912. Total number of pupils 3006	1918. Total number of pupils 21,520
1912. Total number of teachers 61	1918. Total number of teachers 668

In addition to the French and indigenous schools, sewing-schools have been formed for the native girls and have been exceptionally successful.

Moslem colleges have been founded at Rabat and Fez in order to supplement the native education of young Mahometans of the upper classes, who intend to take up wholesale business or banking, or prepare for political, judicial or administrative posts under the Sultan's government. The course lasts four years and comprises: Arabic, French, mathematics, history, geography, religious (Mahometan) instruction, and the law of the Koran.

The "Ecole Superieure de la langue arabe et des dialectes berberes" at Rabat receives European and Moroccan students. The courses are Arabic, the Berber dialects, Arab literature, ethnography, administrative Moroccan law, Moslem law, Berber customary law.

MEDICAL AID

The Protectorate has established 113 medical centres for the native population, ranging from simple dispensaries and small native infirmaries to the important hospitals of Rabat, Fez, Meknez, Marrakech, and Casablanca.

Mobile sanitary formations supplied with light motor ambulances travel about the country, vaccinating, making tours of sanitary inspection, investigating infected areas, and giving general hygienic education throughout the remoter regions.

Native patients treated in 1916 over   900,000
Native patients treated in 1917 over 1,220,800

Night-shelters in towns. Every town is provided with a shelter for the indigent wayfarers so numerous in Morocco. These shelters are used as disinfection centres, from which suspicious cases are sent to quarantine camp at the gates of the towns.

Central Laboratory at Rabat. This is a kind of Pasteur Institute. In 1917, 210,000 persons were vaccinated throughout the country and 356 patients treated at the Laboratory for rabies.

Clinics for venereal diseases have been established at Casablanca, Fez, Rabat, and Marrakech.

More than 15,000 cases were treated in 1917.

Ophthalmic clinics in the same cities gave in 1917, 44,600 consultations.

Radiotherapy. Clinics have been opened at Fez and Rabat for the treatment of skin diseases of the head, from which the native children habitually suffer.

The French Department of Health distributes annually immense quantities of quinine in the malarial districts.

Madame Lyautey's private charities comprise admirably administered child-welfare centres in the principal cities, with dispensaries for the native mothers and children.

VII

A SKETCH OF MOROCCAN HISTORY

[NOTE—In the chapters on Moroccan history and art I have tried to set down a slight and superficial outline of a large and confused subject. In extenuation of this summary attempt I hasten to explain that its chief merit is its lack of originality.

Its facts are chiefly drawn from the books mentioned in the short bibliography at the end of the volume, in addition to which I am deeply indebted for information given on the spot to the group of remarkable specialists attached to the French administration, and to the cultivated and cordial French officials, military and civilian, who, at each stage of my rapid journey, did their best to answer my questions and open my eyes.]

THE BERBERS

In the briefest survey of the Moroccan past, account must first of all be taken of the factor which, from the beginning of recorded events, has conditioned the whole history of North Africa: the existence, from the Sahara to the Mediterranean, of a mysterious irreducible indigenous race with which every successive foreign rule, from Carthage to France, has had to reckon, and which has but imperfectly and partially assimilated the language, the religion, and the culture that successive civilizations have tried to impose upon it.

This race, the race of Berbers, has never, modern explorers tell us, become really Islamite, any more than it ever really became Phenician, Roman or Vandal. It has imposed its habits while it appeared to adopt those of its invaders, and has perpetually represented, outside the Ismalitic and Hispano-Arabic circle of the Makhzen, the vast tormenting element of the dissident, the rebellious, the unsubdued tribes of the Blad-es-Siba.

Who were these indigenous tribes with whom the Phenicians, when they founded their first counting-houses on the north and west coast of Africa, exchanged stuffs and pottery and arms for ivory, ostrich-feathers and slaves?

Historians frankly say they do not know. All sorts of material obstacles have hitherto hampered the study of Berber origins, but it seems clear that from the earliest historic times they were a mixed race, and the ethnologist who attempts to define them is faced by the same problem as the historian of modern America who should try to find the racial definition of an "American." For centuries, for ages, North Africa has been what America now is: the clearing-house of the world. When at length it occurred to the explorer that the natives of North Africa were not all Arabs or Moors, he was bewildered by the many vistas of all they were or might be: so many and tangled were the threads leading up to them, so interwoven was their pre-Islamite culture with worn-out shreds of older and richer societies.

M. Saladin, in his "Manuel d'Architecture Musulmane," after attempting to unravel the influences which went to the making of the mosque of Kairouan, the walls of Marrakech, the Medersas of Fez—influences that lead him back to Chaldaean branch-huts, to the walls of Babylon and the embroideries of Coptic Egypt—somewhat despairingly sums up the result: "The principal elements contributed to Moslem art by the styles preceding it may be thus enumerated: from India, floral ornament; from Persia, the structural principles of the Acheminedes, and the Sassanian vault. Mesopotamia contributes a system of vaulting, incised ornament, and proportion; the Copts, ornamental detail in general; Egypt, mass and unbroken wall-spaces; Spain, construction and Romano-Iberian ornament; Africa, decorative detail and Romano-Berber traditions (with Byzantine influences in Persia); Asia Minor, a mixture of Byzantine and Persian characteristics."

As with the art of North Africa, so with its supposedly indigenous population. The Berber dialects extend from the Lybian desert to Senegal. Their language was probably related to Coptic, itself related to the ancient Egyptian and the non-Semitic dialects of Abyssinia and Nubia. Yet philologists have discovered what appears to be a far-off link between the Berber and Semitic languages, and the Chleuhs of the Draa and the Souss, with their tall slim Egyptian-looking bodies and hooked noses, may have a strain of Semitic blood. M. Augustin Bernard, in speaking of the natives of North Africa, ends, much on the same note as M. Saladin in speaking of Moslem art: "In their blood are the sediments of many races, Phenician, Punic, Egyptian and Arab."

They were not, like the Arabs, wholly nomadic; but the tent, the flock, the tribe always entered into their conception of life. M. Augustin Bernard has pointed out that, in North Africa, the sedentary and nomadic habit do not imply a permanent difference, but rather a temporary one of situation and opportunity. The sedentary Berbers are nomadic in certain conditions, and from the earliest times the invading nomad Berbers tended to become sedentary when they reached the rich plains north of the Atlas. But when they built cities it was as their ancestors and their neighbours pitched tents; and they destroyed or abandoned them as lightly as their desert forbears packed their camel-bags and moved to new pastures. Everywhere behind the bristling walls and rock-clamped towers of old Morocco lurks the shadowy spirit of instability. Every new Sultan builds himself a new house and lets his predecessors' palaces fall into decay, and as with the Sultan so with his vassals and officials. Change is the rule in this apparently unchanged civilization, where "nought may abide but Mutability."

II

PHENICIANS, ROMANS AND VANDALS

Far to the south of the Anti-Atlas, in the yellow deserts that lead to Timbuctoo, live the wild Touaregs, the Veiled Men of the south, who ride to war with their faces covered by linen masks.

These Veiled Men are Berbers, but their alphabet is composed of Lybian characters, and these are closely related to the signs engraved on certain vases of the Nile valley that are probably six thousand years old. Moreover, among the rock-cut images of the African desert is the likeness of Theban Ammon crowned with the solar disk between serpents, and the old Berber religion, with its sun and animal worship, has many points of resemblance with Egyptian beliefs. All this implies trade contacts far below the horizon of history, and obscure comings and goings of restless throngs across incredible distances long before the Phenicians planted their first trading posts on the north African coast about 1200 B.C.

Five hundred years before Christ, Carthage sent one of her admirals on a voyage of colonization beyond the Pillars of Hercules. Hannon set out with sixty fifty-oared galleys carrying thirty thousand people. Some of them settled at Mehedyia, at the mouth of the Sebou, where Phenician remains have been found, and apparently the exploration was pushed as far south as the coast of Guinea, for the inscription recording it relates that Hannon beheld elephants, hairy men and "savages called gorillas." At any rate, Carthage founded stable colonies at Melilla, Larache, Sale and Casablanca.

Then came the Romans, who carried on the business, set up one of their easy tolerant protectorates over "Tingitanian Mauretania,"[A] and built one important military outpost, Volubilis in the Zerhoun, which a series of minor defenses probably connected with Sale on the west coast, thus guarding the Roman province against the unconquered Berbers to the south.

[Footnote A: East of the Moulouya, the African protectorate (now west Algeria and the Sud Oranais) was called the Mauretania of Caesar.]

Tingitanian Mauretania was one of the numerous African granaries of Rome. She also supplied the Imperial armies with their famous African cavalry, and among minor articles of exportation were guinea-hens, snails, honey, euphorbia, wild beasts, horses and pearls. The Roman dominion ceased at the line drawn between Volubilis and Sale. There was no interest in pushing farther south, since the ivory and slave trade with the Soudan was carried on by way of Tripoli. But the spirit of enterprise never slept in the race, and Pliny records the journey of a Roman general—Suetonius Paulinus—who appears to have crossed the Atlas, probably by the pass of Tizi-n-Telremt, which is even now so beset with difficulties that access by land to the Souss will remain an arduous undertaking until the way by Imintanout is safe for European travel.

The Vandals swept away the Romans in the fifth century. The Lower Empire restored a brief period of civilization; but its authority finally dwindled to the half-legendary rule of Count Julian, shut up within his walls of Ceuta. Then Europe vanished from the shores of Africa, and though Christianity lingered here and there in vague Donatist colonies, and in the names of Roman bishoprics, its last faint hold went down in the eighth century before the irresistible cry: "There is no God but Allah!"

III

THE ARAB CONQUEST

The first Arab invasion of Morocco is said to have reached the Atlantic coast, but it left no lasting traces, and the real Islamisation of Barbary did not happen till near the end of the eighth century, when a descendant of Ali, driven from Mesopotamia by the Caliphate, reached the mountains above Volubilis and there founded an empire. The Berbers, though indifferent in religious matters, had always, from a spirit of independence, tended to heresy and schism. Under the rule of Christian Rome they had been Donatists, as M. Bernard puts it, "out of opposition to the Empire"; and so, out of opposition to the Caliphate, they took up the cause of one Moslem schismatic after another. Their great popular movements have always had a religious basis, or perhaps it would be truer to say, a religious pretext, for they have been in reality the partly moral, partly envious revolt of hungry and ascetic warrior tribes against the fatness and corruption of the "cities of the plain."

Idriss I became the first national saint and ruler of Morocco. His rule extended throughout northern Morocco, and his son, Idriss II, attacking a Berber tribe on the banks of the Oued Fez, routed them, took possession of their oasis and founded the city of Fez. Thither came schismatic refugees from Kairouan and Moors from Andalusia. The Islamite Empire of Morocco was founded, and Idriss II has become the legendary ancestor of all its subsequent rulers.

The Idrissite rule is a welter of obscure struggles between rapidly melting groups of adherents. Its chief features are: the founding of Moulay Idriss and Fez, and the building of the mosques of El Andalous and Kairouiyin at Fez for the two groups of refugees from Tunisia and Spain. Meanwhile the Caliphate of Cordova had reached the height of its power, while that of the Fatimites extended from the Nile to western Morocco, and the little Idrissite empire, pulverized under the weight of these expanding powers, became once more a dust of disintegrated tribes.

It was only in the eleventh century that the dust again conglomerated. Two Arab tribes from the desert of the Hedjaz, suddenly driven westward by the Fatimites, entered Morocco, not with a small military expedition, as the Arabs had hitherto done, but with a horde of emigrants reckoned as high as 200,000 families; and this first colonizing expedition was doubtless succeeded by others.

To strengthen their hold in Morocco the Arab colonists embraced the dynastic feuds of the Berbers. They inaugurated a period of general havoc which destroyed what little prosperity had survived the break-up of the Idrissite rule, and many Berber tribes took refuge in the mountains; but others remained and were merged with the invaders, reforming into new tribes of mixed Berber and Arab blood. This invasion was almost purely destructive, it marks one of the most desolate periods in the progress of the "wasteful Empire" of Moghreb.

ALMORAVIDS AND ALMOHADS

While the Hilalian Arabs were conquering and destroying northern Morocco another but more fruitful invasion was upon her from the south. The Almoravids, one of the tribes of Veiled Men of the south, driven by the usual mixture of religious zeal and lust of booty, set out to invade the rich black kingdoms north of the Sahara. Thence they crossed the Atlas under their great chief, Youssef-ben-Tachfin, and founded the city of Marrakech in 1062. From Marrakech they advanced on Idrissite Fez and the valley of the Moulouya. Fez rose against her conquerors, and Youssef put all the male inhabitants to death. By 1084 he was master of Tangier and the Rif, and his rule stretched as far west as Tlemcen, Oran and finally Algiers.

His ambition drove him across the straits to Spain, where he conquered one Moslem prince after another and wiped out the luxurious civilization of Moorish Andalusia. In 1086, at Zallarca, Youssef gave battle to Alphonso VI of Castile and Leon. The Almoravid army was a strange rabble of Arabs, Berbers, blacks, wild tribes of the Sahara and Christian mercenaries. They conquered the Spanish forces, and Youssef left to his successors an empire extending from the Ebro to Senegal and from the Atlantic coast of Africa to the borders of Tunisia. But the empire fell to pieces of its own weight, leaving little record of its brief and stormy existence. While Youssef was routing the forces of Christianity at Zallarca in Spain, another schismatic tribe of his own people was detaching Marrakech and the south from his rule.

The leader of the new invasion was a Mahdi, one of the numerous Saviours of the World who have carried death and destruction throughout Islam. His name was Ibn-Toumert, and he had travelled in Egypt, Syria and Spain, and made the pilgrimage to Mecca. Preaching the doctrine of a purified monotheism, he called his followers the Almohads or Unitarians, to distinguish them from the polytheistic Almoravids, whose heresies he denounced. He fortified the city of Tinmel in the Souss, and built there a mosque of which the ruins still exist. When he died, in 1128, he designated as his successor Abd-el-Moumen, the son of a potter, who had been his disciple.

Abd-el-Moumen carried on the campaign against the Almoravids. He fought them not only in Morocco but in Spain, taking Cadiz, Cordova, Granada as well as Tlemcen and Fez. In 1152 his African dominion reached from Tripoli to the Souss, and he had formed a disciplined army in which Christian mercenaries from France and Spain fought side by side with Berbers and Soudanese. This great captain was also a great administrator, and under his rule Africa was surveyed from the Souss to Barka, the country was policed, agriculture was protected, and the caravans journeyed safely over the trade-routes.

Abd-el-Moumen died in 1163 and was followed by his son, who, though he suffered reverses in Spain, was also a great ruler. He died in 1184, and his son, Yacoub-el-Mansour, avenged his father's ill-success in Spain by the great victory of Alarcos and the conquest of Madrid. Yacoub-el-Mansour was the greatest of Moroccan Sultans. So far did his fame extend that the illustrious Saladin sent him presents and asked the help of his fleet. He was a builder as well as a fighter, and the noblest period of Arab art in Morocco and Spain coincides with his reign.

After his death, the Almohad empire followed the downward curve to which all Oriental rule seems destined. In Spain, the Berber forces were beaten in the great Christian victory of Las-Navas-de Tolosa, and in Morocco itself the first stirrings of the Beni-Merins (a new tribe from the Sahara) were preparing the way for a new dynasty.

THE MERINIDS

The Beni-Merins or Merinids were nomads who ranged the desert between Biskra and the Tafilelt. It was not a religious upheaval that drove them to the conquest of Morocco. The demoralized Almohads called them in as mercenaries to defend their crumbling empire; and the Merinids came, drove out the Almohads, and replaced them.

They took Fez, Meknez, Sale, Rabat and Sidjilmassa in the Tafilelt; and their second Sultan, Abou-Youssef, built New Fez (Eldjid) on the height above the old Idrissite city. The Merinids renewed the struggle with the Sultan of Tlemcen, and carried the Holy War once more into Spain. The conflict with Tlemcen was long and unsuccessful, and one of the Merinid Sultans died assassinated under its walls. In the fourteenth century the Sultan Abou Hassan tried to piece together the scattered bits of the Almohad empire. Tlemcen was finally taken, and the whole of Algeria annexed. But in the plain of Kairouan, in Tunisia, Abou Hassan was defeated by the Arabs. Meanwhile one of his brothers had headed a revolt in Morocco, and the princes of Tlemcen won back their ancient kingdom. Constantine and Bougie rebelled in turn, and the kingdom of Abou Hassan vanished like a mirage. His successors struggled vainly to control their vassals in Morocco, and to keep their possessions beyond its borders. Before the end of the fourteenth century Morocco from end to end was a chaos of antagonistic tribes, owning no allegiance, abiding by no laws. The last of the Merinids, divided, diminished, bound by humiliating treaties with Christian Spain, kept up a semblance of sovereignty at Fez and Marrakech, at war with one another and with their neighbours, and Spain and Portugal seized this moment of internal dissolution to drive them from Spain, and carry the war into Morocco itself.

The short and stormy passage of the Beni-Merins seems hardly to leave room for the development of the humaner qualities; yet the flowering of Moroccan art and culture coincided with those tumultuous years, and it was under the Merinid Sultans that Fez became the centre of Moroccan learning and industry, a kind of Oxford with Birmingham annexed.

VI

THE SAADIANS

Meanwhile, behind all the Berber turmoil a secret work of religious propaganda was going on. The Arab element had been crushed but not extirpated. The crude idolatrous wealth-loving Berbers apparently dominated, but whenever there was a new uprising or a new invasion it was based on the religious discontent perpetually stirred up by Mahometan agents. The longing for a Mahdi, a Saviour, the craving for purification combined with an opportunity to murder and rob, always gave the Moslem apostle a ready opening; and the downfall of the Merinids was the result of a long series of religious movements to which the European invasion gave an object and a war-cry.

The Saadians were Cherifian Arabs, newcomers from Arabia, to whom the lax Berber paganism was abhorrent. They preached a return to the creed of Mahomet, and proclaimed the Holy War against the hated Portuguese, who had set up fortified posts all along the west coast of Morocco.

It is a mistake to suppose that hatred of the Christian has always existed among the North African Moslems. The earlier dynasties, and especially the great Almohad Sultans, were on friendly terms with the Catholic powers of Europe, and in the thirteenth century a treaty assured to Christians in Africa full religious liberty, excepting only the right to preach their doctrine in public places. There was a Catholic diocese at Fez, and afterward at Marrakech under Gregory IX, and there is a letter of the Pope thanking the "Miromilan" (the Emir El Moumenin) for his kindness to the Bishop and the friars living in his dominions. Another Bishop was recommended by Innocent IV to the Sultan of Morocco; the Pope even asked that certain strongholds should be assigned to the Christians in Morocco as places of refuge in times of disturbance. But the best proof of the friendly relations between Christians and infidels is the fact that the Christian armies which helped the Sultans of Morocco to defeat Spain and subjugate Algeria and Tunisia were not composed of "renegadoes" or captives, as is generally supposed, but of Christian mercenaries, French and English, led by knights and nobles, and fighting for the Sultan of Morocco exactly as they would have fought for the Duke of Burgundy, the Count of Flanders, or any other Prince who offered high pay and held out the hope of rich spoils. Anyone who has read Villehardouin and Joinville will own that there is not much to choose between the motives animating these noble freebooters and those which caused the Crusaders to loot Constantinople "on the way" to the Holy Sepulchre. War in those days was regarded as a lucrative and legitimate form of business, exactly as it was when the earlier heroes started out to take the rich robber-town of Troy.

The Berbers have never been religious fanatics, and the Vicomte de Foucauld, when he made his great journey of exploration in the Atlas in 1883, remarked that antagonism to the foreigner was always due to the fear of military espionage and never to religious motives. This equally applies to the Berbers of the sixteenth century, when the Holy War against Catholic Spain and Portugal was preached. The real cause of the sudden deadly hatred of the foreigner was twofold. The Spaniards were detested because of the ferocious cruelty with which they had driven the Moors from Spain under Ferdinand and Isabella, and the Portuguese because of the arrogance and brutality of their military colonists in the fortified trading stations of the west coast. And both were feared as possible conquerors and overlords.

There was a third incentive also: the Moroccans, dealing in black slaves for the European market, had discovered the value of white slaves in Moslem markets. The Sultan had his fleet, and each coast-town its powerful pirate vessels, and from pirate-nests like Sale and Tangier the raiders continued, till well on into the first half of the nineteenth century, to seize European ships and carry their passengers to the slave-markets of Fez and Marrakech.[A] The miseries endured by these captives, and so poignantly described in John Windus's travels, and in the "Naufrage du Brick Sophie" by Charles Cochelet,[B] show how savage the feeling against the foreigner had become.

[Footnote A: The Moroccans being very poor seamen, these corsair-vessels were usually commanded and manned by Christian renegadoes and Turks.]

[Footnote B: Cochelet was wrecked on the coast near Agadir early in the nineteenth century and was taken with his fellow-travellers overland to El-Ksar and Tangier, enduring terrible hardships by the way.]

With the advent of the Cherifian dynasties, which coincided with this religious reform, and was in fact brought about by it, Morocco became a closed country, as fiercely guarded as Japan against European penetration. Cut off from civilizing influences, the Moslems isolated themselves in a lonely fanaticism, far more racial than religious, and the history of the country from the fall of the Merinids till the French annexation is mainly a dull tale of tribal warfare.

The religious movement of the sixteenth century was led and fed by zealots from the Sahara. One of them took possession of Rabat and Azemmour, and preached the Holy War; other "feudal fiefs" (as M. Augustin Bernard has well called them) were founded at Tameslout, Ilegh, Tamgrout: the tombs of the marabouts who led these revolts are scattered all along the west coast, and are still objects of popular veneration. The unorthodox saint worship which marks Moroccan Moslemism, and is commemorated by the countless white koubbas throughout the country, grew up chiefly at the time of the religious revival under the Saadian dynasty, and almost all the "Moulays" and "Sidis" venerated between Tangier and the Atlas were warrior monks who issued forth from their fortified Zaouias to drive the Christians out of Africa.

The Saadians were probably rather embarrassed by these fanatics, whom they found useful to oppose to the Merinids, but troublesome where their own plans were concerned. They were ambitious and luxury-loving princes, who invaded the wealthy kingdom of the Soudan, conquered the Sultan of Timbuctoo, and came back laden with slaves and gold to embellish Marrakech and spend their treasure in the usual demoralizing orgies. Their exquisite tombs at Marrakech commemorate in courtly language the superhuman virtues of a series of rulers whose debaucheries and vices were usually cut short by assassination. Finally another austere and fanatical mountain tribe surged down on them, wiped them out, and ruled in their stead.

VII

THE HASSANIANS

The new rulers came from the Tafilelt, which has always been a troublesome corner of Morocco. The first two Hassanian Sultans were the usual tribal chiefs bent on taking advantage of Saadian misrule to loot and conquer. But the third was the great Moulay-Ismael, the tale of whose long and triumphant rule (1672 to 1727) has already been told in the chapter on Meknez. This savage and enlightened old man once more drew order out of anarchy, and left, when he died, an organized and administered empire, as well as a progeny of seven hundred sons and unnumbered daughters.[A]

[Footnote A: Moulay-Ismael was a learned theologian and often held religious discussions with the Fathers of the Order of Mercy and the Trinitarians. He was scrupulously orthodox in his religious observances, and wrote a treatise in defense of his faith which he sent to James II of England, urging him to become a Mahometan. He invented most of the most exquisite forms of torture which subsequent Sultans have applied to their victims (see Loti, Au Maroc), and was fond of flowers, and extremely simple and frugal in his personal habits.]

The empire fell apart as usual, and no less quickly than usual, under his successors; and from his death until the strong hand of General Lyautey took over the direction of affairs the Hassanian rule in Morocco was little more than a tumult of incoherent ambitions. The successors of Moulay-Ismael inherited his blood-lust and his passion for dominion without his capacity to govern. In 1757 Sidi-Mohammed, one of his sons, tried to put order into his kingdom, and drove the last Portuguese out of Morocco; but under his successors the country remained isolated and stagnant, making spasmodic efforts to defend itself against the encroachments of European influence, while its rulers wasted their energy in a policy of double-dealing and dissimulation. Early in the nineteenth century the government was compelled by the European powers to suppress piracy and the trade in Christian slaves; and in 1830 the French conquest of Algeria broke down the wall of isolation behind which the country was mouldering away by placing a European power on one of its frontiers.

At first the conquest of Algeria tended to create a link between France and Morocco. The Dey of Algiers was a Turk, and, therefore, an hereditary enemy; and Morocco was disposed to favour the power which had broken Turkish rule in a neighbouring country. But the Sultan could not help trying to profit by the general disturbance to seize Tlemcen and raise insurrections in western Algeria; and presently Morocco was engaged in a Holy War against France. Abd-el-Kader, the Sultan of Algeria, had taken refuge in Morocco, and the Sultan of Morocco having furnished him with supplies and munitions, France sent an official remonstrance. At the same time Marshal Bugeaud landed at Mers-el-Kebir, and invited the Makhzen to discuss the situation. The offer was accepted and General Bedeau and the Caid El Guennaoui met in an open place. Behind them their respective troops were drawn up, and almost as soon as the first salutes were exchanged the Caid declared the negotiations broken off. The French troops accordingly withdrew to the coast, but during their retreat they were attacked by the Moroccans. This put an end to peaceful negotiations, and Tangier was besieged and taken. The following August Bugeaud brought his troops up from Oudjda, through the defile that leads from West Algeria, and routed the Moroccans. He wished to advance on Fez, but international politics interfered, and he was not allowed to carry out his plans. England looked unfavourably on the French penetration of Morocco, and it became necessary to conclude peace at once to prove that France had no territorial ambitions west of Oudjda.

Meanwhile a great Sultan was once more to appear in the land. Moulay-el-Hassan, who ruled from 1873 to 1894, was an able and energetic administrator. He pieced together his broken empire, asserted his authority in Fez and Marrakech, and fought the rebellious tribes of the west. In 1877 he asked the French government to send him a permanent military mission to assist in organizing his army. He planned an expedition to the Souss, but the want of food and water in the wilderness traversed by the army caused the most cruel sufferings. Moulay-el-Hassan had provisions sent by sea, but the weather was too stormy to allow of a landing on the exposed Atlantic coast, and the Sultan, who had never seen the sea, was as surprised and indignant as Canute to find that the waves would not obey him.

His son Abd-el-Aziz was only thirteen years old when he succeeded to the throne. For six years he remained under the guardianship of Ba-Ahmed, the black Vizier of Moulay-el-Hassan, who built the fairy palace of the Bahia at Marrakech, with its mysterious pale green padlocked door leading down to the secret vaults where his treasure was hidden. When the all-powerful Ba-Ahmed died the young Sultan was nineteen. He was intelligent, charming, and fond of the society of Europeans; but he was indifferent to religious questions and still more to military affairs, and thus doubly at the mercy of native mistrust and European intrigue.

Some clumsy attempts at fiscal reform, and a too great leaning toward European habits and associates, roused the animosity of the people, and of the conservative party in the upper class. The Sultan's eldest brother, who had been set aside in his favour, was intriguing against him; the usual Cherifian Pretender was stirring up the factious tribes in the mountains; and the European powers were attempting, in the confusion of an ungoverned country, to assert their respective ascendencies.

The demoralized condition of the country justified these attempts, and made European interference inevitable. But the powers were jealously watching each other, and Germany, already coveting the certain agricultural resources and the conjectured mineral wealth of Morocco, was above all determined that a French protectorate should not be set up.

In 1908 another son of Moulay-Hassan, Abd-el-Hafid, was proclaimed Sultan by the reactionary Islamite faction, who accused Abd-el-Aziz of having sold his country to the Christians. Abd-el-Aziz was defeated in a battle near Marrakech, and retired to Tangier, where he still lives in futile state. Abd-el-Hafid, proclaimed Sultan at Fez, was recognized by the whole country, but he found himself unable to cope with the factious tribes (those outside the Blad-el-Makhzen, or governed country). These rebel tribes besieged Fez, and the Sultan had to ask France for aid. France sent troops to his relief, but as soon as the dissidents were routed, and he himself was safe, Abd-el-Hafid refused to give the French army his support, and in 1912, after the horrible massacres of Fez, he abdicated in favour of another brother, Moulay Youssef, the actual ruler of Morocco.

VIII

NOTE ON MOROCCAN ARCHITECTURE

I

M. H. Saladin, whose "Manual of Moslem Architecture" was published in 1907, ends his chapter on Morocco with the words: "It is especially urgent that we should know, and penetrate into, Morocco as soon as possible, in order to study its monuments. It is the only country but Persia where Moslem art actually survives; and the tradition handed down to the present day will doubtless clear up many things."

M. Saladin's wish has been partly realized. Much has been done since 1912, when General Lyautey was appointed Resident-General, to clear up and classify the history of Moroccan art; but since 1914, though the work has never been dropped, it has necessarily been much delayed, especially as regards its published record; and as yet only a few monographs and articles have summed up some of the interesting investigations of the last five years.

II

When I was in Marrakech word was sent to Captain de S., who was with me, that a Caid of the Atlas, whose prisoner he had been several years before, had himself been taken by the Pasha's troops, and was in Marrakech. Captain de S. was asked to identify several rifles which his old enemy had taken from him, and on receiving them found that, in the interval, they had been elaborately ornamented with the Arab niello work of which the tradition goes back to Damascus.

This little incident is a good example of the degree to which the mediaeval tradition alluded to by M. Saladin has survived in Moroccan life. Nowhere else in the world, except among the moribund fresco-painters of the Greek monasteries, has a formula of art persisted from the seventh or eighth century to the present day; and in Morocco the formula is not the mechanical expression of a petrified theology but the setting of the life of a people who have gone on wearing the same clothes, observing the same customs, believing in the same fetiches, and using the same saddles, ploughs, looms, and dye-stuffs as in the days when the foundations of the first mosque of El Kairouiyin were laid.

The origin of this tradition is confused and obscure. The Arabs have never been creative artists, nor are the Berbers known to have been so. As investigations proceed in Syria and Mesopotamia it seems more and more probable that the sources of inspiration of pre-Moslem art in North Africa are to be found in Egypt, Persia, and India. Each new investigation pushes these sources farther back and farther east; but it is not of much use to retrace these ancient vestiges, since Moroccan art has, so far, nothing to show of pre-Islamite art, save what is purely Phenician or Roman.

In any case, however, it is not in Morocco that the clue to Moroccan art is to be sought; though interesting hints and mysterious reminiscences will doubtless be found in such places as Tinmel, in the gorges of the Atlas, where a ruined mosque of the earliest Almohad period has been photographed by M. Doutte, and in the curious Algerian towns of Sedrata and the Kalaa of the Beni Hammads. Both of these latter towns were rich and prosperous communities in the tenth century and both were destroyed in the eleventh, so that they survive as mediaeval Pompeiis of a quite exceptional interest, since their architecture appears to have been almost unaffected by classic or Byzantine influences.

Traces of a very old indigenous art are found in the designs on the modern white and black Berber pottery, but this work, specimens of which are to be seen in the Oriental Department of the Louvre, seems to go back, by way of Central America, Greece (sixth century B.C.) and Susa (twelfth century B.C.), to the far-off period before the streams of human invention had divided, and when the same loops and ripples and spirals formed on the flowing surface of every current.

It is a disputed question whether Spanish influence was foremost in developing the peculiarly Moroccan art of the earliest Moslem period, or whether European influences came by way of Syria and Palestine, and afterward met and were crossed with those of Moorish Spain. Probably both things happened, since the Almoravids were in Spain; and no doubt the currents met and mingled. At any rate, Byzantine, Greece, and the Palestine and Syria of the Crusaders, contributed as much as Rome and Greece to the formation of that peculiar Moslem art which, all the way from India to the Pillars of Hercules, built itself, with minor variations, out of the same elements.

Arab conquerors always destroy as much as they can of the work of their predecessors, and nothing remains, as far as is known, of Almoravid architecture in Morocco. But the great Almohad Sultans covered Spain and Northwest Africa with their monuments, and no later buildings in Africa equal them in strength and majesty.

It is no doubt because the Almohads built in stone that so much of what they made survives. The Merinids took to rubble and a soft tufa, and the Cherifian dynasties built in clay like the Spaniards in South America. And so seventeenth century Meknez has perished while the Almohad walls and towers of the tenth century still stand.

The principal old buildings of Morocco are defensive and religious—and under the latter term the beautiful collegiate houses (the medersas) of Fez and Sale may fairly be included, since the educational system of Islam is essentially and fundamentally theological. Of old secular buildings, palaces or private houses, virtually none are known to exist; but their plan and decorations may easily be reconstituted from the early chronicles, and also from the surviving palaces built in the eighteenth and nineteenth centuries, and even those which the wealthy nobles of modern Morocco are building to this day.

The whole of civilian Moslem architecture from Persia to Morocco is based on four unchanging conditions: a hot climate, slavery, polygamy and the segregation of women. The private house in

Mahometan countries is in fact a fortress, a convent and a temple: a temple of which the god (as in all ancient religions) frequently descends to visit his cloistered votaresses. For where slavery and polygamy exist every house-master is necessarily a god, and the house he inhabits a shrine built about his divinity.

The first thought of the Moroccan chieftain was always defensive. As soon as he pitched a camp or founded a city it had to be guarded against the hungry hordes who encompassed him on every side. Each little centre of culture and luxury in Moghreb was an islet in a sea of perpetual storms. The wonder is that, thus incessantly threatened from without and conspired against from within—with the desert at their doors, and their slaves on the threshold—these violent men managed to create about them an atmosphere of luxury and stability that astonished not only the obsequious native chronicler but travellers and captives from western Europe.

[Illustration: From a photograph from the Service des Beaux-Arts au Maroc Rabat—gate of the Kasbah of the Oudayas]

The truth is, as has been often pointed out, that, even until the end of the seventeenth century, the refinements of civilization were in many respects no greater in France and England than in North Africa. North Africa had long been in more direct communication with the old Empires of immemorial luxury, and was therefore farther advanced in the arts of living than the Spain and France of the Dark Ages; and this is why, in a country that to the average modern European seems as savage as Ashantee, one finds traces of a refinement of life and taste hardly to be matched by Carlovingian and early Capetian Europe.

III

The brief Almoravid dynasty left no monuments behind it.

Fez had already been founded by the Idrissites, and its first mosques (Kairouiyin and Les Andalous) existed. Of the Almoravid Fez and Marrakech the chroniclers relate great things; but the wild Hilalian invasion and the subsequent descent of the Almohads from the High Atlas swept away whatever the first dynasties had created.

The Almohads were mighty builders, and their great monuments are all of stone. The earliest known example of their architecture which has survived is the ruined mosque of Tinmel, in the High Atlas, discovered and photographed by M. Doutte. This mosque was built by the inspired mystic, Ibn-Toumert, who founded the line. Following him came the great palace-making Sultans whose walled cities of splendid mosques and towers have Romanesque qualities of mass and proportion, and, as M. Raymond Koechlin has pointed out, inevitably recall the "robust simplicity of the master builders who at the very same moment were beginning in France the construction of the first Gothic cathedrals and the noblest feudal castles."

In the thirteenth century, with the coming of the Merinids, Moroccan architecture grew more delicate, more luxurious, and perhaps also more peculiarly itself. That interaction of Spanish and Arab art which produced the style known as Moorish reached, on the African side of the Straits, its greatest completeness in Morocco. It was under the Merinids that Moorish art grew into full beauty in Spain, and under the Merinids that Fez rebuilt the mosque Kairouiyin and that of the Andalusians, and created six of its nine Medersas, the most perfect surviving buildings of that unique moment of sober elegance and dignity.

The Cherifian dynasties brought with them a decline in taste. A crude desire for immediate effect, and the tendency toward a more barbaric luxury, resulted in the piling up of frail palaces as impermanent as tents. Yet a last flower grew from the deformed and dying trunk of the old Empire. The Saadian Sultan who invaded the Soudan and came back laden with gold and treasure from the great black city of Timbuctoo covered Marrakech with hasty monuments of which hardly a trace survives. But there, in a nettle-grown corner of a ruinous quarter, lay hidden till yesterday the Chapel of the Tombs: the last emanation of pure beauty of a mysterious, incomplete, forever retrogressive and yet forever forward-straining people. The Merinid tombs of Fez have fallen; but those of their destroyers linger on in precarious grace, like a flower on the edge of a precipice.

IV

Moroccan architecture, then, is easily divided into four groups: the fortress, the mosque, the collegiate building and the private house.

The kernel of the mosque is always the mihrab, or niche facing toward the Kasbah of Mecca, where the imam[A] stands to say the prayer. This arrangement, which enabled as many as possible of the faithful to kneel facing the mihrab, results in a ground-plan necessarily consisting of long aisles parallel with the wall of the mihrab, to which more and more aisles are added as the number of worshippers grows. Where there was not space to increase these lateral aisles they were lengthened at each end. This typical plan is modified in the Moroccan mosques by a wider transverse space, corresponding with the nave of a Christian church, and extending across the mosque from the praying niche to the principal door. To the right of the mihrab is the minbar, the carved pulpit (usually of cedar-wood incrusted with mother-of-pearl and ebony) from which the Koran is read. In some Algerian and Egyptian mosques (and at Cordova, for instance) the mihrab is enclosed in a sort of screen called the maksoura; but in Morocco this modification of the simpler plan was apparently not adopted.

[Footnote A: The "deacon" or elder of the Moslem religion, which has no order of priests.]

The interior construction of the mosque was no doubt usually affected by the nearness of Roman or Byzantine ruins. M. Saladin points out that there seem to be few instances of the use of columns made by native builders; but it does not therefore follow that all the columns used in the early mosques were taken from Roman temples or Christian basilicas. The Arab invaders brought their architects and engineers with them; and it is very possible that some of the earlier mosques were built by prisoners or fortune-hunters from Greece or Italy or Spain.

At any rate, the column on which the arcades of the vaulting rests in the earlier mosques, as at Tunis and Kairouan, and the mosque El Kairouiyin at Fez, gives way later to the use of piers, foursquare, or with flanking engaged pilasters as at Algiers and Tlemcen. The exterior of the mosques, as a rule, is almost entirely hidden by a mushroom growth of buildings, lanes and covered bazaars, but where the outer walls have remained disengaged they show, as at Kairouan and Cordova, great masses of windowless masonry pierced at intervals with majestic gateways.

Beyond the mosque, and opening into it by many wide doors of beaten bronze or carved cedar-wood, lies the Court of the Ablutions. The openings in the facade were multiplied in order that, on great days, the faithful who were not able to enter the mosque might hear the prayers and catch a glimpse of the mihrab.

In a corner of the courts stands the minaret. It is the structure on which Moslem art has played the greatest number of variations, cutting off its angles, building it on a circular or polygonal plan, and endlessly modifying the pyramids and pendentives by which the ground-plan of one story passes into that of the next. These problems of transition, always fascinating to the architect, led in Persia, Mesopotamia and Egypt to many different compositions and ways of treatment, but in Morocco the minaret, till modern times, remained steadfastly square, and proved that no other plan is so beautiful as this simplest one of all.

Surrounding the Court of the Ablutions are the school-rooms, libraries and other dependencies, which grew as the Mahometan religion prospered and Arab culture developed.

The medersa was a farther extension of the mosque: it was the academy where the Moslem schoolman prepared his theology and the other branches of strange learning which, to the present day, make up the curriculum of the Mahometan university. The medersa is an adaptation of the private house to religious and educational ends; or, if one prefers another analogy, it is a fondak built above a miniature mosque. The ground-plan is always the same: in the centre an arcaded court with a fountain, on one side the long narrow praying-chapel with the mihrab, on the other a classroom with the same ground-plan, and on the next story a series of cell-like rooms for the students, opening on carved cedar-wood balconies. This cloistered plan, where all the effect is reserved for the interior facades about the court, lends itself to a delicacy of detail that would be inappropriate on a street-front; and the medersas of Fez are endlessly varied in their fanciful but never exuberant decoration.

M. Tranchant de Lunel has pointed out (in "France-Maroc") with what a sure sense of suitability the Merinid architects adapted this decoration to the uses of the buildings. On the lower floor, under the cloister, is a revetement of marble (often alabaster) or of the almost indestructible ceramic mosaic.[A] On the floor above, massive cedar-wood corbels ending in monsters of almost Gothic inspiration support the fretted balconies; and above rise stucco interfacings, placed too high up to be injured by man, and guarded from the weather by projecting eaves.

[Footnote A: These Moroccan mosaics are called zellijes.]

The private house, whether merchant's dwelling or chieftain's palace, is laid out on the same lines, with the addition of the reserved quarters for women; and what remains in Spain and Sicily of Moorish secular architecture shows that, in the Merinid period, the play of ornament must have been—as was natural—even greater than in the medersas.

The Arab chroniclers paint pictures of Merinid palaces, such as the House of the Favourite at Cordova, which the soberer modern imagination refused to accept until the medersas of Fez were revealed, and the old decorative tradition was shown in the eighteenth century Moroccan palaces. The descriptions given of the palaces of Fez and of Marrakech in the preceding articles, which make it unnecessary, in so slight a note as this, to go again into the detail of their planning and decoration, will serve to show how gracefully the art of the mosque and the medersa was lightened and domesticated to suit these cool chambers and flower-filled courts.

With regard to the immense fortifications that are the most picturesque and noticeable architectural features of Morocco, the first thing to strike the traveller is the difficulty of discerning any difference in the probable date of their construction until certain structural peculiarities are examined, or the ornamental details of the great gateways are noted. Thus the Almohad portions of the walls of Fez and Rabat are built of stone, while later parts are of rubble; and the touch of European influence in certain gateways of Meknez and Fez at once situate them in the seventeenth century. But the mediaeval outline of these great piles of masonry, and certain technicalities in their plan, such as the disposition of the towers, alternating in the inner and outer walls, continued unchanged throughout the different dynasties, and this immutability of the Moroccan military architecture enables the imagination to picture, not only what was the aspect of the fortified cities which the Greeks built in Palestine and Syria, and the Crusaders brought back to Europe, but even that of the far-off Assyrio-Chaldaean strongholds to which the whole fortified architecture of the Middle Ages in Europe seems to lead back.

IX

BOOKS CONSULTED

Afrique Francaise (L'). Bulletin Mensuel du Comite de l'Afrique Francaise. Paris, 21, rue Cassette.

Bernard, Augustin. Le Maroc. Paris, F. Alcan, 1916.

Budgett-Meakin. The Land of the Moors. London, 1902.

Chatelain, L. Recherches archeologiques au Maroc: Volubilis. (Published by the Military Command in Morocco).

Les Fouilles de Volubilis (Extrait du Bulletin Archeologique, 1916)

Chevrillon, A. Crepuscule d'Islam.

Cochelet, Charles. Le Naufrage du Brick Sophie.

Conferences Marocaines. Paris, Plon-Nourrit.

Doutte, E. En Tribu. Paris, 1914.

Foucauld, Vicomte de. La Reconnaissance au Maroc. Paris, 1888.

France-Maroc. Revue Mensuelle, Paris, 4, rue Chauveau-Lagarde.

Gaillard. Une Ville d'Islam, Fez. Paris, 1909.

Gayet, Al. L'Art Arabe. Paris, 1906.

Houdas, O. Le Maroc de 1631 a 1812. Extrait d'une histoire du Maroc intitulee "L'Interprete qui s'exprime clairement sur les dynasties de l'Orient et de l'Occident," par Ezziani. Paris, E. Leroux, 1886.

Koechlin, Raymond. Une Exposition d'Art Marocain. (Gazette des Beaux-Arts, Juillet-Septembre, 1917).

Leo Africanus, Description of Africa.

Loti, Pierre. Au Maroc.

Migeon, Gaston. Manuel d'Art Musulman, II, Les Arts Plastiques et Industriels. Paris, A. Picard et Fils, 1907.

Saladin, H. Manuel d'Art Musulman, I, L'Architecture. Paris, A. Picard et Fils, 1907.

Segonzac, Marquis de. Voyages au Maroc. Paris, 1903.

Au Coeur de l'Atlas. Paris, 1910.

Tarde, A. de. Les Villes du Maroc: Fez, Marrakech, Rabat. (Journal de l'Universite des Annales, 15 Oct., 1 Nov., 1918).

Windus. A Journey to Mequinez. London, 1721.

Edith Wharton – A Short Biography

The extraordinary American writer Edith Wharton was born Edith Newbold Jones on January 24th, 1862 to George Frederic Jones and Lucretia Stevens Rhinelander at their brownstone at 14 West Twenty-third Street in New York City. Her parents already had two older sons, Frederic Rhinelander, and Henry Edward.

Edith was baptized April 20, 1862, Easter Sunday, at Grace Church. To her friends and family she was apparently known as "Pussy Jones".

The 1860's were a time of Civil War in America but by the time Edith was three the war was over and a more normal life among Americans could resume.

From 1866 to 1872, the Jones family visited France, Italy, Germany, and Spain and Edith became fluent in French, German, and Italian. She was taught by a succession of tutors and governesses. Her thirst for learning was apparent at even this early age. So too was a streak of rebelliousness as she pushed back at society's standards of fashion and etiquette that were thought to be needed to help these young women marry well and to be displayed at balls and parties. She thought this superficial and oppressive.

Although he mother forbade her to read novels until she married (Edith it seems complied with that instruction) she read from her father's library and that of friends.

Edith first step to becoming a writer was inventing stories when she was around six. She would walk around the living room holding a book and reciting her story.

In 1872 at age ten, Edith was taken ill with typhoid fever while the family was at a spa in the Black Forest. The family returned to the United States that same year to begin a cycle of winters in New York and their summers in Newport, Rhode Island.

The following year, 1873, Edith wrote a short story and gave it to her mother to read. It was heavily criticised and Edith retreated to writing only poetry. Despite a child's need for a mother's approval and love, it was rare that she received either. This core relationship was indeed a troubled one.

By the time Edith was 15 she had translated a German poem "Was die Steine Erzählen" ("What the Stones Tell") by Heinrich Karl Brugsch, for which she was paid $50.

However her family did not wish to see her name in print (upper class women of the time only appeared in print to announce birth, marriage, and death). Consequently, the poem was published under the name of a friend's father, E. A. Washburn, a cousin of Ralph Waldo Emerson and a supporter of women's education and a great encourager of Edith's talents.

That same year, 1877, Edith had also secretly written a 30,000 word novella "Fast and Loose". Her central themes came from her experiences with her parents. She was very critical of her own work and would even write public reviews criticizing it. The following year, 1878, her father arranged for a collection of two dozen original poems and five translations, Verses, to be privately published.

In 1880 she had five poems published anonymously in the Atlantic Monthly, a much revered literary magazine. Despite these early successes, she was not encouraged to publish by others but did continue to write.

Edith was courted by Henry Stevens from 1880 and after two years they became engaged. A month before their marriage the engagement abruptly ended.

In 1885, at age 23, she married Edward (Teddy) Robbins Wharton, who was 12 years her senior. He was from a well-established Boston family, a sportsman and a gentleman of the same social class and shared her love of travel.

However this desirable match was blighted. From the late 1880s until 1902, he suffered acute depression. At that latter time his depression manifested as a more serious disorder, after which they lived almost exclusively at their estate; The Mount.

In October 1889 her poem "The Last Giustiniani", was published in Scribner's Magazine.

At age 29 Edith finally had her first short story published. "Mrs. Manstey's View." It had very little success, and another year was to elapse until she published again.

She completed "The Fullness of Life" following her annual European trip with Teddy. Burlingame was critical of this story but Wharton did not want to make edits to it. This story, along with many others, speaks about her marriage. She sent Bunner Sisters to Scribner's in 1892. The editor in chief, Edward L Burlingame wrote back that it was too long for Scribner's to publish. This story is believed to be based on an experience she had as a child. It did not see publication until 1916.

After a visit with her friend, Paul Bourget, she wrote "The Good May Come" and "The Lamp of Psyche". "The Lamp of Psyche" was a comical story with verbal wit and sorrow. After "Something Exquisite" was rejected by Burlingame, she lost confidence in herself.

By 1894 she had decided to write about her travels. This allied with her other interests of garden and interior design came to a publishing point in 1897 with a co-authorship on The Decoration of Houses, the first of several design books.

Her thirst for travel and to explore eventually meant some sixty trips across the Atlantic to travel across Europe and even Morocco.

Her husband, Edward, shared this love of travel and for years they would spend four, or more, month abroad until his illness deteriorated their quality of life such that they remained in America.

In 1888, the Wharton's and their friend, James Van Alen, took a cruise through the Aegean islands. Wharton was 26. The trip cost a substantial amount: $10,000 and lasted four months. Edith kept a travel journal during this trip that was later published as The Cruise of the Vanadis, her earliest known travel writing.

In 1901, Wharton wrote a two act play called "Man of Genius". This play was about an English man who was having an affair with his secretary. The play was rehearsed, but was never produced. One of her earliest literary endeavors (1902) was the translation of the play, "Es Lebe das Leben" ("The Joy of Living"), by Hermann Sudermann. "The Joy of Living" was a short lived Broadway production but was, however, a successful book.

She collaborated with Marie Tempest to write another play, but the two only completed four acts before Marie decided she was no longer interested in costume plays.

In 1902, she designed The Mount, her estate in Lenox, Massachusetts. Edith wrote several of her novels there, including The House of Mirth (1905), the first of many chronicles of life in old New York. At The Mount, she entertained the cream of American literary society, including her close friend, novelist Henry James, who described the estate as "a delicate French chateau mirrored in a Massachusetts pond".

Although she spent many months traveling The Mount was her primary residence until 1911.

With her marriage falling apart, due mainly to Edward's illness, she decided to move to Paris, living first at 53 Rue de Varenne, Paris, in an apartment that belonged to George Washington Vanderbilt II.

In 1908 her husband's mental state was determined to be incurable. In the same year, she began an affair with Morton Fullerton, a journalist for The Times, in whom she also found an intellectual partner.

She divorced Edward Wharton in 1913 after 28 years of marriage.

In 1914 Edith was preparing for her summer vacation when World War I broke out. Many fled Paris, but she moved back to her Paris apartment on the Rue de Varenne and for the next four years was a tireless, ardent supporter of the French war effort.

In August 1914 at the onset of War she opened a workroom for unemployed women; here they were fed and paid one franc a day. Thirty women started and this soon doubled to sixty, and their sewing business began to thrive. When the Germans invaded Belgium in the fall of 1914 and Paris was flooded with Belgian refugees, she helped to set up the American Hostels for Refugees, which gave shelter, meals, clothes and then an agency to help them find work. She raised and collected more than $100,000 on their behalf.

In early 1915 she organized the Children of Flanders Rescue Committee, which gave shelter to almost 900 Belgian refugees whose homes had been bombed by the Germans.

Aided by her influential connections in the French government, she and her long-time friend Walter Berry (then president of the American Chamber of Commerce in Paris), were among the few foreigners in France allowed to travel to the front lines. She and Berry made a total of five journeys between February and August 1915, which Edith described in a series of articles that were first published in Scribner's Magazine and later as Fighting France: From Dunkerque to Belfort, which became a bestseller. Travelling by car, they drove through the war zone; one decimated French village after another. She visited the trenches that were within earshot of artillery fire. She wrote, "We woke to a noise of guns closer and more incessant...and when we went out into the streets it seemed as if, overnight, a new army had sprung out of the ground".

During the war years Edith worked tirelessly in charitable efforts for refugees, the injured, the unemployed, and the displaced.

On 18 April 1916, the President of France appointed her Chevalier of the Legion of Honour, the country's highest award, in recognition of her dedication to the war effort.

Edith also kept up her own work during the war, which was now a prodigious output of novels, short stories, and poems, as well as reporting for the New York Times and keeping up her enormous correspondence. She urged Americans to support the war effort and to enter the war with its enormous resources of industry and men. She wrote the popular romantic novel Summer in 1916, the war novella, The Marne, in 1918, and A Son at the Front in 1919, (though not published until 1923).

When the war ended, she watched the Victory Parade from the Champs Elysees' balcony of a friend's apartment. After four years of intense effort, she decided to leave Paris in favor of the peace and quiet of the countryside. She settled a few miles north of Paris in Saint-Brice-sous-Forêt, buying an eighteenth-century house on seven acres of land which she called Pavillon Colombe. Edith would live there in summer and autumn for the rest of her life. She spent winters and springs on the French Riviera at Sainte Claire du Vieux Chateau in Hyeres.

Edith was a committed supporter of French imperialism, describing herself as a "rabid imperialist", and the war solidified her political views. After the war she travelled to Morocco as the guest of Resident General Hubert Lyautey and wrote a book, In Morocco, about her experiences. Wharton's writing on her Moroccan travels is full of praise for the French administration and for Lyautey and his wife in particular.

During the post war years she divided her time between Hyères and Provence, where she finished The Age of Innocence in 1920, which won the 1921 Pulitzer Prize for literature, making Edith the first woman to win the award.

Edith returned to the United States only once after the war, receiving an honorary doctorate degree from Yale University in 1923.

Edith included in her intellectual circle many of the great artists of her day; Henry James, Sinclair Lewis and Jean Cocteau were among her guests at the time. Theodore Roosevelt and Kenneth Clark were also friends. Of particular note was her meeting with F. Scott Fitzgerald, described as "one of the better known failed encounters in the American literary annals".

In 1934 Edith's autobiography A Backward Glance was published. This glossed over much of the problems in her life barely registering the criticism of her mother, her difficulties with Teddy, and her affair with Morton Fullerton.

On June 1, 1937 Wharton was at the French country home of Ogden Codman, working on a revised edition of The Decoration of Houses, when she suffered a heart attack and collapsed.

Edith Wharton died of a stroke some months later on August 11, 1937 at Le Pavillon Colombe, her 18th-century house on Rue de Montmorency in Saint-Brice-sous-Forêt at 5:30 pm. At her bedside was her friend, Mrs. Royal Tyler. The street is today called rue Edith Wharton.

Edith was buried at the Cimetière des Gonards in Versailles, "with all the honors owed a war hero and a chevalier of the Legion of Honor....a group of a hundred friends sang a verse of the hymn "O Paradise"...." She is buried next to her long-time friend, Walter Berry.

Edith Wharton – A Concise Bibliography

BOOKS
The Touchstone, 1900 (novella)
The Valley of Decision, 1902
Sanctuary, 1903 (novella)
The House of Mirth, 1905
Madame de Treymes, 1907 (novella)
The Fruit of the Tree, 1907
Ethan Frome, 1911 (novella)
The Reef, 1912
The Custom of the Country, 1913
Bunner Sisters, 1916 (novella)
Summer, 1917
The Marne, 1918
The Age of Innocence, 1920 (Pulitzer Prize winner)
The Glimpses of the Moon, 1922
A Son at the Front, 1923
Old New York: False Dawn, The Old Maid, The Spark, New Year's Day, 1924 (novellas)
The Mother's Recompense, 1925
Twilight Sleep, 1927
The Children, 1928
Hudson River Bracketed, 1929
The Gods Arrive, 1932
The Buccaneers, 1938 (unfinished)
Fast and Loose: A Novelette, 1938 (written in 1876–1877)

POETRY
Verses, 1878
Artemis to Actaeon & Other Verse, 1909
Twelve Poems, 1926

SHORT STORY COLLECTIONS
The Greater Inclination, 1899
Souls Belated, 1899
Crucial Instances, 1901
The Descent of Man & Other Stories, 1903
The Hermit and the Wild Woman & Other Stories, 1908
Tales of Men & Ghosts, 1910
Xingu & Other Stories, 1916

Old New York, 1924
Here and Beyond, 1926
Certain People, 1930
Human Nature, 1933
The World Over, 1936
Ghosts, 1937

NON-FICTION
The Decoration of Houses, 1897
Italian Villas and Their Gardens, 1904
Italian Backgrounds, 1905
A Motor-Flight Through France, 1908
Fighting France, from Dunkerque to Belfort, 1915
French Ways and Their Meaning, 1919
In Morocco, 1920
The Writing of Fiction, 1925
A Backward Glance, 1934

AS EDITOR
The Book of the Homeless, 1916

CINEMA
The House of Mirth (La Maison du Brouillard), a 1918 silent film adaptation (6 reels).
The Glimpses Of The Moon, a 1923 silent film adaptation (7 reels)
The Age of Innocence, a 1924 silent film adaptation (7 reels) (of the 1920 novel)
The Marriage Playground, a 1929 film adaptation (70 minutes) (of the 1928 novel The Children)
The Age of Innocence, a 1934 film adaptation (9 reels).
Strange Wives, a 1935 film adaptation (8 reels) (of the 1934 short story Bread Upon the Waters)
The Old Maid, a 1939 film adaptation (95 minutes) (of the 1924 short novella)
Ethan Frome (99 minutes) directed by John Madden. 1993,
The Age of Innocence (138 minutes) directed by Martin Scorsese. 1993,
The Reef (88 minutes) directed by Robert Allan Ackerman. 1999.
The House of Mirth (140 minutes) directed by Terence Davies. 2000.

TV
Ethan Frome, a 1960 (CBS) TV US adaptation.
Looking Back, a 1981 TV US adaptation of two biographies of Edith Wharton.
The House of Mirth, a 1981 TV US adaptation.
The Buccaneers, a 1995 BBC mini-series, starring Carla Gugino and Greg Wise.

THEATRE
The Man of Genius in 1901
"Es Lebe das Leben" ("The Joy of Living"), by Hermann Sudermann in 1902 - Translator.
The House of Mirth was adapted as a play in 1906.
The Age of Innocence was adapted as a play in 1928.

www.ingramcontent.com/pod-product-compliance
Lightning Source LLC
Chambersburg PA
CBHW071352170626
46811CB00003B/1111